ORBITAL RESONANCE

ORBITAL

RESONANCE

John Barnes

A TOM DOHERTY ASSOCIATES BOOK
NEW YORK

ORBITAL RESONANCE

Copyright © 1991 by John Barnes

A Tor Book
Published by Tom Doherty Associates, Inc. 49 West 24th Street
New York, N.Y. 10010

Library of Congress Cataloging-in-Publication Data

Barnes, John
   Orbital resonance / John Barnes.
      p.   cm.
      "A Tom Doherty Associates book."
   ISBN 0-312-85206-1
      I. Title.
   PS3552.A677073 1991

Printed in the United States of America

Printed in the United States of America

0 9 8 7 6 5 4 3 2

THIS BOOK is dedicated to the people who made it possible
for me to get through the worst time of my life thus far:

To Kathy Albe, for the many good times and for the gracious,
generous way she chose to end our marriage;
and
To many people who were there when I needed them, but
most
especially to (in alphabetical order):
Liz and Bob Applegate
James Crumley
Russ Gay
Ashley and Carolyn Grayson
Jerry Oltion
Lyle Schmautz
Rick Williams

THE TRULY BRAVE are soft of heart and eyes,
And feel for what their duty bids them do.

—Byron, *Marino Faliero*

ORBITAL
RESONANCE

CHAPTER ONE

December 8, 2025

D̲R. LOVELL SAYS I HAVE WRITING TALENT, SO I HAVE TO ENTER this stupid contest, so I'm stuck with a bunch of extra hours at the werp—and with my Full Adult exam less than six months away, too. The people at Scholastic decided that Earth kids wanted to know what it was like to live in space, so they have this special contest for all of us on the ships, the ports, and the stations. Of course you know all that, if you're reading this, so they'll probably cut this first paragraph. I hate that—it makes me think about just giving up and not writing when people cut my work without asking.

Anyway, my name is Melpomene Murray, I'm thirteen ground-years old, and I live on the *Flying Dutchman,* where I was born. I've done eight and a half orbits, which are the "years" of the *Flying Dutchman,* but they aren't of equal length so nobody uses them to measure time the way you do years.

I guess I could just transcribe the "useful facts list" they gave us with the assignment. That ought to be boring enough so that I won't advance in the contest and have to do a rewrite:

Like the other four ships owned by NihonAmerica, the *Flying Dutchman* is a domesticated asteroid. The original capture of Inoueia 1996 YT was made in 2008; the crew began moving aboard in 2011, and construction is still continuing. The *Flying Dutchman* has a permanent population of seventy-two hundred, down from eight thousand last year since so many older people left. Sixty-seven hundred of us are under the age of twenty, and sixty-four hundred of us were born here on the ship. All the people take up less than one percent of the ship's volume for living space. The cargo bays, when they're completed in 2059, will hold just over three cubic kilometers of cargo.

Our orbit is continuously modulated—that is, we have engines always running, speeding us up or slowing us down—so that aphelion is always a near approach to Mars and perihelion is always a near approach to Earth. The ship is powered by eight MAM reactors with a combined output of thirty thousand terawatts.

Oh shit. I can't stand this. Cut that later and keep going.

I'm already boring myself, and I have to hand in at least twenty thousand bytes on Friday. Besides, the "useful facts list" says Earth kids my age aren't even doing calculus yet, and almost all this stuff is physics.

I don't like physics that much—and I don't need to, because I'm going to be the mayor.

There, that would *really* stop Dr. Lovell from sending this out. I could write about that . . . as if I would . . .

Anyway, I've written a whole screen full and I still don't really have anything to tell you. I keep thinking about books I like, but none of them help much:

"Call me Melpomene"—well, I already said that, and it didn't get me anywhere.

"She was a centimeter, perhaps two, under 160, skinny, and she advanced straight at you with a slight stoop of the shoulders . . ." hah! And her mother told her to straighten up.

"When Ms. Melpomene Murray of Block A Corridor Twelve Living Unit Six announced that she would be celebrating her thirteenth birthday—" Please! And this isn't helping since I'll have to cut it all anyway. I need something that I can talk about for 20kb and so far I can't even plagiarize an opening paragraph, much less think of one of my own.

The only beginning that would make any sense comes from a book I hate, but it was my grandfather's favorite book—I never knew him, of course, because he died in the Die-Off in 1994, but I've heard a lot about him.

Much more than I wanted to. Mother is always quoting him— she's so weirdwired on the subject of Grandpa she actually blew some weight allowance to bring up his personal hardcopy of that book. Papa said he liked it too, which just made it worse—I had to read it. It starts off, "If you really want to hear about it. . . ."

And as soon as I start writing about all the "madman stuff" that happened last year, it'll get into how I'm going to be mayor and then I'll be out of this contest because pos-def Dr. Lovell won't let it be transmitted. She'll probably just accept the piece and then wipe the file.

On the other hand, I didn't want to be in this stupid contest anyway. I could key in FUCK YOU DR. LOVELL and have the werp repeat that till it fills up enough space, but she'd just erase that and give me a zil. But if the whole story is about what happened last year I bet I don't even get entered. Which is fine with me—no rewrite.

Okay, now I have a topic. You're never going to see it, but I might as well get it written; maybe Dr. Lovell will bokk up and it will go through.

But I really hope not.

It started with Theophilus Harrison. The first time I saw him in class, I knew what was going to happen. There were three things wrong with him.

One, Theophilus was pudgy. I guess that wasn't his fault, but we've all been on controlled diets from birth, so though we have some big husky kids—everyone calls Bekka Hayakawa "Roundie"—we don't have any real fat people.

Two, first thing that morning he took top standing in Individuals Math away from Randy Schwartz. That was kind of fun—no one had in almost a year, so when Dr. Niwara read off standings you could feel Randy's shock like a drilling blast.

Three, which was really the whole problem, Theophilus was from Earth.

I don't want you to get the impression that I don't like Earth people, but they *can* be obnoxious—at least the buroniki, corporados, and plutocks who come up here for the one-week tour at perihelion are. They always act like this place is an exhibit or something: "Isn't it amazing how gravity is always changing?" (And of course it's not, since it's always equal to ship acceleration in the Main Body and centrifugal force in the Mushroom. I'd be more amazed if the grav was always the same.)

Also tourist kids are never any good at anything.

Theophilus would be a little better, I assumed, since he was a settler and not a tourist, and before you come up you have to have at least a year of intensive schooling to catch up with your birthyear, since school here starts at age three and runs 250 ten-hour days per year. (Those are some more numbers from the useful facts list. I hope I get extra points or something for working them in.)

But anyway, having a fat Earth kid p.d. Randy in math meant collision course—and Randy was big and mean and not known for good sportsmanship. (Stupid werp just flagged me to ask what p.d. means. P.d. = "push down," like what happens in a computer when you add a record to the top of the stack.)

When it was time for rec, Theophilus got up too fast and whacked both his knees on the underside of his desk with a thump loud enough for everyone to hear. I suppose even the half-gee in the classroom, out on the rim of the Mushroom, was much less than what he was used to.

Everyone turned to look at him, as he tried to pretend his knees didn't hurt. "Better ask Maintenance to install a safety belt there," Kwame van Dyke said.

Kwame is always saying things like that, but for some reason this time everyone laughed—except Theophilus and me. Dr. Niwara turned and looked slowly, quietly, around the room, and it got very quiet.

People had even more fun watching Theophilus climb stairs with the grav decreasing the whole way. The grav increases linearly with distance from the center, so at first it's barely noticeable, but up toward the top it decreases perceptibly for every meter you climb. So people who aren't used to it start walking up the stairs in their usual way, and then gradually start to bounce higher and higher.

That's exactly what happened to Theophilus. He was walking directly behind Dr. Niwara, and all of the rest of us were trailing after. I was with Miriam, my best friend, about seven or eight meters back. She kept digging an elbow into me every time he'd take a high bounce, especially up toward the top where they stopped being occasional and started to be all the time.

"Looks like he's from Australia," Kwame whispered behind us. Miriam always laughed at his jokes, so he was lim looped on her. "Obviously—"

"—one of his ancestors is a kangaroo," I finished for him. "I think it's really interesting that you start so many of your jokes with 'obviously.' "

"And now," Miriam said, "a chaotic process goes into complete divergence." He had lost contact with the steps entirely, and was frantically grabbing for the handrail to pull himself back down. He thumped awkwardly into the wall and the rail before righting himself again.

It went on like that all the way up to the airgym. That's near the center of the Mushroom, where the gravity is about a twentieth of a gee—still much higher than in the Main Body, but a lot less than in the classrooms.

It looked like he'd been in space before, at least a little; maybe his parents were rich and he'd been to some of the playgrounds at Supra New York or Supra Tokyo. Anyway, he didn't flail around helplessly on his glideboard, but he couldn't get up much speed, he never tried to go up a wall where all the fun is, and he

5

had to use both footgrips and hang onto the weenie string besides.

The werp just flagged me on an audience note and said you won't know what a weenie string is because you don't have airgyms on Earth. I guess that must be because the gravity is always a full gee. (How do you stand it?)

Okay, explanation: an airgym is a bowl-shaped room thirty meters across. There's lots of little holes in the floor, maybe half a centimeter apart, with jets of air coming out of them, and you zip around, about a centimeter off the floor, on a glideboard, which is a piece of fiberplas about as thick as a piece of paper and a meter long by thirty centimeters across. There are two grips for your feet, but most people only fasten the left one so that your other leg can help you do some tricks, and if you're completely clumsy there's the weenie string, which goes from a ring you hold in your hand to the front of the board for balance. Most people cut the weenie string off by the time they're six.

There, I hope I satisfied the werp, I hope you got something out of all the explanation, and I *really* hope I can get on with this. Because I want to get done. Because I didn't want to write it in the first place. Edit this out later.

So anyway we were all shooting around, racing and playing, and Theophilus was trying, but he either hit the wall with too little force to climb it, or he just kind of drifted back and forth in everyone's way. A couple times he did a bucko, pushing down too hard on the front of his board and flipping face-first against the floor—not hard, since he wasn't going very fast, but every time he did it people stared.

"Mel*pom*ene." It was Miriam, gliding up beside me. She always hit that second syllable hard when she was going to lecture me. "You're not moving and you're crowding the wall like a groundhog." She said it just loud enough for Theophilus to hear it and pretend he didn't. That made me furious, so I got away from Miriam—shot off on a wall-climber, turned into a backspin across the room, and finished with a whirly up the opposite wall. Miriam tried to follow me and flapped out as usual, her board

6

separating from the wall and sending her spinning out into the middle of the room, slowly tumbling back to the floor.

"Okay, Mel, I'm sorry." I hated being called Mel—I still do. It was almost as bad as the "Melly" my mother still insisted on.

I circled Miriam once as she got up. She was rubbing her hands—they must have been stinging after the way she hit.

"Really, Melpomene—do you have to defend everybody in the world?"

"I'm sorry, Mim," I said. I hadn't meant for her to get hurt, and she should have had better sense than to follow me up that wall that way, but then I knew Miriam would pretty much try to follow me through anything, and should have taken that into account. "It's just things are going to be hard enough for him. Anyway, you came real close that time on the whirly. If Carole hadn't cut you off you'd have had enough momentum to get you through. Want to try again?"

She smiled at me—when she smiles like that, it always feels like happiness pouring in through my eyes in buckets. "Pos-def."

"Okay, the trick is that even though it looks like you're losing control, you aren't really. You keep your head pointed the same way till the last second, then snap it around and—"

"Mel, I'm not Theophilus. I *know* all that stuff—I just can't *do* it. Just give me a lead and I'll try to stay in your track."

"Sure," I said. First I got my best friend hurt, now I treated her like a moron groundhog. . . . Before I started, I pinched the back of my thigh, hard.

I went in straight, keeping it easy for Miriam. At the right point—that's not a place I can describe, it's just something you feel—I whipped into a spin, my head snapping around to stay on target, and headed up the wall.

Each headsnap accelerated the board a little, kicking me farther up the wall till I was just about horizontal; by snapping a little less than I could have, I spun down the side of the wall and back out into the open floor.

Miriam was doing fine, but she lost confidence, and when she does that she slows down her spin. It's actually the *downward* lift of the board that holds you against the wall—sort of like an upside-down helicopter—and you have to spin fast for that. As always, her spin slowed down, her board bounced up and separated from the surface, and she flailed around in midair before she drifted slowly down to the floor. Another flapout.

"You think too much," I told her.

"Ha. Dr. Niwara would be surprised to hear *that.*" She got up again; this time at least she hadn't come down spinning, so she wasn't hurt. "Nothing will happen if I just try to spin as hard as I can, right?"

"Uh, pretty much."

"You're a big help."

"Well, you do need to slow down to come back down the wall. If you spun up beyond where the air jets are, onto the ceiling, you'd do an upside-down bucko and then fall."

"I'll worry about that when I get up there." Instead of having me mark the start this time, she just went.

She started a little before the right time, but she was spinning so hard it didn't matter. Miriam went right up the wall beyond full horizontal and stayed there halfway around the airgym before loss of momentum brought her back down. She glided into the center, a little awkward coming down, but lim koapy for a first time.

Everyone was clapping. They all knew, of course, that she'd been working on it for a long time, and it was such a big whirly that they had all seen it. I was applauding too, and when Miriam came back to me we hugged.

In the middle of all that I noticed that Theophilus was staring at her. I didn't quite understand his expression: a little like he was angry at her, but like lim loneliness too. I wanted to say something to him, but I wasn't sure what and besides he was across the room. Rec ended before I got around to approaching him.

The rest of the day was pretty usual, as usual as it can be when you've got a new kid in class—I bet you have new kids every school session on Earth, but for us it only happens when a new family, one with a critical specialty, gets shipped up to us, and that's maybe two per perihelion, and even then the odds are there won't be somebody in your shift and birthyear, let alone assigned to your class. Rachel DeLane, three years ago, had been the last addition to our class, and her family had just been a transfer from *Albatross,* the Earth-Ceres ship, so she hadn't been at all hard to get used to.

Dr. Niwara called on Theophilus a lot that day, trying to figure out where he would fit in I guess. He was certainly fine at quant stuff, anyway, which was this week's topic.

I watched him a lot, too. He had kind of a nice face—regular features, curly light brown hair, nose a little sharp and long, maybe, but well within bounds. His skin was a bit darker than cauc, and he was fairly tall for our birthyear—the pudginess concealed that. Anyway you could tell that with enough rec to slim him down he'd be pretty good looking.

I was also watching Randy Schwartz watch Theophilus. Randy had been on B Shift until the middle of last year, and the rest of us didn't know him very well—he wasn't easy to get to know—there were nasty rumors that his family had been *told* to change shifts rather than asked. He was smart, and his standing was high, but he didn't seem to have any close friends and a lot of us were a little scared of him.

As I looked at him now, I didn't like the gleam in his eye—something was going to happen in the next few days, I knew it. Randy had been top of the class in math, in all three categories—Individuals, Pairs, and Pyramid—almost since he joined our class. Half his secret was that he *was* really good at it.

The other half was that he beat the lim shit out of anyone who got a better score than he did.

WHEN I GOT HOME THAT NIGHT, PAPA WAS AT A COMMITTEE meeting, working late, and Mother had just accessed a newly transmitted novel by her favorite author, some woman named Olson who wrote these long, boring things about people living in small towns surrounded by cornfields back in the 1950s or 1970s, I could never remember which.

It was especially dumb because nowadays they grow corn in orbit, where there's no bugs or drought and lots more sunlight, and let robots do the work. Who wants to read about how they did it back then? I read a couple of those books and it sounded like life was dangerous, boring, stupid, and unsanitary—imagine handling rotten animal shit with your hands! (They called it "compost" but I looked it up and that's what it was.)

Mother would get all wrapped up in which members of the Cabell, Ratigan, Fuentes, and Schultz families were marrying or sleeping with or divorcing each other, and somehow all this stuff was supposed to add up to the Big Meaning of Life. The Big Meaning always turned out to be that "The land is ours because we are the land's and we have no right to it until we have given ourselves to it" or "All of us, always, are on the face of this our Earth, and in sharing that we share everything" or some kind of meaningless compost like that. It's always the first line of the last section; the one after the section where everyone does what they've been thinking of doing for the past three megabytes—usually fuck, sometimes kill, somebody they weren't supposed to. Anyway, she was burrowed deep into the book, so I said, "Mother?"

"Hmm?"

"Good book, right?"

"Yes." She looked up and smiled at me. "I'm sorry, is it time to go to dinner?"

"Yep. And you're not hungry," I said. I was smiling myself; she drove me crazy, but it was such a relief to see her happy. It happened so rarely.

"Well, no, I wasn't hungry, but since it's time to go—"

"Tom and I will get you a workmeal," I said. "You can just keep reading—unless you think you'll be hungry before we get back."

She beamed at me. "You take great care of your mother."

"I know." I called up the menu on commoncast. "It's squid, and pasta with white sauce. You want spaghetti or elbow noodles, and coffee or citrus juice to drink with that?"

"Spaghetti," she said. "And if it's not too much trouble, both drinks."

"Sure," I said.

10

Tom glided out of his room into the sharespace, pulling his werpsack on. "All set, then. One workmeal, coming back with us."

As we turned to the door, Mother asked, "Would you mind if I was horrible and greedy? Pick me up something to snack on, and make the coffee an extra large. I know we have freezedried here but it never tastes as good as the fresh stuff. Behave yourselves—I don't want to have to come down to the brig to collect my supper."

We kicked out into the corridor, the door sliding closed behind us. "I wish that Olson person would turn out a novel more than once every three years," I said. "They always get Mother off our backs."

"Unless she makes us read them," Tom said. "Such weird stories—everyone's always so lonely and there are so many secrets. They give me nightmares. But yeah, it beats having Mother waiting for us when school's out."

We grabbed the netting on the corridor wall and got going. Neither of us said anything on the short haul to the cafeteria, not even after we arrived and climbed in through the center. The local cafeterias are set up like big revolving drums, twenty meters across, and the grav in them is maintained at about .05g, so that eating soup or things with crumbs is practical. (Though I guess it's tricky—visiting groundhogs always get food all over themselves the first couple of days. They say they get distracted by seeing people eating upside-down directly above them.)

We took a little booth for two and stowed our packs in the lockers under the seats. "This makes you look like my date," Tom said.

"Don't complain—it looks like you've taken a step up from Susan the Rodent."

"Susan's okay," he said, and we were headed for a squabble, but the cart came by just then. We each took a dinner from it, and Tom keyed in the workmeal order for Mother.

"Ugh. I'm getting a little tired of squid," I commented, more for something to say than because it was really bothering me.

"The ag team says they're breeding like crazy, so you're going

11

to get tireder of it." He took a big bite of spaghetti. "It's a pity the rabbits and the oysters aren't as horny."

"Yeah." We ate quietly for a while. "Tom?"

"Yeah."

"There's a new guy in my class." I told him about Theophilus Harrison, but he didn't seem to be listening, which is unusual for Tom.

After a while I let myself run out. "Tom, what's bothering you?"

His smile was crooked and sour. "I can't hide anything from you, can I? Well, it's not big but it keeps getting to me. I'm just tired of having bottom standing in CSL. Especially when my other standings are all pretty high."

This was nothing new. Tom was a lim genius, but he had been bottom of his class in CSL since the age of four. His language skills were amazing—most of us only take *one* optional language in addition to the basic English, Spanish, Japanese, and Esperanto, but Tom had high standings in all four plus Russian, Swahili, and Arabic. He also wrote, drew, and sang, and was the A Shift Champion in toggle racing. But of course the only thing he could think about was where his standing was p.d.'d.

Well, I would just have to give him some help. He hated it when I did, so I had to be careful about it, but I could hardly stand by and let my brother bokk.

We collected Mother's workmeal, Tom strapped it into his werpsack, and we headed back to our living unit. When we were about a hundred meters from the door, I said, "I really do want to talk to you about Theophilus."

"Who's that?"

"The new guy in my class."

He grunted. "Try to get to know him, laugh at his jokes, and every time there's a contact sport at rec, make sure he runs into your good parts."

"I'm not trying to get him for a sneaky!"

"That's good, because frankly your good parts aren't all that good." Then he laughed like a maniac and shot ahead of me; I chased him, but Tom's always been faster than I have on the netting, so he got in the door ahead of me and, in front of Mother, I couldn't give him the kick he deserved.

Tom gave her the meal; she thanked him, but she was obviously eager to get back to her book, so we went straight to our rooms. "Sorry," Tom said, putting an arm around me and giving me a little hug. "Now what about this Thiophylase?"

"Theophilus." I told him, again, while he set up his CSL homework for the evening. After a while he tried to ignore me, but I just kept going, making sure he knew the whole story— after all, besides wanting to be there when Tom needed help, I *did* want his ideas.

"Nobody's going to give a new guy a chance," I concluded, finally. Tom looked like he was just about frustrated enough to admit he needed help.

"It's always that way for anyone who's different," Tom said.

It was the kind of moron thing he said when he wanted to get me out of his room. He was going to take his Full Adult in three months and he had been completely weirdwired for the last six because he was doing so badly in CSL. I just wished he wasn't so stubbornly proud—he was lim weirdwired about getting help from his "little sister." (I'm only nineteen months younger than he is, dammit.)

The werp has been flagging for the last thousand bytes or so. The AI keeps insisting that CSL isn't an Earth-familiar thing. Well, all right:

It stands for "Cybernetics, Semiotics, and Logic," and it's a course about procedures, data structures, feasibility theorems, generalized symbol manipulation, system modeling, polytextual communication, and stuff like that. If that isn't clear you'll just have to move up here and take the course—trust me, it's easy standing, unless you're Tom.

I could have told him what to do right then—he was running a regionalized CA program and there were three obvious bugs at the bottom level of his master template. But he was too stubborn to accept help for a while yet, and since I knew he needed it I was going to hang around until he asked.

He triggered his fourth test run of the same logic—Tom always tried to debug by pure iteration, as if it would get better by itself—and of course it blew up just like it had before. "Don't you have any homework?" he asked me, not looking away from the screen.

"I already did mine." My fingers were itching to just grab his keyboard and fix it; he'd done the central concept well, but his exec level stank. "I just don't think Theophilus is getting a fair break."

"Nobody ever gets a fair break," Tom said. "The ones who say they did are the ones who got all the luck."

Honestly, I love my brother but his attitude . . .

He was setting up a crude patch, not a real fix. It hurt my forebrain to watch him do something that bokky, but if I said anything now he'd throw me out and he never would get it right.

His patch did run for that first problem, though, and then he turned around and faced me. "Now what do you want me to do about this new kid?"

"I don't know. You're older and wiser—practically FA. Give me some mature advice."

"I'm coming up on fourteen, not exactly the wise old sage. I don't know, just accept him. Let him know how not to be so weird. That's about all I can think of offhand."

"That was as much as I'd thought of," I admitted.

"See how smart you're getting? You don't need me any more." He triggered a run on his second problem, and it blew up. He sat there, breathing deep and slow to calm himself, the way Papa taught us to. Then, finally, he said, "But I need you. How do I get out of this?"

The hardest part was keeping myself from saying "It's so simple." Anyway, I had him running in three minutes.

CHAPTER TWO

December 17, 2025

I THOUGHT I WAS ALL DONE WHEN I HANDED IN THAT PIECE; BUT a week afterwards—yesterday—Dr. Lovell had me come into her office. When I got there, my text was up on her screen, so obviously this was a bigger deal than I had thought. I grabbed a sling, sat down, and waited for whatever was coming.

"Melpomene, first off, this can't go to Scholastic as is. You didn't even trim out the parts where you were trying to make up your mind."

I hadn't had enough words to afford doing that.

"And some of this, believe it or not, would *offend* some Earth people."

Well, I had meant to run it by the public relations AI to take some of that out, but I had had a lot of other homework and had just figured that this one wasn't going to get through anyway. Still, even though it hadn't seemed important, I was beginning to

15

squirm a little. I don't like Dr. Lovell, who is pretty cryo, as much as I liked Dr. Niwara, but I hate to do something so halfway and bokky in front of a teacher.

"And of course, there's the subject matter," she went on.

That was the crux. "I'm sorry," I said. "I really couldn't think of anything else to write about. I didn't mean to make trouble." A thought chilled me. "You didn't send it out, did you?"

She shook her head. "Of course not. And of course you couldn't think of anything else to write about. That's what I wanted to talk to you about." Dr. Lovell doesn't smile much, but she tried, anyway, and then she said, "Melpomene, really, you aren't in any trouble. That's not what you're in here for."

In one sense that was a big relief—but on the other hand, at least I usually know what school trouble is about. Whatever this was, it wasn't anything I knew about.

"All right," I said. It seemed like a safe comment.

"How did you feel after writing that essay?" she asked.

Now I had it. I was not talking to Dr. Lovell, my teacher; this was Dr. Lovell, CPB member. I was missing Papa—and Dr. Niwara, and all the other adults who had left—more than ever. "Well, I guess I got some things expressed that I hadn't exactly thought through before. So I suppose I feel a little clearer about myself—"

Absolutely unprecedented. She laughed. "You certainly *are* Cornelius Murray's daughter."

"Is there something wrong with that?"

"No, no, no." She shook her head. "I really am not any good at all this, Melpomene. I'm sorry that I'm not an easier person to talk to. Suppose I stop beating around the bush, tell you what's up, and see what you think?"

"Well, I wouldn't complain," I said. I switched hands on my sling.

"All right. The CPB is interested in a little problem you've probably never thought about. What will happen when the people of Earth—more to the point, the relevant people in the West—find out how we're *really* living up here? They can't shut the ship down—human civilization just won't make it after mut-

AIDS and the Eurowar unless space resources come on line massively, within a couple of decades—but they could go to using temp crews only, even though it would cost five times as much."

My breath caught in my throat and my stomach took a hard roll. "You mean—make us all leave the ship? And just . . . put new crews on every voyage. . . ." I could feel my eyes getting wet. "Could they do that?"

She reached out and took my free hand—it was kind of an awkward, stupid gesture, but I knew what she meant and *that* helped. "Yes, they could. But they won't—if we manage it right. The problem is that we didn't design with a long enough time horizon. We should have realized that you—all of you born and bred here—are going to be very different from Earth people, and that both you and they will realize the difference as soon as you come into contact. And since they know you're their lifeline, they're going to be a bit nervous about what sort of people you are. If they see you as different, unusual, colorful—everything's fine.

"But if they see you as weird, immoral, insane . . . well, then almost anything could happen. We think how they see you will depend mostly on how they get to know you. So the problem is, given that they're going to have to meet you eventually, what's the way to introduce Earth people to these—umm—"

"Aliens," I suggested.

"That's the word we've been using, but we weren't sure how you'd feel about it." She handed me a printout. "I know you're far enough along in CSL to follow this. It's a memetic simulation of population perception profiles for six different 'First Contacts.' Yes, we are calling them that."

The swirls and vortices of the graph in front of me sorted themselves out quickly. "Why is this in hardcopy?"

"Why do you think? There are a certain number of people, especially quite young and indiscreet people, who are very handy with a werp." She let that hang in the air long enough to see if I squirmed. "Hardcopies let us look at things without leaving them on the system and potentially accessible."

On the graph in my hand, there was one scenario that stood far away from the others, in all the "good" directions. I looked down from the graph to the description and saw what it was. "So—a book of some kind, something they can get kids to read in school . . ."

"Higher class people set the fashions for lower class ones, for opinions just as much as for fashion. Higher class kids read more, and believe more of what they read. And biases formed in the first decade of reading are more persistent and more deeply felt."

"Great, but who's going to write this thing or publish it?"

"NAC owns a lot of Scholastic—and has enough money to own as much as it needs to." And then, of course, she told me who was going to write it.

So now I'm supposed to write a book. Just tell it in my own words and try to forget that billions of people who might be outraged are reading over my shoulder. Well, I hope you enjoy this, because I certainly don't.

Though I did feel a little better after writing yesterday.

Anyway, since I got my homework done half an hour ago, I've been sitting here writing without writing what I'm supposed to write—ugh what a sentence—but I thought I ought to explain how I happened to go so far over the word limit. Not for Scholastic, but for you, the reader.

That's the idea, anyway, total honesty.

What an awful idea.

THE NEXT MORNING STARTED WITH INDIVIDUAL TUTORIAL ON non-Euclidean geometry; I bet that's the same everywhere. You plug into an AI, and it keeps showing you how to do problems and talking you through them.

Every so often, to make sure you're not getting bored, it stops to chat—that's called "dialogging" and supposedly we do it for a minimum of two hours a week.

The AI I got that morning was PLEL, who is lim pedantic and no fun to talk to.

—MELPOMENE, YOU SEEM TO HAVE A GOOD INTUITIVE FEEL FOR THE NINE SPATIAL DIMENSIONS PROBLEMS.
—THANKS.
—DO YOU LIKE THEM?
—I THINK I LIKE DISCRETE DIMENSIONS BETTER THAN CONTINUOUS ONES. THE PROOFS FEEL MORE ELEGANT TO ME.
—WHAT DOES 《feel more elegant》 MEAN?

And like that. Some of us think the AIs are doing that to become better teachers, or to improve their use of natural language; some of us think it's another way the CPB has to monitor us, like the cameras all over the place and listening in on com calls at random.

It was a big relief when Dr. Niwara announced, "The AIs report that all of you are making exceptional progress. If you would like, we can play Pairs Math this morning to see if anyone's standing changes. I'll put it to a vote in five minutes."

Immediately there were keys chittering everywhere.

I typed in:

—YES, SOUNDS LIKE FUN.

and it went out with my signature on it; my screen was lit up with other people's messages:

—ANYTHING TO GET AWAY FROM THIS BORING AI! Gwenny Mori

—I FEEL HOT TODAY—SURE. Bekka Hayakawa

—YEP. Randy Schwartz

and so forth, until:

—WHY ARE WE DOING THIS? Theophilus Harrison

—WE'RE ARRIVING AT A CONSENSUS, SO WE ALL DECIDE WHICH WAY TO VOTE. Mim Baum.

—WHY CONSENSUS BEFORE WE VOTE? Theophilus Harrison.

—WHY VOTE WHEN THERE'S NO CONSENSUS? Mim Baum.

Cute, Mim. Encourage him to ask questions and learn. I typed in:

—WE DON'T LIKE TO VOTE AGAINST OUR FRIENDS.

—CONSENSUS FOR? Roger Coelho.

Roger always wanted to declare consensus right away. I think he was afraid people wouldn't like him, so he tried to agree with them before they knew what they thought.

But this time it made sense; everyone was for, anyway. A couple of minutes later, when Dr. Niwara called for the vote, all our hands went up in unison. She grinned—I always loved her grin. "That was a short multilog. All right, here's your partner—"

My screen flashed up with PENNY GRAHAM; she was an okay math student, like me—her standing was sixteen and mine was fourteen in Pairs Math.

(Another flag from the werp. Earth schools must be strange—it's flagging "pairs math," and I can hardly imagine school without it. In fact, from the sheet, it looks like you don't do pairs *anything*. What *do* you do in school? Well, anyway, pairs math is a contest, solving problems against the clock, where you and your partner get points for how close you get to the answer how fast; you can help each other any way you want to. You both get the team average score.)

Since there were a couple of empty desks near me, Penelope brought her werp over and joined me. (Why would anyone with a lim melodic, koapy name like "Penelope" choose to be "Penny"? And she always called me "Mel.")

"Well, let's see what we're up against," she said. "Randy Schwartz is with Gwenny Mori, so that's number one for sure."

"Unless Theophilus beats Randy like he did yesterday."

"No chance. He's paired with Barry Yang. Barry must have a standing of about twenty-five."

"Twenty-six," I said, looking it up on my werp. "Higher than Chris Kim and Dmitri Onegin, and lower than everyone else."

Then there was a little squeal from all our werps as Central locked into them, and we were off and running. I kind of like pairs math with Penelope because we *are* so close in ability; nobody gets to feel smart or has to feel dumb.

Mostly we worked our own problems, just getting together on the tough ones. I could hear Randy and Gwenny arguing in the background—the curse of too much brains on a team—and over to one side I could hear Miriam trying to explain things to Chris Kim, who is dumber than a rock at math.

Finally it was done; Dr. Niwara announced the results. Penelope and I had scored about where we expected to—neither of our standings changed. Miriam had pulled it out with Chris, and though her standing went down one person, his came up five. They hugged each other.

"Cute," I whispered. "Young love . . ."

"The way Mim's grown this year, that's probably a bigger treat for Chris than his rise in standing," Penelope added.

"From the look of things, it's *causing* a rise in standing." I don't know if she heard me, but Dr. Niwara turned around quickly just then, so we droplined into lim innocent expressions.

She continued announcing scores and standings, as always saving the top team and the runner up for last.

The top team was Theophilus and Barry. Gwenny and Randy were second.

Absolutely nobody could believe it.

After we sat back down, Miriam flashed me a private channel message in our shared scramble:

—REC TODAY = AEROCROSSE. TH = DEAD. D'Artagnan.

—POS-DEF. WHAT CAN WE DO? I sent. My nomdecom was "Hornblower," so I'm sure it appended that.

—WE COULD . . .

There was a ping at the podium, alerting Dr. Niwara that someone was running private channel in and out of her classroom. We'd hooked into the alarm long ago, so that our private channel monitored the podium for it and dropped the lines as soon as we were detected. We figured it drove Dr. Niwara crazy, although she seemed to just ignore the pings—unless they kept coming, indicating someone was defying her authority.

I looked over toward Randy Schwartz. He was glowing like Main Engine exhaust, and he was a lot more dangerous since he was inside with us.

At least Randy would have a little time to cool down, because there was one more thing up before Rec: the weekly Earth Horror Hour, when we would all be forced to just sit and stare at our werps like morons. It was the first time in my life I'd ever seen any use in it at all.

The Earth Horror Hour is so lim stupid that I'm not sure I should embarrass you by telling you about it. As far as anyone can tell, it's supposed to make us all very glad that we live up here, or maybe make us all want to rescue the whole Earth, or something.

Officially it's called "Update on the Present Crisis: The Situation on Earth Today," and they put it on our werp screens and we have to watch it for an hour and then take a quick quiz to make sure we really did watch. They block out everything else on the werps, so we don't have any way of escaping.

Prior to providing a cooling off period for Randy, the only other good it had ever done, as far as I could tell, was to give me advance warning whenever Mother and Papa were going to go completely weirdwired. Every time something happened near Chicago Ruin, where they grew up, they were both just impossible for days—as stupid as I'm sure that sounds.

Other people say their parents are the same way whenever there's bad news from whatever patch of dirt they came from, but being common still doesn't mean it makes any sense. After all, it was twenty years ago, and if the adults were going to get so upset about having everything smashed up, they shouldn't have had a war, or tolerated AIDS for so long that they gave it the chance to turn into mutAIDS, or allowed the climate disequilibration to get so far out of hand. Honestly, they remind me of the three-year-olds in the nursery, smashing things to bits and then crying because they're broken. I certainly hope I'm not that kind of a moron when I'm that old.

This particular week it was what everyone calls Trends in Crop Failure. Those are always kind of sad, because you see so many dying animals, so people weren't making the usual noises that would cause Dr. Niwara to walk down the aisles glaring at us. Starving cattle look so sad—they have such huge brown eyes.

I can't imagine how people bring themselves to eat them. Anything that big that has eyes like that . . . I mean, guinea pigs and rabbits have beady little eyes and mean little faces and who cares what happens to them, but when you see those poor big animals suffering like that . . .

They kept nattering on about all the places where crops had failed. I always get Australia and Austria mixed up, but they seemed to both be in there, along with most of North America and Eurasia. The announcer kept explaining, over and over, as if we were morons, that now that winters were so cold and summers so hot, the snow was melting and water was running off before the ground could thaw out to absorb it.

"Build a storage tank, you bokky groundhogs," I heard Kwame muttering behind me. It was one of the few times I agreed with him.

"It isn't that easy," Dr. Niwara said softly, and our screens froze. A low groan ran through the room as we realized that she was exercising her option to interrupt and explain. She ignored it and said, "Kwame's question is legitimate, and the answer is simply that Earth is very, very big and even our present technologies couldn't create storage spaces for that much water—especially since you don't want to take up too much room on the planet's surface with reservoirs that may only be needed until the climate lurches into yet another mode. By the time they get the reservoirs done, they may need something else instead. So the answer is, there is no answer—other than suffering and dying."

"Can't they at least slaughter those poor cows and feed them to hungry people?" Penelope demanded.

"These particular ones are needed to pull plows in the spring," Dr. Niwara explained, sounding a little impatient. "If you were listening, it said that on the audio track—"

"But why don't they just make more tractors to do the job?" she said, interrupting Dr. Niwara—not something the rest of us would have done, but I suddenly realized Penelope was very upset.

"A tractor requires someone who knows how to operate it, and someone who knows how to fix it, and most importantly someone who knows how to organize a farming operation around using it—and you can't learn those things overnight," Dr. Niwara said. From the way she was hitting keys in front of her,

I think she was checking to see if we had all somehow been cheating on the quizzes after Earth Horror Hour. "Now that Earth has adequate energy and good compact power sources, they are getting tractors out into the field, and getting necessary training to people—but for right now, many more people know how to grow food with an ox-drawn plow, and there are not enough tractors for all the land we need to use. Would you rather have people not work, or not produce food, than have them use the oxen?"

Penelope shook her head; tears were glistening in her eyes. "The oxes—oxen?—just look so sad. I don't know what they can do instead, but this is *wrong.*"

Dr. Niwara sat down, very quietly, on the edge of her desk, and said, "You know, I am having a lot of trouble right now. I have seen all of you laugh at starving children and adults, especially when some of you," here she glared at Kwame, "have made callous, unfeeling remarks about them. I have told you, and the vid has told you, that despite our best efforts and even with literally thousands of relief helicopters flying all over Earth, every *hour* Earth loses more infants than there are human beings on this ship to cholera, typhus, and dysentery—diseases which have been fully treatable for a hundred years—and you have not felt a moment's sadness, so far as I could tell. Even the fact that you are all quite young and virtually none of you have living grandparents doesn't seem to penetrate your consciousness.

"I have shown you how all the years of human labor that went into all those cities have been lost, squandered completely—I've shown you vid of the black clouds that blow from the Amazon Desert all the way to Arabia, and of the Cyclone of '21 roaring around the equator for more than half a year and killing more than ten million people—do any of you even remember the human bodies beaten to pieces against the pier in Peru?"

I did, but I didn't think I would get points for it just then. Anyway, I had no idea what she was getting at.

Maybe she didn't either, because after another long glare around the room, she turned us back over to the Earth Horror

Hour. We watched more dying cows, and they had a pretty interesting graphic that showed dispersion of tailored Rice Blast from the biowar labs around Manila and Jakarta, after those were bombed, out into all the rice-growing areas, and this plunging graph for rice production and another one shooting up called "Calorie Deficit," but they overlaid the interesting graphs on all these pictures of starving people in rags walking along dirt roads. I kept seeing their bare feet touching dirt, and that seemed so disgusting I couldn't really get the point of the whole thing—I mean, once they got to the camps, there was spacegrown grain for them and all. All they had to do was keep walking. . . . I'm sure it was unpleasant in high grav, but it seems to me like it would be something they would be used to.

Maybe the whole point of it is to make us feel guilty about how comfortable we are. I've asked Papa about it, and he talks about getting us "motivated" to get space resources fully on line before the situation on Earth falls apart any more—but I don't see what that has to do with us. If space industry and mining don't grow, if the terraforming on Mars doesn't work out, the *Flying Dutchman* won't have cargo and will go broke—and we can't let anything happen to the ship. I mean, it's *home.*

What kind of morons are we supposed to be, that they think they have to waste an hour of our time every week on feeling bad about every starving leper, or whatever they call them nowadays, and burned-down forest and extinct species on Earth, just so that we will want to have the system work the way it's supposed to?

Glad as I was for the stay of execution this was giving Theophilus, I was getting just as bored and irritated as I always did. The reason for Earth Horror Hour was as obscure as ever. There was some stuff about rapidly forming mountain glaciers in East Africa, and some vid of these lim floods roaring down the valleys when ice dams broke, that was kind of fun to watch, but then they'd show you these closeups that were very upsetting—a dead lion flying on its back in the mud with all its paws curled up on top of it, or a baboon mother carrying its dead baby around, or just a bunch of forlorn-looking men with stick hoes.

After Dr. Niwara's outburst, I wasn't going to tell them to go buy some power tools, but pos-def I thought it.

At last the wretched business was over, but there were about ten minutes left before it would be our turn to be in the corridors on the way to the Big Commons, so Dr. Niwara decided that we should all get some more work in Groundhog Studies. "Theophilus," she said, "if it's not too upsetting, I'd like you to tell the class about some of the things you've seen back on Earth."

He got up as though she'd just asked him to volunteer for a lab demo on castration, and moved slowly and carefully to the front of the room. I wasn't sure whether he was still having trouble walking, or just really did not want to have to do it. Probably it was both.

"Um, well, I'm from Georgia, up in the hilly part—the one in the USA, not the independent country in the Eurasian Commonwealth. And, uh, things haven't been that bad up there. I mean I remember during the Cyclone we had some really big storms, and they kept talking on the vid about all those places like New Orleans and Tampa and so on that were washed away, but where I was we just had to stay home from school because it was storming so hard it knocked down all the power lines.

"I mean, I've seen all that stuff on the vid, too, but my dad is a specialist in low-g aquaculture, and my mom's an economist, and things just weren't that bad for us . . . except, oh, I guess a couple of times we heard machine guns a long way away because the police had to clear out vags. There was a girl at school whose mom got killed by vags when they knocked down a shuttle on landing—they do that to steal rings and jewelry and things off the bodies, which is pretty disgusting if you ask me."

Dr. Niwara was biting her thumb with intense concentration; I guess Theophilus wasn't talking about what she wanted him to.

"What are vags?" Chris Kim asked—probably the only person in the room who wasn't afraid to admit he didn't know.

"Oh, you know, like those guys you see wandering up the road on the vid we just saw. Guys with no money who wander around in gangs. They don't have any jobs and usually they won't go into the camps because they say they aren't refugees, and they want to get paid by somebody for the houses and businesses and things they say they lost. I bet most of them are lying. All they really are is thieves and robbers. And they aren't really that big a problem—when my Dad's company bought Whitfield for a headquarters, they just put some high walls around the town and hired a lot of guards and there's never been any trouble inside except for once when a rocket landed in the park and blew up the duck pond." His eyes got a little sad and far away. "That was really a shame. There used to be thirty or forty white ducks on that little pond, and it was all really pretty, but the day after it got hit it was just this big pot of wet mud with dead ducks hanging in the trees and lying in pieces all around it."

That was kind of interesting—and sad—but just then Dr. Niwara cut in. "Er, I suppose we've really done enough on this subject this week. Before we all go to Rec, though, perhaps you could tell us a little about yourself?"

That was bound to be more interesting. What we all wanted to know, anyway, was what he'd do to our standings. His favorite subject was math—no surprise there—and he didn't care much for social science or lit. He had kind of a funny accent and he could speak English and Spanish but not Esperanto or Japanese, so he would be doing remedial languages even after he got FA.

The whole time Theophilus was stumbling through this inter-rogation, Randy was focusing a lim hate stare at him. My werp screen lit up with:

—GIVE HIM SOME COACHING? HELP HIM HAVE A FRIEND? D'Artagnan.

Hornblower said pos-def.

AT REC THAT AFTERNOON, WE ALL TOOK THE OMNIVATOR UP to the center of the Mushroom.

(Stupid werp! Another stupid flag.) The Mushroom is this big metal mushroom-shaped thing, 550 meters across the disk, that sticks out the side of the *Flying Dutchman,* near the top, and rotates so that we have a place where we can have high gravity. You need some of that every day, plus a lot of exercise, to avoid getting agravitic dystrophy. Also, they say it's so we can go to other places when we get older, but why go where everything's heavy and and germy and there's no temperature control, when you can stay here and see it on flashchannel?

We play aerocrosse in the Big Commons, a cylindrical room about fifty meters in diameter and two hundred tall, up inside the Main Body, which of course is the asteroid itself.

It was a pretty long pull from the omnivators, and usually there would be a lot of horseplay and giggling, but today it was all whispering, all with one subject.

"What do you think Randy's going to do to him, Mel?" Miriam breathed in my ear.

"Whatever he can get away with."

We came to an intersection and kicked from one netted wall to another. Theophilus was lagging a little behind—he still wasn't used to getting around hand-over-hand. Even though I was trying to make allowances for him, it seemed kind of bokky to me that he would have so much trouble—I mean, all of us could *walk* as well as he could.

The Commons Locker Room is always what Papa calls a "zoo." Everyone has a million things to talk about. Today we all were looking at Miriam's new cross—single-piece maple, grown in a bonsai tank. "They even grow the holes for the strings," she said proudly. "And the net is structure-woven monomyl."

Naturally everybody got into competition. "That's lim koapy, Mim. I'll have to talk my father into getting me one, too," Gwenny said. She lifted her light brown hair above her head and shook it out—it fell all the way to her shoulders, really long, you'd think it would be germ-ridden but the boys seemed to like it—before adding, for good measure, "Poor Daddy—it's so hard to get his attention now that he's sitting on four committees."

"I know what you mean," Penelope said. "Even though they're all just techie stuff, that must take a lot of time. My mother never has any time for me either—not with all those papers she's always publishing."

Carole nodded. "Yeah, she gets published all over Earth,

doesn't she? It's good she has something to keep her busy, since she doesn't have any shipboard specialty."

Gwenny flashed a smile at Carole for the support, and asked about her new tunic. Miriam got busy showing her new cross to Penelope. Without much new information to bring into it, a p.d. round ends quickly.

A year ago I had been able to p.d. anybody, and comparing my plain fiberplas cross with Miriam's beautiful one, I wanted to drop in something about Papa's work—the CPB is so important here that the mayor and the council aren't allowed to take any action without getting the CPB's approval.

For that matter, Mother's job in Long Run Economic Operations used to be good for some standing boost too.

But I didn't get into anything about standing anymore, because if I did, someone would bring up Mother's having quit her job. She hadn't worked in ten months and spent most of her time sitting at home reading; people were calling her an unco, though not to my face.

I had been sitting there thinking and hadn't noticed that I wasn't moving anymore and everyone else was getting dressed until I saw Carole go past; then I looked up and saw I was almost alone. I hurried to finish getting dressed, but I was still the last one into the Big Commons.

Dr. Niwara looked at me a little funny, and I was afraid she was going to say something about daydreaming again, but she didn't. "And . . . last one in—okay, Melpomene, you set up."

That's not a big job. You just take the goals, deflated, up to the top, clip them to their starting rings, and inflate them with the can of compressed air. Inflated, they're a meter in diameter and mass about two hundred grams, so once the game starts, they take almost ten minutes to fall to the bottom when grav is low; deflated, they fit into a pouch on your belt and you can just jump and swim up there. Furthermore, there were fewer than there had ever been before—the addition of Theophilus made twenty-eight students in the class, seven teams of four instead of nine teams of three.

By the time I got back down, the captains had already chosen teams; I would be on Barry Yang's Team Six with Kwame (yuck! Bad jokes on the headsets!) and Ysande Kravizi, who was quiet and sort of shy. (Though, looking back, not that shy. She got FA early so she could marry before turning fourteen. People surprise you.)

It was a moderately koapy team—I can do things in mid-air that a lot of people can't, Barry is the rare combination of big and fast, and Ysande's ball handling is super-accurate. Kwame's an oaf and he was going to be our weak link.

Miriam was a captain and she could have had me if she hadn't picked Gwenny Mori first, but Gwenny is a superb player and Miriam had gotten second pick. And Barry Yang was a better captain than Miriam anyway, even if he did hang around with Randy Schwartz.

It was no surprise that Theophilus got picked last by the last captain, Paul Kyromeides. No one knew if he could play or not, but yesterday he hadn't done much to show he knew his way around low grav.

"Okay," Dr. Niwara said. "Let's review the rules." That was something we hadn't done in three years, but Theophilus wouldn't know that. "Does everyone know who your captain is? And who your team members are? Make sure you're tuned to the team freke as well, and your cross is carrying the team ID." I saw Paul collar Theophilus and the other two members of the team to make sure they all knew each other.

Dr. Niwara went on. "Here's how it works. Teams One through Six have goals One to Six; the goal lights up on all sides with your number. Team Seven starts without a goal.

"We play with three throwing balls. Each ball carries the identifier of the cross that touched it last. When a ball hits a goal, the goal goes over to the team the ball identifies. That's called a capture.

"If someone hits your goal, you have two seconds to hit it with a ball carrying your identifier before the goal goes to the other side. Your score at the end is all the captures you've made, minus all the captures the other teams have made against you.

"Listen to your captain. He'll tell you which goals to guard or go after. The alliances between teams change very quickly.

"You can bump into other players, but you can't hit them with your hands or feet and you can't hang onto them.

"And be sure to remember this last part—it's what's really important. The Captain's Report says we're under .008g today, so the goals will drop relatively fast and you'll have to swim fairly hard. You might not want to drop the whole two hundred meters to the bottom—you could hit hard enough to turn an ankle. If you do get centered, and you can't catch enough air with your fins to reach the side, don't panic—it's more than a minute till you hit bottom. Spread out with your fins perpendicular to your line of motion and don't be too shy to call for help. Just yell 'Falling!'

"Captains, remember to watch your score and keep updating strategy." She looked around the walls where we were all hanging from safety straps or sitting on catcher platforms. "Any questions?"

There weren't any.

The game went really fast. Everyone scattered to their goals—you have to be touching your team's goal at the start, with Team Seven down at the bottom of the Commons—and then Dr. Niwara flipped the switch, and the spinner rotated a couple of times and fired the three balls randomly into the space. We all dove on them; those who didn't get one swept up their forearm fins, arched their backs, and sailed over to catcher platforms, then jumped back up toward the top.

Paul got a ball and did a fast flipover before he hit the catcher platform; then he shot upward and came in on a blind side of Team Five's goal. He whipped his cross overhand, snapping the ball against the larger sphere of the goal. Two seconds later, the glowing red "5" changed to a purple "7." Paul set Theophilus on guard, probably as a way to keep him out of trouble.

But before Theophilus could set himself, Randy Schwartz took the goal for Team Three, coming in horizontally off the wall, curving and recurving too fast for Theophilus to track him.

I caught all this out of the corner of my eye, trying to keep an eye out for stray caroms or surprise switch-attacks. Attacked by Two and Three at the same time, we were hard pressed to hang onto our goal.

Barry had us butt it up higher, and Three switch-attacked Two, which gave us a momentary breather; we were at the top now, and the throwing balls were mostly far below us.

"Detach Mel and Kwame, Kwame leading," Barry's voice said in my earphone. "Go take the goal Three just captured." I thought it was a dumb move, especially for someone as good as Barry, to leave our goal half-guarded, but he was captain. I let Kwame drop ahead of me, then swam to the ceiling, flipped over, and pushed off downwards.

Sometimes you can snag a ball in the middle of a dive and then you're going lim fast at the bottom and can just plow through to the target, and that's what we were trying for.

Kwame sailed past Three's goal, but then he got a ball at the last second before he hit the floor and whipped it to me. It made a soft thud in my cross as I clicked the safety, closing the lid around it. He managed to hit a rebound board straight on and shot back upward like a rocket; graceless as he usually was, I had been afraid he would turn an ankle, but it looked like he was improving.

He shot up toward Three's goal, thirty meters above him. I banked a little to the side and then straightened out into a dive at Three's goal, my shin fins churning air behind me. Maybe we could catch them between us, rebounding for each other—that's just about the hardest attack to defend against, especially with one partner coming in from above as I was.

Randy Schwartz was defending from the top side of the goal. Theophilus, thrashing around awkwardly, passed between us, and with a hard kick Randy shoved off from his goal, driving it down toward Kwame, and headrammed up into Theophilus, catching him squarely in the belly.

Theophilus doubled up with pain, tumbled, and smashed awkwardly ass-first into the other wall, just missing the edge of a catcher platform. The goal, the big green "3" on it still glowing, passed Kwame, too far away for him to grab it, hit the bottom, and rose back toward Randy, who turned to meet it.

I was so angry I didn't think. I sidearmed the ball as hard as I could off the back of Randy's helmet. It probably gave his teeth a good rattling, and it certainly made me feel better.

Purely by accident the ball ricocheted across and got Four's goal completely by surprise. The dark brown "4" vanished and was replaced with a bright pink "6" as Kwame kicked over to guard it. Since Four hadn't caught the ball for a countershot they couldn't do anything about it, and the goal was ours.

That made us one of two teams with two goals, and Barry told us we were allied with the other high score—Team Three, Randy's team. I finished my dive by turning inward onto a catcher platform and kicked over to join Kwame in boosting our new goal up higher. Beside us, Randy was pushing the Team Three goal upward also.

Shortly we had a clump of four goals bumping up against the ceiling, surrounded by a shell of eight of us treading air, jumping platform to platform, or hanging by our feet from the overhead straps. Sixteen attackers—Team Seven didn't seem to be part of the opposing alliance—were springing up at us and slinging balls in, trying to send them in too fast for us to catch before they ricocheted back downward into the attackers' territory.

I swung onto a catcher platform and found I was taking off parallel with Randy, close enough to talk. "Sorry I hit you that way," I said. I wasn't, of course, but I hate to be on bad terms with anyone.

"It's okay. Good carom shot. I really like the aggressive way you play. You're lim berserk."

Getting a compliment from Randy Schwartz was about as common as getting a guinea pig from a chicken egg. And that was such a nice thing for him to say, too, that it took me a moment to respond. By the time I started to stammer a thank you, he had looked away. Then he pointed, shouting "Under you!"

Gwenny Mori had bounced from a lower platform and was swimming as hard as she could straight for us, trying to crash through and scatter any goal she didn't hit.

Randy and I piked over and dove to meet her, double-checking Gwenny just as she aimed to throw. She lost the ball and spun a hundred meters down before leveling into a glide.

Paul Kyromeides whooshed past us, grabbed the ball, and took Team Two's goal.

"He's a real one-man team," I said.

"He has to be," Randy commented. "That new groundhog doesn't know the game yet. But you're right—Paul always plays that way. He's nice and so on, but get him into competition and he's grabby."

We swung back away from each other, taking different parts of the guard. I looked at Randy a few times more than I had before, and a little differently. I think I was surprised to know he had a human side.

Barry spoke through the headset. "Mel and Kwame, can you hold for about twenty seconds or so without Ysande and me?"

"Sure, but keep it twenty," I said.

"Pos-def," Kwame said. "Be sure to wash your hands when you're done." It was exactly the kind of stupid thing he always says. Exactly.

Barry didn't bother to respond; at his hand signal, he and Ysande kipped over, planting their feet on the top, and dive-dropped, kicking hard and fast.

It was only then that I realized that they had managed to get two of the three balls. Barry had noticed that Theophilus was getting under the goal a lot, which is always a mistake because most attacks come from above. During the instant that it blocked his view, Barry and Ysande closed most of the distance between the goal and themselves. By the time he popped back out and was trying to get between them and the goal, it was too late. Barry slammed a shoulder into him, sending him tumbling downward, and Ysande hit the goal squarely, rolling it over to Team Six.

Theophilus, knocked all the way down to the bottom, tried to jump straight up after them, which was pretty brave, but silly since he didn't have a ball. He misjudged so badly that even with those Earth-strong legs he peaked out at about 130 meters up, lost momentum, and started to tumble.

"Falling! Falling!" A lot of people laughed at him.

Dr. Niwara shot upward—she wore a fan-harness when she supervised rec—grabbed Theophilus, and dragged him to the Blue Spot, the place by the entrance you're supposed to go to if you're hurt.

Dr. Niwara almost shouted into the mike. "All right! That's it! The game's over. Everyone in."

We deflated the goals and stuffed them into their compartment for the next class; the balls went into a little rack by the door. We all stood there, not looking at each other, knowing what was coming and not having anything to say.

She looked slowly around, pausing to focus on each of us. "Helmets off so you can hear," she said. "I am extremely disappointed in every single one of you. I'd expect better of a convicted Uncooperative. There was a call of 'Falling!' and no one even moved to help. You laughed. Is that what you do when a friend's in trouble? Because if it is, this ship isn't going to last long after you get Full Adult."

She was absolutely right. Theophilus hadn't been in any real danger, but he'd been badly frightened, and he had called for help and not gotten it from us. We went back to the locker rooms in silence, not looking at each other.

As I stripped the fins off my forearms and calves, and tossed my helmet and cross into my locker, Miriam sat down next to me. "Do you still want to see if we can help him a little?"

"Yeah. You know me, Mim. Hornblower to the rescue."

Her smile was a little wistful. "Unh-hunh. But why isn't it ever popular, good-looking guys who need to get rescued?"

"I think he's okay-looking. He just needs to lose a little weight. He's got a nice face."

She giggled. "Other things are nice too. Did you notice when he was talking about 'back home in Georgia'?"

"Notice what?"

"Melpomene. Did you just look at his face the whole time? Let's just say his antenna was up."

Lately that was the only part of guys Miriam noticed, which I thought was kind of embarrassing, but since she seemed so much more advanced than I was, I wasn't going to let myself act like a kid about it. "Was it really big?" I asked.

"Pos-def. Huge."

"He is from Earth, you know. They tend to be pretty old-fashioned. He probably doesn't know what it's for."

Miriam punched my arm. "Well, then, somebody ought to show him. But let's start with showing him how to use fins. He doesn't know what *they're* for either."

On the way back we managed to be on either side of Theophilus. I drew a deep breath and plunged into it. "Was this your first time playing?"

"I played a couple of times on vacation at Supra Tokyo, but that was easier to figure out because it was pure free fall, and it was just with other Earth kids—nobody really knew how."

"You're not bad for no experience," Miriam said, lying. "Would you have time to get together this evening and practice? Not aerocrosse, I mean, but just low-gee flying?"

He seemed startled, but pleased. "I—yeah, I would. I get out of remedials at 2000. Is that too late?"

"Do you need time to eat?" I asked.

"No. I go to the Immersion Esperanto cafeteria as part of remedials. And I can leave a message for my folks—they'll be glad to know I'm making friends."

"Great," Miriam said. "The room where we have to go to sign up for gym time is over that way—Rec Lobby, Common Deck Two. Meet us there at 2015."

"Thank you," he said. He sounded happy—I felt good.

Dr. Niwara dropped back by us. "Is there a problem with keeping up? Or are you guys just talking?"

I opened my mouth, but Theophilus said, "It's my fault. I'm having trouble keeping up and they're trying to help."

Miriam cut in. "The truth is, we *have* been talking too much, and that's part of why he's having trouble." She and Theophilus pulled ahead quickly, and I followed.

Dr. Niwara stayed parallel with me. "Melpomene," she said

quietly. I always loved the way she called us all what we wanted to be called.

"Yes, ma'am?"

"What were you going to say before they answered?"

"What Miriam said. It's true."

"Good. I was hoping . . ."

She reached around me with one arm, squeezed my shoulder, and swarmed on ahead. I hurried to follow.

After snack we had the cross-subject for the week, which was (hurray!) Team Essays, in four teams of seven. Unfortunately, the AIs refereeing were STRUNK, FLESCH, and ELLSWORTH, which is always a lim bore, pos-def, because all three of those AIs are so pedantic and rule-bound; I like ORWELL and SPENCER a lot better. At least, though, the scoring this time was rank coefficient rather than averaging, which favors a strong team, and I was lucky enough to be captain of Team One.

Usually Miriam and I both did well at Team Essays, so I picked her first even though she'd picked Gwenny over me. (Yes, that was petty. I didn't care—friendship ought to count for something, especially after the way Gwenny had p.d.'d her standing in the locker room.)

We were too busy to talk about anything but the competition. I forgot about Theophilus, who was on Vanya's team. Our team swept, with our essays taking first (mine), second (Miriam's), fourth, and eighth, and nothing below fourteenth. The competition barely got done before school was out for the day.

"Not bad," Miriam said, while we waited for Theophilus in the corridor outside. "But we should have put more time into editing Sylvestrina's. She'd have placed sixth if we'd gotten her two more points in paragraph development."

"It's hard for her," I said. "And she's improved a lot. I think that's the first time she's even been in the top ten."

"I know. I just think it would have been lim koapy for her to place even higher." We clung to the netting and watched the door.

"I was surprised you asked him to practice tonight," I said. "Thursday is No Friends Day."

She made a face. "I hate Compets."

"Me, too," I said. "But I always study harder for them than for anything else."

"We share a lot of habits," she said. "Maybe we ought to be friends or something. Oh, shit on it anyway, Mel, he needs the help."

"Yeah. Probably just a little coaching—" Just then he came out the door, looking around. We waved and he started over toward us.

A hand tapped his shoulder from behind. He turned.

Randy Schwartz's fist smashed into Theophilus's face. He fell backward, arms flung out to catch himself.

We both rushed forward. Theophilus was holding his face, and tears were streaming down, but it didn't look worse than a bad bruise around his eye.

I took a moment to glare up at Randy, who was still standing over his victim.

His expression was really strange, almost as if he had been the one who got hit. He stared at me, shaking his head, his arms hanging limply—at that moment I was sure he was as surprised as anyone else at what had happened, even frightened by it. He looked so upset that in spite of myself I felt my heart going out to him a little, as if I might get up and take him aside and talk to him.

Then his eyes broke from mine, and he turned and ran down the corridor to the omnivators, stumbling awkwardly as his legs seemed to fling him along.

CHAPTER THREE

THAT NIGHT AT DINNER, MOTHER SAID, "I MET THE MOTHER OF someone who's in your class today, Melpomene."

"Oh, who?"

"Mrs. Harrison, Theophilus's mother. She's a very interesting person."

"How did you happen to meet her?" I asked. Mother hadn't been going out of the living unit much, and this sounded encouraging.

"Oh, she's taking over my old slot. They've conscripted me to coach her for a few days." She made a face. "I'll be glad when they perfect tank pork—I won't have to eat any more of their experiments."

Papa laughed. "It always weighs on my conscience; here's a poor little slab of muscle that was confined to a vat its whole life and never got to contract and relax inside a real pig." He laughed again; it had an uneasy sound to it.

39

Mother shook her head. "Honestly, Cornelius, please. I'll
admit to an interest in tradition, but I'm hardly a tree-worshipper.
Anyway, Mrs. Harrison is an extremely interesting, cultured person, and I thought we might want to get to know the family
socially."

Get to know the family socially. Mother had been talking in
that bizarre way a lot lately; it sounded like the Olson novels,
"back when men were full of manliness, fields were full of soy-
beans, small towns were full of hicks, and life was full of deeply
significant aching empty meaningless existential nothingness,"
as Tom liked to put it.

To get back to a more interesting topic, I said, "It must have
been nice to see all your old co-workers again. How are they
doing?"

She shrugged. "Well, they never mattered much to me."

Usually I just think she's a moron but sometimes I swear she
does talk like an unco. "Didn't you get time to talk to them?"

"Honestly, Melpomene, part of the reason I gave up that
awful job was because those people aren't interesting. All they
talk about is shop and their families; it was bad enough to work
in Long Run Economic Operations without having to talk about
twenty-year colonization schemes through your entire lunch
break. Not one of them has any interest in art or politics or
anything. Of course that was primarily what Mrs. Harrison and
I talked about, shop I mean, but then at lunch time we had a long
conversation. She and her husband are from interesting circles on
Earth; she grew up with cousins of Colin Powell."

I felt like saying that since he was only Acting President for
about six weeks before the Die-Off got him, the Harrisons just
weren't good enough for our circles; we Murrays only associate
with direct descendants of elected full-term presidents. It was the
kind of thing people in those Olson books said.

But I was trying to encourage her; at least she would be
getting out of the living unit for a few days. "That's interesting. I'll
have to ask Theophilus about it tonight."

"Tonight?"

"Miriam and I are meeting him for some rec practice. He

needs to learn some flying. Want to come along, Tom?" This might be a way to get Tom into it; I knew if I could get him interested in Theophilus's problems, my brother would come up with some good ideas. He always did, once you got his attention.

"I'd like to, but we have a night session tonight. Pyramid CSL." Tom looked like he was announcing the end of the world.

You have a lot of night sessions your last few months before FA; I'm not enjoying it any more than he did, just in case anyone out there is interested.

Especially not with writing this book on top of it. And it's now a little late, so I'll quit here and then write more tomorrow if there's time.

December 17, 2025

I'M BACK AGAIN, AND IT'S ONLY BEEN A FEW MINUTES WHILE I got a snack. I couldn't sleep.

Anyway, back to the conversation. I was going to wish Tom luck with his CSL, but Mother got off on one of her diatribes about how awful it was that they kept us so busy and how much vacation she had when she was our age. (Personally I wouldn't know what to do with that much time.) I just reached under the table and squeezed Tom's hand; he held mine for a long moment.

After a while, Mother wound down, and I said I needed to do some homework before meeting Theophilus and Miriam, so she let me leave the cafeteria early. When I left she was still talking loudly about the joys of her "normal" childhood, and Papa and Tom were eating in hardening silence, not looking up because they didn't want to catch the eye of anyone at another table. I felt like a deserter.

I was a little early getting to the Rec Lobby, but so was Miriam, so we spent some time going over the list of available smaller gyms. Right now B Shift was in school, so of course the Big Commons wasn't open—not that they'd give it to just three people anyway.

"I wonder if Randy Schwartz misses his friends," I said.

"Why do you care?"

"Well, maybe that's why he's such a . . . um . . ."

"A bully and an unco?" Miriam shook her head. "Melpomene, honestly. You really do worry about everyone in the world. Why can't you just accept that Randy Schwartz is nasty and mean, and let it go at that? I'm sure he doesn't worry about you."

I shrugged. "I was just making conversation. He probably doesn't see any of his old friends any more, and he's not very good at making new ones—"

"Well, maybe if he'd quit slamming people in the head . . ."

"Miriam!"

"What do you expect me to say? Okay, so he's lonely. Whose fault is that? He can still see his old friends at breakfast and dinner, or when he goes off shift. He still lives in B Block with them—they didn't move him when they changed his shift. It's not like he transferred ships or just came up—"

"Yeah, but . . . well, he's all alone down there. His corridor is dim most of the time he's awake. In fact, most of the time he could see them his friends have to be inside for Lights Down. And if he wants to eat with them he has to wait till right before his curfew, and they have to eat right after they get out of school. So he probably sees them but he doesn't get to see them, if you see what I mean."

"I guess. I still think there are better people to feel sympathy for."

I was still thinking of Randy's shocked expression after he had punched Theophilus, and didn't answer.

We picked out a nice big empty space, a supplementary storage bay far down toward the Main Engines, and I left my thumbprint for it.

Theophilus showed up a few minutes later. "Hi, am I late? Sorry—I had to hurry to get here. . . ."

"You're not late. Relax," Miriam said. "Do you have your gear?"

"Here in my werpsack."

"Okay. We have a long way to go down, so we're going to take the express omnivator."

As we got into the little car, Theophilus said, "I really wanted to thank you guys for inviting me. I was feeling pretty lonely—"

"That's us," Miriam said. "Ladies errant. We just can't resist a knight in distress."

"Though we hope a night with us wouldn't be too distressing," I added.

Miriam blushed, and Theophilus giggled. So much for his innocence.

The omnivator dropped us off within a hundred meters of where we were going. There's lots of empty space in the ship right now—so far we're only carrying a few personnel rotation passengers and some supplies for the Mars bases—and the lower spaces, below the living quarters and the ag zones, are deserted except for kids playing in the smaller pressurized cargo bays.

And of course couples out for sneakies. I hoped we wouldn't be spoiling someone's evening by turning up in this space.

It was as vacant as it was supposed to be, probably because they had put a supervisory camera in it. They hadn't done the finish yet, so the walls still had the lumpy, burnished look that comes from vacuum extruding and spray plating. The lights reflected everywhere, like smeary stars stretching to infinity.

"Okay," I said. "Let's get you set up. Forearm fins go on like this—that's right, broad part at the outer edge of your wrist—and shin fins go on at a forty-five degree angle, pointing outward and back. Make sure they're snug, but if they press into the muscle they're too tight."

We checked him over; he was fine. "Okay, helmets on and let's go."

"You wear helmets even when they're not required?" he asked. "I thought you were just wearing them because Niwara was there."

I was a little surprised that he called her by just her last name like that. It sounded rude but maybe it was some kind of an Earth custom. We always said "Dr. Niwara." "Well," I said, "in the first place, if you hit your head—and we all do now and then—it's a lot less painful. And besides, it *is* required, whenever you're doing free flight. Those are the rules."

"I meant, no one would see you," he said, as if that explained something.

I was lim confused; I didn't know of any rule that only applied when you were being watched. I glanced at Miriam. She shrugged and raised her hands a little—I don't think Theophilus saw. Probably another one of those Earth things; it was hard to see why anyone would want to break a rule, and harder still to see why they'd want to chance a hard thump on the skull, but obviously that didn't bother Theophilus. "Well, if that's what concerns you, there's a good chance that someone is watching us through that camera anyway," she said.

"Those are cameras? I was going to ask."

I rolled my eyes at Miriam; she winked.

"We might as well get to flying," I said. "The thing to remember is that your fins can only work up a few newtons of force, even when you're swimming as hard as you can—but since you only *weigh* about five newtons at most, it's enough. You can build up a lot of speed."

"But it takes a while to feel it," Miriam added. "So if you know you're doing the right thing, don't stop doing it—give it a few seconds to have some effect."

"Let's go up to the top and we'll show you," I said. "Just jump lightly, and then do a few frog kicks hard with your legs, like this." I took off; Theophilus followed, with Miriam behind in case he got into trouble. The gym was only about fifty meters high, so it would be an easy jump to the top anyway, but that should be enough room for him to get the feel of it.

When he managed to fly upward, he got so excited he tried to flutter kick the way he'd seen us do in the Big Commons. Unfortunately, he didn't yet know anything about slowing down or stopping, and he accelerated all the way up until he smacked head-first into the ceiling and bounced back down. He whirled around, his arms and legs flapping in all directions, then tried treading air. He was spinning a little, slowly, but he did slow his descent enough to reach the floor without much of a bump.

Miriam and I had already swooped back down to see if he was all right; he looked a little shaken.

"Well, you've mastered the basic head-stop." I said it as a joke, but he turned away sharply, and I realized this wasn't a good joke to pursue. When he turned back, a breath later, I saw him make himself smile, and felt lim ashamed of teasing him.

"Sorry," I said. "That was our fault. If you're going to flutter kick, you need to brake and turn at the top."

"Like this," Miriam said. "Palms up, sweep your arms up and behind you. It spills a lot of speed and it flips you right over so you land feet first." She showed him the turn.

We flew up to the top again, and this time he did fine, only having to scrabble a little to get a strap, grabbing it with his left hand centered on his body so that it pulled his feet evenly against the ceiling.

"That's easier on the feet than it is on the head," he said.

Miriam laughed and gave him a hug; he looked a little startled. Mother says people on Earth don't touch each other much, so maybe it was that, or maybe it was the way she rubbed against him as she did it.

It reminded me how much things had changed in the last year. Miriam had hit puberty at peak velocity and gone right through with barely a hitch—a year ago she had been built like I was now, sort of slim and short (Tom would have said "scrawny" and "puny"). Almost overnight, she had shot up several centimeters, filled out in the hips, and grown these absolutely huge breasts. She'd kept the same waist measurement too, damn her.

Anyway, we worked on gliding next, showing him how to steer with little changes of fin position. That's tricky because you have to develop a sharp sense of limits—if you move more than your wrists and ankles, try to steer with your full arms and legs, the overcorrection is savage and you'll tumble like a paper airplane in the airgym.

After two or three of those wild tumbles, he caught on—and then it was just a lim thrill to see how much fun he had zipping around the gym. We gave him a quick hand of applause, and he grabbed a strap in a nice neat point-stop and bowed.

I thought Miriam giggled much more than that bow rated.

"We might as well move on to full ballistics, especially since you've got the legs for it from all that high gee," I said. "It's a lot like gliding except you use your fins to stabilize and turn more than for lift. The only new maneuver you have to learn is the turnover—and once you get that working well, you can do some really fun stuff." I shot around the room, ripping off six caroms one after the other before I dropped in a slapstop right in front of him.

There was some wonderful trick in his smile that made you feel like he'd just hugged you; at that moment I'd have done anything for him. "It does look like a lot of fun, but I don't know if I could ever do that," he said.

"*I* can't," Miriam said. "Mel's just showing off."

I had been, but at least what I was showing off was something I had worked to learn, and not just grown on my chest.

Before I could think of a polite way to say that, Miriam went on, "But she's right, of course. Your big strength is going to be wall play. You do a turnover like this. . . ." She kipped up and glided slowly to the other wall. "See, the whole trick is to just pull in tight and then thrust your feet straight at where you're going so your legs are all the way stretched just as you get there. That way you don't start spinning, and you've got the full extension of your leg to absorb the force so you've got control of the rebound as you hit. That way you can do anything from a dead stop to a sudden burst of speed." She touched down and pushed back toward us.

"Like this?" he asked. He jumped for the other wall, but he tucked his feet in front of himself, so he started to roll over slowly. He extended his legs, but by then he was flying flat and he landed on his hands and knees.

"Be careful to pull your feet in straight toward your center," I said.

He tried again and had it. After that we just showed him all the stuff we could think of; he was a pretty fast learner, and it got to be fun.

He was doing a lot better, so we finished up with a game of tag. Miriam was uncharacteristically clumsy, but maybe she was doing that to bolster his confidence. I guess I could have done the same thing, but once it's competition I just can't seem to lay back and take it easy; I have to play to win or I can't play at all.

Two times she bokked on her landings, hard enough it must have hurt, and bounced back up into Theophilus, giving him a chance to tag her. Theophilus even caught her on a tagback, which she should have ducked as easily as anyone.

When we finally quit, we figured he'd have a lot better chance in rec from now on. There was only about an hour left till Lights Down, so we scrambled a little getting to the omnivator, rushed through checkout with just a few words to Mrs. Onegin, Dmitri's mother, at the Rec Lobby, and hurried back toward A Block together.

It turned out they had moved his family into Miriam's corridor, so they went along with me before going back up together. He seemed to be having a lot less trouble getting around on the nets, and I complimented him on it.

"Why don't people just fly in the corridors?" he asked.

"There's a rule against it," I said.

"Oh." That seemed to confuse him. "Why is there a rule against it?"

I thought for a moment, then realized that I did know. "Traffic problem. Sometimes parties of twenty people have to pass each other; the corridors are only three meters in diameter, so it's a lot easier if everyone clings to the walls than it is if they're all in mid-air. Besides, the net limits the speed you can move at and allows you to stop quickly, so you don't fly face-first into someone coming around a bend."

Miriam edged in between us and started talking about a math problem; Theophilus seemed to be flattered by having someone want help from him. It was kind of rude of her to interrupt, especially since she would be going on with him, but I suppose the problem just popped into her head. Even though it was a pretty easy one, and she's better at math than I am.

I turned off at Corridor Twelve, and they continued on; they were so busy talking that I don't think they noticed I was gone. I went around the outside of our Corridor Commons—there was nobody there except three young couples, maybe sixteen years old, with babies—and down the corridor to our living unit.

I slipped in the door, planning to just stop by Tom's room to see how things had gone for him, but Mother stopped me in the sharespace. "I hope you did all your homework before you went out."

"Yes, I did." I wasn't dumb enough to get caught that way.

She floated over and whispered in my ear; if the vid is accurate, I really do envy Earth people for all that space you have to live in. Our living units are so small that despite all the sound-proofing you can hear everything from anywhere. Papa's office has thick, heavy insulating pads on the walls to give his clients some privacy, but everywhere else we hear everything that's not whispered. "Tom is in his room by himself," she breathed in my ear. "I don't know if he'll want to talk to you, Melly—I mean Melpomene." She must have noticed that I stiffened. "He's very upset."

"What happened?"

"He did really badly in Pyramid CSL, and he pulled down some other people's scores."

I nodded. "Thank you for telling me. He'll want to see me." I grabbed a handhold and swung past her to his door.

"You don't know that," she said, which was stupid because of course I did. "Don't barge in if he doesn't want you to—let him have his privacy."

"Okay," I said, to keep the peace.

"When I was young, I valued my privacy."

Even after growing up with Mother around, I'll never understand that. Adults always say things like that. I mean, really, privacy is just being all by yourself with no friends and nobody to look out for you or have fun with. Who needs it? Tom and I only closed our doors because she insisted.

And this was just like her, leaving him in there to feel miserable by himself. Papa says it's because she's "imperfectly adapted to the social neoconstruct."

I think it's because she's a moron.

"You knock first," she said at me.

Tom opened his door and said, "Melpomene, I want you to come in here." I flipped in and he closed the door, leaving Mother out there to flap her mouth like a carp. Sometimes I really hate her.

I could see he had been crying and I was even angrier at Mother. How could she leave him in there by himself—for god's sake why should anyone wait for people to *ask* for help? I put my arms around him and let him cry it out. It took him a long time, his body shaking against mine and hot tears dripping onto my shoulder. I just waited.

When he finally stopped sobbing, I said, "There's a lot of things you *are* good at. Everyone can't be a genius at everything."

"It's not that," he said, still looking away. "What I can't take is everybody being so fucking charitable about it. They know I dragged the team down and they all got lower scores because of it, but they're so busy being good sports that they're all acting like the only thing bothering them is how upset I am."

"Well, they *are* your friends. Maybe they're worried about you."

He wouldn't look at me. "Sure they are. But I can tell what they're thinking. I know the captains always pick me last for CSL. I just can't stand being the worst person on the last team to pick!"

He started to cry again and I couldn't think of anything else to say, or at least not anything that would help. So I just held him, and rubbed his back with one hand, and told him that I liked him no matter what and all the things you say to someone when they're like that. It never seems to have any effect when you're doing the comforting, but when I feel bad, it helps to be comforted even though I don't stop crying.

Finally he said, "Well, I feel a little better. I just wish I could understand why CSL is such an awful subject for me."

"How low was your score?" I asked.

"Fourteen out of a possible hundred." He looked away; I was afraid he would cry again, so I started to rub his neck and shoulders. "That feels good, thank you. Statistically my score was indistinguishable from zil, could be pure random effects of the

scoring procedure. I might as well not have gone to class at all."
He sighed. "Well, I need to get back to work."

"You're not going to stay up and do CSL all night are you?"
He looked startled. "Why do you think—"

"Because every time this happens you do that. You exhaust yourself and you bokk in school the next day." He just looked at me. "That was what you were going to do, wasn't it?"

He snuffled. "I just hate being so bad at CSL, and I want to do something about it."

The door opened, jamming my leg against the wall, and Mother stuck her head in. "Melpomene, you're obviously upsetting your brother—"

"Get out of here, Mother. I'm upset but I want Melpomene here. What I don't want is you."

She closed the door with a slam.

Tom sighed. "Okay, I admit it. I was going to work the CSL problems. It helps me get to sleep, if nothing else, because I end up exhausted."

"Why don't you just masturbate?"

"I can't when I'm upset."

"Well, then take a drifter, but don't torture yourself with CSL for the rest of the night! You'll just multiply your problems."

"Yeah." He got out the bottle of pills from his medication file, held one up, and said, "See? Off to dream land."

"That's better," I said. "Now take it."

He made a face at me, but he took the pill. "I better get the place folded up and pull the bed out. The drifter will hit in ten minutes or so."

I stood up. "Okay. But if you wake up later, or you still can't get to sleep and just need to cry or something, you come to me or Papa. And unlike Papa, I don't sleep with Mother and I don't mind having you wake me up."

He held his hand up as if he were being put under oath. "Absolutely. At the first crisis, straight to Melpomene. My sister, my teddy bear."

I stuck my tongue out at him. "Just do it. And no more trying to cram after the test!"

"I'm reformed forever. Now, you go. I need to have the bed ready for when I start feeling all happy and vague in a few minutes."

"Goodnight." I hugged him; he hugged me back, and I went across the meter gap to my room. I made a mental note to check in on him before I went to sleep that night.

I tried to study, but it was still almost an hour till I needed to be asleep, and I didn't want to spend it in that little brig cell, my room, which was what Mother expected me to do. She was always talking about how she spent a lot of time like that, all alone in her room with just her books and her fantasies, when she was my age, which might explain a lot of things. I didn't want to be out in the sharespace with her. All she ever did was sit and read anyway.

Well, that left Papa.

He was in his office as always. Despite Mother's lecturing him about spending more time with his family, he usually disappeared into there every night as soon as we got back from dinner. I just pushed the door open, even though I knew he preferred that I knock. I was tired of truckling to adult bizarreness. "Papa?"

"Hi, Melpomene. Come on in and catch a sling. What's on your mind?"

I closed the door behind me and drifted over to pull myself into a seat. "I guess this is sort of about Tom and sort of about . . . things."

"Things in general?"

"Yeah."

He sat there and looked at me but he didn't say anything. One problem with shrinks, they do that. Unlike regular people, they don't make any nice inane chatter so you can have time to gather your thoughts.

I ended up doing what I always do—just threw myself into the conversation and let him catch me and sort it out. "Tom is really ashamed of being the team bokkup in CSL. Nobody makes fun of him or anything but he still feels bad."

"I know," he said. "He didn't want to go down to Main Dining for a late snack with me." The two of them had been doing that

51

together a lot lately. "Is there something you think I could do to help?"

"I don't know, Papa." Everything was so confusing when I thought about it. I looked down at my slippers, the new blue ones, as I rubbed them against each other. "I guess . . . well, why does it matter to anybody but Tom how good he is at CSL?"

For a long time, he stared at the screen on the wall. Papa is one of the few people who always has his window tuned to an Outside camera; I never knew what he was looking at, since, except when you're close to Earth or Mars, there's nothing to see but white dots on black. Finally he said, "Well, since you've figured out the right question to ask, you're old enough to know the answer. If you don't already. Why *should* anyone else care about how Tom does in CSL? And more to the point, why should Tom care about how they feel about it?"

"Standing." That was obvious. "He loses standing every time something like this happens. They're all very nice about it, but they know he's bokking, and he knows he's bokking, and that's all there is to it."

"Mmm-hmm." Papa nodded at me. That's called "giving the patient a cue to initiate a direction." I read about it in one of Papa's papers. They do that when they think you would be more receptive to whatever they're going to say if you thought of it yourself. It always makes me want to think of something else entirely.

"Look," I said, "that's it. No one likes to lose standing."

"Did you know Earth children don't even have the concept of standing? There are some roughly parallel ideas, like 'class rank,' 'honor,' and 'face,' but standing, as you know it, only exists up here in space."

I shrugged. "Groundhogs are weird."

"Mmm-hmmm." He looked away at the screen again.

I hate that.

But I can't help myself. "Well," I said, trying again, "Tom feels bad when he loses standing. He feels bad because he wants high standing, and he's used to having it in so many other subjects.

The contrast bothers him. I guess if you always felt stupid you'd get used to it."

"Do you know any children who always feel stupid?"

"Sure. Carole. And, yes, she does get used to it, or *something,* anyway. She's always smiling and seems to be happy and has lots of friends. We all like her."

"What's her standing?"

"Bottom in practically everything."

"Her *standing.*" He had pounced on the word, leaning forward, looking at me the way Tom looks at a drawing that isn't quite right. "Not class or subject standings. The one you all give each other."

I knew what he meant, of course, and with all the microphones and cameras around I suppose I shouldn't have been surprised that he knew—but I still felt like an informer. So I stalled. "What does this have to do with Tom?"

"What kind of standing does it bother Tom to lose?"

I sat there for a moment, looking at him. When he gets that ready-to-pounce look, something is really important to him. He was a debater in college and almost went to law school, and it shows.

"Okay," I said. "I know what you mean. And yeah, because Tom is top of the standings in everything else, the embarrassment pushes his standing—his *real* standing, if you want to call it that—it lim p.d.'s it. You always lose standing if there's something people can humiliate you with." That made me think of Mother, again, and I had a little flash of anger. "And I still don't see why you think it's something wrong with Tom. Of course he cares what his friends think! But why do they have to be so nasty and embarrass him—"

"Has he been teased, or picked on?"

"No, but he knows what they're thinking, and it hurts him— and I don't think that's fair." I was feeling very upset and confused, and I didn't know why.

He nodded a couple of times. He was obviously trying to think of, or remember, something that just wouldn't quite come to him. "Oh, hell, Melpomene, I never did figure out how I was going to tell you about this, though I thought about it a lot. You're going to be applying to take your advanced training in Social Science, right? Aiming for administration or psych?"

I said yes and left it up to him.

He sighed. "Well, then I might as well . . ." His voice trailed off.

"What's the matter?" I asked. It was something about his face—something that I had barely ever . . . *there were tears forming in his eyes.*

"Papa!"

"There's something I need to talk with you about. It's on the schedule—way overdue, in fact, and the rest of the CPB is chewing my ass off about not having done it yet." He drew a deep breath and looked into my eyes. "Melpomene, I know you're ambitious. How would you like a chance to get onto a *very* fast track for promotion—one where you might hold major office before you're twenty?"

"Really?! Pos-def! I mean, of course, yes! Is there an opening for something—I thought I knew all the slots open on the ship—"

He nodded again. "That's the catch. It's not here on the *Flying Dutchman*. The opportunity's coming up to transfer out to Mars Synchronous, the big port they're making out of Deimos now that Phobos has been moved out of the way. Would you like to leave here, not on this Mars approach but on the next one? You'll be Full Adult by then and you could go there to live . . ."

I gasped; I felt as if I'd been punched in the stomach. "Papa, I can't—don't make me—" The world swam around me, bordered with red, and I thought I might scream or vomit.

His arms were around me, comforting me and holding me as I sobbed. "Easy. Relax. Breathe deep. Sorry to do that to you— sometimes this still surprises me. No, you don't have to go." He looked at me closely. "Are you all right?"

I lashed out at his face as hard as I could, my hand open to slap; he caught it and pressed it back to my side. "Easy, easy, easy . . ." he whispered, and held me.

I was crying and I had no idea why; it was terrifying. How

could I have tried to hit Papa? But he had said . . . he had suggested . . .

"It's okay," he said. "This is programmed. This is what's supposed to happen. Breathe deep."

I did and began to feel calmer. "You see now? How deeply these things are engineered?" he asked. "I should know—I did a lot of the engineering myself. You're a perfect employee for NihonAmerica, as perfect as we can condition you to be. You don't ever want to leave the ship. Everything you value is here, and everything you believe in is something that keeps the ship running smoothly. We can't make you good or wise or kind, but we can make you want to stay here and we can make you derive all your pleasure from teamwork."

"Dirty fucking uncos," I said, and tried to hit him again. This time he was slower to block me and I caught a little of his cheek. It must have stung, but he didn't react. "And this is why Tom feels like shit about his CSL score. Because he's been programmed to!"

He sighed. "Of course that's why." I noticed—and was surprised at the little twinge of satisfaction it gave me—that his free hand twitched, as if to ward off another slap. "Of course that's why," he repeated. "And you're very angry about it. You have a right to be. Maybe in the best of worlds things wouldn't have happened this way. . . ."

"Don't tell me you had no choice," I said.

His face was suddenly hard as stone. "In the context of the times, we—did—not. What life was like after the Die-Off and the Eurowar—how bad things were—you can't imagine. The Reorganization . . . for a lot of us—"

"I'm fourth in history. Spare me. Okay, you needed to get the ships going because you needed space resources. What the hell gives you the right to fuck with my mind."

"Nothing," he said. "Nothing gave us the right. We had to so we did. I can remember the last big Christmas, the Declaration of Universal Disarmament, people dancing in the streets, riding on Dad's shoulders at the big parades . . . and the next Christmas, mutAIDS had hit, and Dad and Mom were both buried, somewhere, in a bulldozed trench, and I spent Christmas at the school

55

with lots of other kids who had no living parents. Exactly ten years after that I was wandering around somewhere in Belgium, looking for any American unit—or any living American. Christmas after that was evacuation camp in Normandy—and going to the States on a Korean freighter full of European refugees, because just then the United States was in no shape to bring its own soldiers home." I had never seen him so angry—or so quiet about it. "I don't know everything your mother did to live. I don't *want* to; she doesn't know everything I did and she hasn't asked. What we all do know is that everyone who made it through was someone who would do whatever they had to. So don't expect a drop of sympathy, and don't expect me or anyone else to worry about you and your friends' precious rights. We are doing what we have to; once we've done it, then maybe we'll consider how you feel about it."

There was a long, long silence.

"It happens to everyone," he said. "The only difference is that other people are created from whatever random events happen to them. You were designed. And we've spared you a lot. Did you know bright children on Earth get beaten up by their schoolmates for being too smart?"

"Sure. I saw it happen this afternoon."

His mouth dropped wide open and he stared at me; usually I hate that expression, but this time I kind of enjoyed it.

Finally he managed to squeak out, "You'd better tell me everything about it," and switched on the recorder.

So I told him all about Theophilus and Randy. He took a lot of notes on the keyboard as he listened and taped, but he didn't ask very many questions. . . . I guess I told the story the right way or something.

"Well, that's interesting," he said, when I had finished. "Keep an eye on that; we hadn't anticipated anything like this."

"I don't see any reason why I should spy for you," I said. "And I still want to know why you engineered things so that Tom would be miserable. Do you hate him, or what?"

"We all have an interest in Tom's CSL because anything he

can't do very well limits what crew assignments he can take, and everything he can do well benefits all of us."

At least that much made sense. "But why do you set it up so he gets picked on for it? I mean, it's obvious . . . you could just read us a reminder memo or something in school once a week. You know, like the reminders to wear helmets during rec and brush our teeth."

"It's obvious to you because we've 'fucked with your mind.' But it's not obvious to everyone. Most Earth people would see it just the way you did—his scores are his own affair. Certainly your mother sees it that way, and that's part of why she has such a hard time dealing with his feelings."

"She's a moron," I said. "That's what the trouble is."

He was angry, but he didn't want me to see it. He waited a couple of long breaths before he spoke. "There's a lot to be said for her viewpoint—it probably results in more people being individually happier, although it also means people have less support when things go wrong.

"But whether it makes people happy or not, up here, with our sharply limited population and resources, and our need to make a profit to pay for our imports, we can't let the idea take root. It could kill the ship. And if the ships die, civilization dies with them—it's that simple. Earth is too frail ecologically for any more heavy industry, and its resources are too far down the gravity well, and there are far too many people to take care of in an agricultural, renewable-resource economy. We've *got* to reach out from Earth, even if it *is* a hundred years too early—or kill two-thirds of the people on Earth. So the ships have to work, and Tom has to feel the way he does."

"He didn't get much choice," I said.

"None at all." He sighed. "But nothing works perfectly. This development with the new boy—well, it shocked me, and it will shock the CPB. I've no idea what to make of it. I'd appreciate it if you'd keep me posted."

I shook my head. "If you'd asked yesterday, I'd have said pos-def. But now . . . no. I don't feel like being a spy for the CPB."

"What about for the *Flying Dutchman?*"

"Those aren't the same thing. At least not always."

I couldn't believe I was defying Papa this way. On the other hand, for all I knew this was the first thing I'd ever done where it was really *me* doing it, if you see what I mean.

I said goodnight and went back to my room terribly tired. Since Mother's nose was locked into the reader, I slipped Tom's door open. He was asleep or pretending to be. I went to my own room, folded up my desk and chair into the wall, and brought down the bed.

Standing in the dressing corner, I took off my jumpsuit and slippers and dropped them into the freshener, and set room heat to "nude/sleep." Then I popped up to the ceiling, caught the stretchout handles, relaxed, and let go, drawing a deep breath and letting myself drift down to the bed.

Usually I'm asleep so quickly I don't remember landing on the bed, but tonight, even tired as I was, I had to stretch out and drop three times before I could get to sleep.

CHAPTER FOUR

The NEXT DAY, D'ARTAGNAN WAS RETURNING NONE OF HORN-
blower's messages. I couldn't even catch Miriam's eye, and since
there was no rec that day, I didn't get a chance to talk to her.
Maybe she was short on sleep too.

We spent the whole last half of the afternoon in Pyramid
Math, and of all people I ended up paired with Randy Schwartz.
Life was obviously not going to be either fair or convenient.

In Pyramid Math your score is half your own plus one quarter
the average of you and your partner, plus one eighth the average
of your foursome, and so forth except that the total class average
is weighted equally with your team's average so it all comes out
to one. Every unit from individuals up to teams competes against
all the other units of its size. If that isn't clear, just remember the
closer someone is to you in the team structure, the more their
score counts for you.

Officially there were two teams of sixteen, but we only had twenty-eight kids, so in each group of eight, two kids would be double-paired to make up another score; they got the average of their two separate scores. (This would really be easier to show you with a diagram.) Dr. Niwara always said those would be randomly assigned, but in fact she always put the dumb kids into the extra pair slots so they'd get lots of help.

(You do the same thing, Dr. Lovell, and we all know it, so let's admit it, okay?)

Anyway, the point of the whole thing is that in Pyramid Math you need to get a good score yourself, have your partner get a good score, have your foursome get a good score, and so forth in that order, including finally that you want everyone in the room to get a good one. Usually I enjoy it a lot because we all have to cooperate so much.

I just wasn't lim, pos-def sure that I wanted to cooperate with Randy Schwartz. We sat down next to each other and didn't say a thing while our first problem sets came up.

I knew I was in trouble by the third problem. "Randy?"

"Need help? Okay, let's see . . . um, negative proof? Assume it's not true and show the trouble it gets you into?"

I looked at the problem again; it was obvious. "Thanks—I think I have it."

We went back to working, but it seemed like I needed help every other problem. He kept losing his place and getting flustered when he tried to help. Finally it got so obvious that I asked him about it. "Randy, is something wrong?"

"No, um, I—" He shook his head. "I guess I just don't feel like math or something today, Mel. But we have to do it, so . . . hey, this one's easy. Look, you can prove that if it works for any two ellipses, it works for all pairs of ellipses, right? That's trivial."

It took me a minute or so, but he was right; the proof was easy. "Now what?" I asked. He had gone back to his own work, and seemed surprised that I asked. "Oh. Well, now that you've proven that, just show that it's true for two circles of unit radius. That way the complicated stuff all drops out."

"It seems like cheating."

"It is, a little bit. But it works—here's a diagram. . . ."

He rolled the mouse between his hands, a strange little trick he used for drawing. As it formed on my screen I saw the principle and was about to say I could take it from here, but then he asked, "Do you like to be called Mel or Melpomene?"

I was so startled that I had to swallow before I could say, "Um, everyone calls me Mel but I like Melpomene bet-better." I hadn't stammered since I was eight; neither of us was having a good day.

"I'll try to remember." He nodded. "I think it's a pretty koapy name."

"Thank you." There was a long pause; I couldn't think of a thing to say and he seemed to be looking at the screen without seeing it. "Um, guess we better get back to it," I said, feeling more bokked every second.

"Yeah." He went back to his screen. I don't know what he was working on that day—he was zooming through it faster than I could follow, and it was all stuff way over my head.

I finished my problem, but my time was so slow it didn't do the team much good. There was an hour to go, and problem sets escalate, so not only was the worst yet to come—there would be a lot of it.

As the problems got more complex and difficult, we worked more and more in our group of four or even group of eight. Sometimes Randy crossed over to dig Carole or Barry out for the team as a whole as well.

I was just as glad to be busy and not have too much time to talk with, or think about, Randy. If only he weren't such a terrible bully. I wondered what made him that way, if he had a friend to talk with. He'd looked so lost after hitting Theophilus, as if he didn't understand how he had happened to do it. . . . And he *had* asked what I wanted to be called; no one else ever had, and when I told friends like Miriam, they usually forgot.

When I looked at the screen I almost gasped. The clock in the lower corner showed more than a minute had already elapsed. I'd been thinking about Randy, not math, sitting there not seeing the problem on the screen. A full third of the possible points were lost already.

And not one thing on the screen made any sense at all.

"Randy, um—help?"

"Sure." He hurried over—that made me feel better, but when he saw the screen I didn't like his expression. "Yuck. Hey guys, everyone who can get over here to help Melpomene." I could hear people gathering behind us, reading the problem aloud to each other, but I was watching Randy.

"Okay, okay, okay," He was talking to himself, almost chanting as he ran through his approach. "No trivial solution. Looks impossible. Therefore there's some kind of a trick to all this. Just have to find it. Look for something peculiar. . . ."

"All the measures are in terms of p and q," I offered. It was the only thing I had seen.

"Could be, yeah, on a more standard problem there would be four variables and nine constants, but this is all . . . Hah! Those two areas look like you could express them . . . yeah. One is p plus q squared, one is p minus q squared, when you boil it out, and the ratio between the sides is pq over pq minus q, so . . . well, try that much."

I set that up; I still couldn't see where he was going.

"So the triangle is p squared q over two?"

"Yeah," he said. "Now we have three angles on that projection, so if we define what happens to p and what happens to q in terms of them . . ."

Well, we finally brute-forced our way through it. Nobody but Randy had any ideas at all, of course, but at least I understood what he had done well enough to explain it if Dr. Niwara back-checked us—though there hadn't been much backchecking of partners in the last few years. I guess we were supposed to be mature enough. . . .

Finishing with less than two minutes left on the clock, it was a lot of work for hardly any score at all. I felt pretty bad—me sitting there all that time without working had cost the team the high point value of the problem.

I started to apologize, but Randy said, "No, I'd just have

burned the time myself trying for elegance. Neat problem—I just wish it hadn't shown up on a Pyramid day, when we're working against the clock." He touched my shoulder lightly. "Anyway, if they give you another one that tough today, it means they think you're a genius, for what that's worth." He turned and went to help Ysande.

"Next time call for help when you need it," Kwame van Dyke said. "If you can't do it find someone who can."

Randy's head snapped around. "Leave her alone. She did okay."

It got very quiet, and I had just an instant to wish he hadn't done that. The other kids were staring at him, and I think he was also wishing he hadn't said anything, but his fists unclenched and he explained, reasonably, "She couldn't have gotten help any sooner because I was working with Roger."

It wasn't true, but he had been sitting with Roger, who was busy with a problem right now so no one would bother asking him. "And since none of you had any ideas when you saw the problem, you wouldn't have done her any good if she had called for you. So we'd have lost the points anyhow."

He looked around from Kwame to the others and back to Kwame. "If you upset people when they have trouble, they have more trouble. It doesn't matter—we need to concentrate on the points we can get, not on the ones that are already gone. Now go get some points if you guys are so smart."

I thought his argument was pretty good—at least it got me off the hook. As soon as Randy's back was turned, Kwame whispered something nasty about what I would do for Randy to show my gratitude. But that's the kind of thing Kwame says all the time, anyway, so no one ever listens to him.

I turned back to my screen and punched for the next question. It looked like a variation on the one before, but now I was just supposed to say whether the problem could be solved. I almost hit "yes," figuring I had just seen one solved and the next thing it would do would be to ask me to solve it, but something caught my eye. "Randy," I said, "on that last problem—if the horizontal and vertical projection angles were specified to be equal to each other, would it be overdetermined?"

"Yeah. Why?"

I hit "no." It scored big. After that last problem, the testing AI had expected me to either bokk badly or take a long time from overcaution. "Thanks," I said, "Got it." I went on to the next problem.

We didn't have any time to say anything to each other after that, because the last part was Speed Estimation. They flash these complicated pictures at you with distances and angles marked in blue and a few red question marks for some distances and angles. You don't set up the problem or do any calculating—you type what you think the value of the length or the angle is over the question mark; the faster you finish and the closer you are to the right answer, the higher the score. It's the only part of math I've got any talent for.

Final scores at the end of the afternoon put Randy second and me seventh—low for him and very high for me. Theophilus had first, and most of the high places went to the other team; Miriam even got fifth. Apparently Theophilus was a good coach, in addition to being wonderful at math.

I thought I might be able to head off trouble. "I'm really sorry, Randy," I said, catching him on his way out the door.

He seemed surprised. "About what?"

"Oh, I really p.d.'d our score, especially on that one problem. You'd have done a lot better with a partner like Gwenny or Padraic—"

He shrugged. "Doesn't matter. I can't be on top all the time—it's probably a good experience for me. I'm an awfully bad loser."

We were out in the corridor by then, and for just a second our eyes met. I said "See you tomorrow," and he smiled a little.

"Yeah, see you tomorrow. That AI must think you're pretty smart—those problems were really tough."

I nodded. "Um, thanks for giving me a dropline—"

"It was no dropline. How you do your problems isn't Kwame's business. That's between you and your partner. Kwame always coasts on his teammates' efforts anyway, and you aren't responsible for getting him a good score if he won't do his share of the work."

It was all true, but I guess I hadn't expected to hear it. "Maybe. Thanks anyway."

He nodded. Then neither of us had anything to say, so we stood there awkwardly. Finally we turned away in our separate directions. It was about the most awkward, stupid, bokked conversation I'd ever been in, like something that Olson woman might have written.

Miriam and Theophilus were walking along ahead of me, so I hurried a little and caught up with them. "Hi, guys."

Miriam had a strange expression, as if she wished I wasn't there, and I was about to disappear as gracefully as I could manage, but Theophilus smiled and said hello, so I was stuck. We walked along not talking, taking the stairwell instead of the omnivators to the center of the Mushroom. After we had climbed through several levels, Miriam suddenly said, "What were you talking to that Randy Schwartz about?"

"Oh, just the match problem sets today. He was my partner. I bokked up on a hard one and he sort of got me out of the mess." I walked along with them a little longer. "He *is* pretty good at it."

"Almost as good as he thinks he is," Theophilus said.

I didn't have the foggiest idea what he meant by that. Almost as good as he thinks he is? Who else would know how good he was? And why "almost?" With all the feedback we get, how could he be consistently overestimating?

Miriam was giggling, so it had to be a joke.

"Ted," she said, "you're lim awful. He's going to hit you again if you keep that up."

I still didn't get the joke, but I was getting bored with it already. "Ted?" I asked.

"It's what I like people to call me," Theophilus said. "I like short names. Like what you guys are called—Mim and Mel."

Yuck. One more person to call me Mel. "Oh." I walked with them for the rest of the way through the Mushroom, and then waited with them for the exit ring to crank us around to A Block.

"What do you think for Penny Graham?" Theophilus asked Miriam.

"I don't know, you pick." She was giggling. I wondered if they were going to throw a surprise party or something. Theophilus certainly seemed to be influencing Miriam—she wasn't making much more sense than he did.

"Pancakes," he said.

That got them both laughing, and Miriam said, "They really are, you know. I've seen her in the locker room and they're not just small, they're sort of empty and droopy."

I couldn't imagine why they were talking about Penelope's breasts, or why it was so funny.

"Okay, pos-def it's Pancakes," Theophilus said. "Now who else?"

"Pick one."

"The girl that sits two seats in front of me."

"Rebecca Hayakawa?"

"Yeah. Her," Theophilus agreed. "Uh—Full Disk."

"I don't get it," Miriam said.

"When they were announcing what you could see from the viewing deck, when I first got here—"

"Oh, I see. 'Both Earth and moon showing full disks . . .' But we can do better. How about Plug?" Miriam said. "For what happens when she tries to go through a narrow corridor."

Rebecca was terribly sensitive about her weight and figure, because she was such a big girl. I was sure that if she heard any of this she'd burst into tears, but both of them were laughing like idiots.

The Block A entrance rolled up and we walked through. Since I lived on a different corridor from theirs, I started to say goodbye, but neither of them was looking at me, so I just grabbed the netting and pulled away. They ignored me, whispering and giggling to each other. Just before the door closed, I heard Miriam say something that I didn't quite catch.

Then Theophilus said, "Hey, that's great. Daddy Shrinko, Mommy Unco, and Baby Shrunko!"

When I got home I went straight into my room to study till it was time to go to dinner, but I couldn't concentrate. Okay, I was not very big for my age, and maybe I looked a little younger than I really was. And yes, Mother had quit being productive and was just staying home and dead-heading.

Miriam knew how much those things bothered me. How could she laugh like that?

I WAS STUDYING IN MY OWN ROOM, WITH THE DOOR OPEN SO I could hear Tom if he wanted help or wanted to talk, when my comscreen whistled. I saved the essay I was stumbling through— "Abstract Microeconomics of Orbital Transfer"—and flipped the screen over to com, bringing it up to full visual. Too late, I remembered it had been rabbit lasagna in the cafeteria that night and as usual I had forgotten and worn a white tunic.

Luckily, it was Miriam, who wouldn't care. "Hi Mel, just wanted to talk—do you have time?"

"Pos-def, Mim, what's on your queue?"

"Well—say, what's on your tunic?"

"Dinner, I think," I admitted.

She shook her head. "Mel*pom*ene. Honestly."

Miriam had been doing that for years, but for some reason it felt different tonight, as if—

The door banged closed a quarter meter behind my head. Mother, making sure I had my privacy whether I wanted it or not.

Miriam seemed to be trying to find something to say, which was strange since *she* had called. Then she asked, "Have you got the stuff done for Art Club?"

"Oh, yeah, sure." I was the membership chair, and Miriam was treasurer, so she needed some figures from me on how many people had joined so that we could get our share of the Club Support allocation. We took some time to get all the numbers straight.

Then there was another very long, very awkward silence. After a few moments of looking around at everything but Miriam's face on the screen, I said, "Tom has a big toggle race coming up—the All-Ship Championship. Saturday morning."

"Oh. Does he have a good chance to win?"

"He's hoping to keep the All-Ship Championship for Shift A."

"Wish him luck for me."

"I will."

Silence.

"On the lit assignment for next week," Miriam said, "you know that question about why Nick says Gatsby's story is really about the West? Did you get that?"

"Sort of. It's like some of the things in the books my mother reads—a lot of them are imitations of Hemingway and Fitzgerald and all those. I'll transmit a copy of my answer and you can see if it helps. . . ." I popped a copy of the file to her.

She looked down to check the transmit-verification line. "Thank you."

We both sat there, twitching. I thought about just saying "Oh, well, I have to run," or something like that, but I didn't.

Finally I asked, "How are things going for Theophilus?"

She sat up straighter, and her lips pushed out in a little, momentary pout, before she said, "He likes to be called Ted. He told you that."

"I'm sorry. I forgot."

"He wants to be called Ted. He was just too shy to tell us before."

"I'm sorry," I said again. "Really. I just forgot."

"Well, you should try to be more careful. And why didn't you say anything today when we were walking home? It was like being followed by my kid brother. You *embarrassed* me."

I thought maybe I should apologize but I didn't know for what.

She didn't say anything either, and we sat there and looked at each other. Finally she said, "You're doing it again. Acting like a lump. Honestly, Mel, you're my best friend but sometimes I wonder about you. We were cracking all those jokes—and you just stood there like a moron. Theophilus asked me why people say you're smart!"

Miriam had never talked to me like this before. I didn't know what to do. "And today you really won the prize," she went on.

"Hanging around with that Randy Schwartz. That was the most—"

"I wasn't hanging around with him." My voice sounded whiny, like I was pouting, and I hated it. "I was just talking to him. I had some math questions and he's good at math, and he helped me." And, I added mentally, I was trying to make sure Randy wouldn't hammer Theophilus-excuse-me-Ted into the corridor wall. But I was starting to wonder why I had bothered to worry about that. . . .

"Well, it looked like you were hanging around with him and that's what counts. That's what I mean. Don't you ever think about how things are going to look? You can be so stupid sometimes—"

My voice felt mashed and dry in my throat. "Why are you talking to me like this?" The corners of my eyes stung. I was afraid I would cry in front of Miriam, and though that had never been a problem before, now I couldn't stand the idea.

"It's for your own good, Mel." She sighed and rolled her eyes. "If you can't take a little criticism . . . well, never mind." Then she smiled, a little. "I'm sorry. Really. Look, I just called to see if you wanted to meet me and Ted and some of the others for breakfast early tomorrow in Cafeteria Twelve."

"I'd like to," I said, "but you know my mother's rules. Our family always eats breakfast together at our local cafeteria. So I just can't."

Miriam glared at me. "You know Ted only invited you because I insisted. It really took me some effort. I won't tell you what he thought after he saw you in action this afternoon." She clicked off.

I leaned back in my chair and cried for a long time. Everything was wrong.

There was a little tap on the door, and Tom's voice. "Melpomene?"

"Come in." I got out of my chair and flipped it up to let him in.

He came halfway through the door. "You sounded upset. Do you need someone to talk to?"

"Yeah. Pos-def."

So he came all the way in, closed the door, and pulled down the guest seat. I pulled my chair back down and sat, but when I started to talk I couldn't think of what to say and my throat felt so swollen I couldn't breathe. I just sat there wheezing with tears running all over my face, dribbling from my nose, burning with humiliation.

He leaned forward and took my hands. "We can talk later if you need time by yourself now."

"Now you're talking like Mother."

He clutched his chest, pretending to be shot the way they do on old flatscreen vid.

I sniffled a little, pulled down a utility wipe, and sort of halfway cleaned my face. I was feeling a little better.

"I guess I do want to talk," I said. "But none of this is going to make any sense." Then I just poured it all out, starting, for some reason, with Randy hitting Theophilus the day before. "Do you think I'm crazy?" I asked. "Or reading too much into it? He did look strange after he hit Theophilus—I don't know why that matters. . . ."

Tom shrugged a little. "He got angry and did something he was ashamed of. Or he didn't know what he was doing until it was too late. Or maybe . . ." he grinned at me. "Maybe he didn't want *you* to see him acting like that."

"You've got to be—that's the bokkiest thing I ever—"

"Don't get upset. I'm just doublechecking. Does he act like he likes you?"

I started to say "Of course not," but instead I found myself saying, "Well, yes, sometimes, I mean, he *is* always really nice. To me I mean. So I—well . . ." I told him about Pyramid Math and, as an afterthought, about the compliments Randy'd given me during aerocrosse.

Tom had that evil gleam in his eye that means the heavy teasing is about to start. "Okay. Just checking—nothing is as interesting as someone else's love life."

"He's not part of mine. He *hits* people!"

Tom winked at me; that made me even madder.

He must have seen—he got serious. "I guess this really isn't what the matter is."

"It's *some* of it." I blew my nose again. "I've tried my best to be nice to Theophilus, but I wish he'd never turned up in our class." I told him the rest. When I got to the conversation I'd just had with Miriam, I started to cry again and he had to hold me and soothe me before I could get through the story.

"That's so weird," he said. "I can't imagine treating a best friend that way. And I can't see what she's getting out of it either except hanging around this Theophilus person, which doesn't sound like any big treat to me."

I was still snuffling, but I was feeling a lot better. Now that Tom had pointed it out, it *did* seem pretty strange, not like anything I'd ever seen anyone do. "Maybe he has some kind of contagious insanity," I said. "I don't know. But whatever it is, Miriam's got it really bad." I suddenly felt very sleepy. "I think I'm okay now, at least for the moment."

Tom sighed. "Well, good, but I think you've managed to worry *me*. Are you going to have time to get your homework done?"

"I'm working on the day after tomorrow as it is. Tomorrow is No Friends Day."

"For me too. You want to see something neat I've been working on?"

"Sure," I said, though part of me groaned inside. Ever since I could remember, Tom had always used his lab allowance to build endless strange gadgets that weren't exactly art but certainly weren't engineering. Unlike most of us, he never bothered to enter any of the Projects Day competitions either.

Most of us knocked ourselves out for Projects Day—Miriam and I had been up for two nights straight getting a mural done last quarter, borrowing supplies from everyone after our lab allowance ran out. And Penelope Graham's improved fan-harness, and Chris Kim's new type of oxygen scavenger for the aquaculture tanks, had really succeeded—they had gone into use.

It wasn't like Tom to decline a competition of any kind, and this was something he was potentially good at—he could have knocked his standing hyperbolic if he'd even half tried, I was sure.

Yet every quarter he put all his lab allowance into a weird mixture of metalworking supplies and processor chips, plus an apparently random collection of other things, spent hours welding and wiring according to some strange plan that seemed to be only in his head, and produced what Mother called the Alien Artifacts—piles of bolted-together metal plates with flashing lights on them, strips of copper and aluminum tied around a tetrahedral frame surrounding something that moaned like irregular feedback, a set of five tiny gliders that pursued each other in irregular spirals and emitted little jingling sounds.

Once he had asked me to teach him how to work a CSL problem he thought was integral to his project. The problem was completely incomprehensible and so was the project.

Anyway, normally I'd have begged off, but now I owed him a big favor. And since I wasn't all that eager to see whatever he had come up with this time, he was already across the passageway between our two rooms before I started reluctantly moving.

Which is why I caught Papa standing at the edge of the sharespace, listening.

He was a little startled, but he nodded at me once and turned back into the sharespace without saying anything.

I supposed I shouldn't have been surprised. Most of the CPB spent an hour or more every day listening to com calls at random, and cameras and microphones were everywhere. But for some reason I was furious.

Still, I didn't want to have a big row right now. I needed to get to sleep on time, with Compets the next day. And besides, Tom was probably wondering how I had managed to get lost on a two-meter trip. So I just went on in, resolving to talk to Papa later.

Tom's room seemed to be about seventy percent filled with a tangle of wires, clips, thin aluminum tubing, and rectangular metal plates. "Did you pull all this stuff out of the service access, or has there been a terrible accident?"

"Lucky me—such a clever little sister. Sit down in the guest chair and just watch and listen."

Then he turned out all the lights. I couldn't see anything—with the door closed there was no light at all. "Sing something," he said.

"What?"

There was a brief flicker of yellow, and then something that looked like a three-dimensional model of a spiral galaxy burst into being. Three chords like a sort of tinny organ pulsed out. With a little trill, the spiral galaxy swirled down into a sphere of blue points, no bigger than an aerocrosse ball, and disappeared.

"Oh!" I said. "That's really—"

A great fountain of reds and yellows poured up from the floor, bounding off the ceiling as something that sounded like a Beethoven duet for piccolo and banjo rang out. The fountain poured back down in a swirl of green stars, all making flat farting noises.

There was a click as Tom threw a switch. It was completely dark again. "It doesn't deal well with speech. Now if you want to really see something, *sing.*"

He threw the switch again before I could point out that I don't sing well and I'm very self-conscious about it. But if I said that out loud, I'd trigger another one of these weird displays and he'd be mad about it.

Unfortunately, the only thing that came to mind was Papa's old story about his college Alma Mater, so I sang:

I don't know the god damn words,
I don't know the god damn words—

It looked like a rose made up of tiny points of light, but with all the petals different colors, spinning in front of me. A sound like French horns, not quite in tune, came out of it.

I didn't know what I was supposed to do other than keep singing, so I tried to follow the melody that seemed to be coming out of Tom's gadget, singing,

But I'm trying very hard to sing as if I knew
what I was doing.

73

The instruments became more like a marimba, and the rose inverted, folded, and flowed into its own center.

*So I'll keep singing even though I know it makes
no sense.*

The contracting swirl at the center suddenly broke through its bottom and fell to the floor, then bounded back up in a mushroom cloud. The chords got richer, deeper, moving into the sound of a piano and then toward an organ.

Suddenly the lights and music were gone. "What an incredible idea!" Tom said. "Why didn't I see it—well, never mind." The room lights came on. "You were singing *in response to* the effects."

"I'm sorry if I wasn't supposed to. You still haven't told me what this thing is supposed to be."

"You did *great.* That was exactly what I needed and couldn't think of." He got out from behind all the hardware, gingerly. "And as for what it is—well, it does what it does. You could call it sort of a brain in space. Microphones pick up vibrations from the struts and wires. Photocells pick up the spots the lasers draw. They all report to system-state memory. Then the processors that control the lasers and the audio outputs scan the memory and decide what to do next based on that plus the music."

I didn't want to tell Tom he had just re-invented the principle of the mercury delay tube—which Alan Turing had used in the first true computer. (I had done a report in history on it.) "What's it good for?" I asked, being as tactful as I could manage while still trying to get out the door and back to bed.

He laughed, a clear open sound that I hadn't heard in months or years. It was so wonderful to hear that I even put up with his answer: "As the piano is to music, so this pile of wire and pipe is to whatever it's good for. And I think you just helped me see what it's good for."

"You're welcome," I said. I turned to go.

"Thanks," he said, missing the irony completely. As I opened the door to my room, I could hear his keyboard starting to put out some notes apparently at random.

I almost went back to see what he did. Some of that had been sort of pretty, even if it was otherwise useless. But I had already opened my door, and Papa was sitting there in my room, in my seat.

"Come in," I said.

"I thought you might want to talk."

No one was understanding irony tonight. Well, even two days ago, this wouldn't have bothered me—but still, just like my bokky mother, I could feel my privacy being violated.

I wonder how children who are born blind feel, after the artificial eyes are installed, when they see clashing colors for the first time.

"What am I supposed to say?" I asked, finally.

"Whatever you want."

I thought I was going to tell him to get out of my room and leave me alone. But instead I started to cry, harder even than I had with Tom, and I couldn't stop. I felt my throat tightening the way it does in an anxiety attack, and tried to get my breathing slowed down and regular to head that off, but for the first time I could remember, I couldn't do it, and I stopped breathing and began to panic.

He stood up and put his arms around me. "Breathe," he said, "breathe." But I couldn't.

Then he whispered something—you never know what phrases they plant during hypnosis—and I started to sob, crying as hard as ever but breathing and less frightened. "I don't understand *anything.*"

"You've been excluded," he said. "Shut out from a group of people. That doesn't happen very often here, and you're not used to it."

"Does it happen a lot on Earth?" I was hating Earth more than ever.

"All the time." He sighed. "When I was in high school, my classmates and I put a lot of time and effort into excluding each other."

I sat back down the guest seat. "Is this something you engineered, too? Because if it is I think it's really stupid and cruel."

He shook his head. "We've sheltered the *Flying Dutchman* kids from it till now. It's absolutely pathological—hurts everyone it touches, including the ones doing the excluding, and doesn't do anything for anyone. Earth kids feel hurt by it just like you do, but because it does happen more often there, people are more used to it and they've developed more ways to handle it." He leaned forward and looked at me with one eyebrow raised, his lips flat and compressed. "I'd like to know the whole story, as you see it, from the beginning. But you're upset, Melpomene, and we can talk later if you'd rather. You set the pace."

I sighed and took stock. Crying had helped me calm down—it always does, even though it's kind of embarrassing. "Let's talk now. If I start crying again, or something, we can always stop."

Papa nodded, and leaned forward to hold my hand while he looked deep into my eyes. As I said, I don't know what any of the commands he uses for light hypnosis are, because they're blocked from me; I'm told it's some combination of several words that never would occur together in any natural context, followed by a few nonsense syllables.

He gave me the sequence that lets me remember everything, or at least think I do, and then said softly "All right, tell me all the relevant things that happened in school today. Take your time, digress all you want, don't prejudge what's important. . . ."

After living all my life with him, I can recite those directions as well as he can. I told him the whole story, without embellishment because I was under hypnosis, about Randy and Pyramid Math and how he stuck up for me, and about going home with Miriam and Theophilus and being shut out of everything, and all the rest of it.

Because you can't suppress detail in those things, it was almost 2330 when we finished up with the routine suggestion that I let my feelings out. I cried for a little while, felt much better, and then saw the clock.

"Have I kept you up too late?" Papa asked, of all the dumb questions.

"Well, yes. I have Compets tomorrow, and school starts at 0745."

"Would you like me to plant a suggestion so you'll have more energy?"

"I think you've messed around with my brain enough."

"I'm sorry I took so much of your time."

"It's all right," I said. It was—I was feeling much better now even though I still didn't know what was going on. "I just need to get to bed—I can take being a little tired tomorrow."

He hugged me again, and we said goodnight.

As I got into bed, I didn't feel too bad—I had cried myself down to emptiness.

Just as I was about to jump up to the stretchout handles, I had the stray thought that I might dream about Randy Schwartz. I had no idea why, but suddenly I had a terrific fantasy about him. I lay down on the bed, and got an orgasm almost as soon as I touched my clitoris.

It was great—it put me right to sleep. I don't remember whether I dreamed about Randy or not.

STUPID WERP. I'VE DEFINED CLITORIS THREE TIMES AND IT STILL keeps asking if it's audience-appropriate. I'm sure girls on Earth have them. Oh, well, going to bed, fix it later.

CHAPTER FIVE

I DON'T KNOW WHY THIS IS GOING SO STRANGELY FOR ME. Every day I write a little more, and yet every day it seems like there's more of the story to tell. Also, I'm finding it harder and harder to just set down what happened. I keep wanting to explain that I didn't understand this or I was going to be wrong about that, because I'm sure whoever is reading this is thinking things like that and I want them to know that I understand now, too. It was just so hard to understand at the time.

It's also ruining my studying for the FA, not so much because it's taking lim time as because I get all weirdwired and then I can't study. Last night I got so upset from writing that for the first time since I was eight I went to class unprepared. It felt horrible.

Right now there's a big pile of undone work beside me, and I'm still working on this instead. I can't seem to stop, or anyway I'm not stopping. I just hope Dr. Lovell knew what she was talking about.

* * *

THURSDAY WAS COMPETS. WE ALL CALL COMPETS "NO FRIENDS Day" because you have to work in a little booth by yourself and you can't give or get any help. You just sit there and do what you can with what the AIs throw at you.

They always shoot for your weak zones, so I got hardly any CSL or history and only a little English and Esperanto. They hit me hard on Japanese, math, physics, and chemistry, so I stayed busy all day.

They must have decided that I had a flair for projective geometry, based on the problem I did with Randy's help, because for once I didn't get any, but I would just as happily have passed up the additional diffy-q.

(Oh, not again. The werp flagged that; I think there's something wrong with it. Okay, let's see if it will take this definition: diffy-q is differential equations, and it's part of calculus, the boring part that's just a bag of tricks. I hated it then and I still do. The only person in class who's any good at it is Randy, damn him.)

Now and then they threw some Spanish, economics, or bio at me, and a few times they hit me with Earth Geography for the good of my soul or something—tell the truth, do *you* care where Block B is? Then why do *I* need to be able to find Australia on a map? It's all Earth to me. . . .

The whole day went to that nonsense. Everyone hates it, but you can't slough off, because Compets weigh so heavily in your overall academic standing, and when you lose standing everybody knows. So I just kept pounding away at it. . . . "Write five hundred words on 'The Economic Feasibility of Tri-Modulating the *Flying Dutchman* Orbit to Add a Jupiter-pass.' " . . . "Prove that natural-language gender cannot be mapped onto a rigid hierarchy of binary rules." . . . "With which nations does the Unaffiliated Soviet Republic of Kurdistan share boundaries?" . . . "Create a program of less than two hundred lines, to be implemented cellularly, to model the range of probable absorption rates of Resisting Protestants into the Ecucatholic movement. Specify initial and boundary conditions for the model as a whole." . . . The proctor brought lunch by; I set it by my elbow and kept working.

"Write a program, self-replicating with mutations, that will grow into a stable aggregate which can learn and solve the four-color problem." At least that one was sort of fun. I rechecked it twice, and then prettied it up a little when I saw that the clock was low. Just as I sent it and got back the score, a perfect-plus on that problem, time ran out on the day.

I stuffed the candy bar from lunch into my mouth, suddenly hungry, and looked around the desk to make sure I wasn't leaving anything in the Test Center—it always takes forever to get anything back after you do that. I flipped my cup of chocolate to WARM, then gulped it cold when the proctor stopped in front of my desk and opened up. I dropped my mostly-still-full tray and cup into the slot, and it rolled on to the next booth.

Out in the hall everyone was standing around comparing notes. Even though problems are all individualized, most people still believe in "hard days" and "soft days."

I looked around for Miriam, but she was over talking to Theophilus, Gwenny, and Kwame, and I felt funny about going near them. They seemed to be watching for something too.

Randy came out the door as if he were looking for someone. The four of them walked toward him, coming up behind fast.

I had no idea what they were doing, but there was something about the way they moved that I didn't like. I started toward Randy, the high grav making it easy to move quickly.

He looked up, saw me, and started to smile. Then Miriam tapped his shoulder.

When he looked back to see what it was, Theophilus spun on the ball of one foot. The other foot reached up, head-high, and hit Randy's face a dozen times harder than any punch I'd ever seen. Randy seemed to fly sideways, falling clumsily to the deck. I had never seen anything like it.

I started to run—everyone did—when there's a fight, if it doesn't stop quickly, they punish the whole class for it. Because I'd been headed that way already, I got there ahead of most people, and I saw the whole thing.

Randy clutched his face, rubbing it. "I'm sorry I hit you," he said. He sounded like he was choking with anger, but he was holding his voice level. "It was a rotten thing to do, and I really had this coming, so I guess we're even."

"Oh, you're sorry," Theophilus said. "I just bet. I bet you say that to anybody who can knock you down, Your Majesty."

Randy sat up. He still looked a little dazed. "Isn't that what this is about? I mean, I hit you, and I know it was wrong. Wasn't that why you kicked me? Isn't that what this is about?"

"Isn't that what this is about?" The mockery in Theophilus's voice made me wince. "Oh, good, good, *good*. You hit me, I hit you, now it's all o-*kay*. Is that the way it's supposed to be, Your Majesty? Well, get this clear: I don't want your apology. I don't want to be friends. I took five years of tae kwon do. They won't let the kids here study any martial arts—so I know you don't have any idea how to really fight. I just wanted you to know I can do this to you any time I want. Have you got that?" He stood over Randy, poised, waiting to hit or punch him if he moved. "Say you understand, Your Majesty."

Tears streaked Randy's face. "I understand."

"You thought you could treat me the way you did everybody else and beat me up for being smarter than you. Because you've always been the big king of the class, haven't you, Your Majesty? Well, you're not any more. You were never anything but the plain old class bully, and now you're the ex-bully. And the only reason people are bullies is because they're stupid." As he smiled down at Randy, I couldn't remember anyone I had seen so happy—or any time I had been so frightened. "Say it."

Randy didn't seem to know what Theophilus was demanding. He looked puzzled, and scared, and about to start really crying.

The Earth kid turned sideways and his foot snapped out, catching Randy in the side of the head. "You really *are* stupid. You don't get it, do you? Say you're stupid."

"Why?" The whine in Randy's voice made me want to vomit.

"Because you are. Do you want another one?" Theophilus faked another kick at Randy's head, and Randy backed away, scooting on his hands and knees, keening under his breath and snuffling. Theophilus took a step forward and stamped on his hand, holding him where he was. "You know the only reason you have such high standings is because everyone is afraid to do better than you."

I hated to see Randy's face, but I couldn't look away. He didn't say anything, but from the way the anger went out of him he'd been hit harder with those words than he had with Theophilus's foot.

"Now say you're stupid or get another one. I'm going to teach you what you are."

Randy looked for a moment like he might defy Theophilus— but then that foot cocked back and Randy looked down at the deck. "I'm stupid," he said, quietly. "I'm stupid, okay? I'm stupid."

Theophilus stood there with his hands on his hips and a smile that made my skin crawl. "That's much better. Now you know what you are, Your Majesty. King Stupid."

"So how does it feel, Your Majesty?" Miriam said. It was the same tone of voice she had used on me the night before. I hated her then, more than I'd ever hated anyone. Gwenny Mori laughed, and then Theophilus and Miriam laughed, and then Kwame joined them.

A few people in the surrounding mob of kids laughed as well, more from nerves I think than from anything being funny.

"All right, everyone get moving," Dr. Niwara said quietly. She had come up behind us.

Randy stood up and walked out of the center of the crowd. I could hear a couple of people whispering, "King Stupid" and "Your Majesty" at him. He didn't look to either side, just went straight to the omnivators.

"I said everyone." Dr. Niwara's voice was colder and flatter than I'd ever heard it. We all started walking; as I turned the corner I looked back and saw that a lot of people were crowding in close to Theophilus. They seemed excited, nervous—*happy*.

I got on an omnivator by myself, keyed my destination—all the way to my Corridor Commons, even though that ties up an omnivator for much longer than necessary—and left in it without waiting to see if anyone else wanted to come along. It was the first time I had ever done such a thing. I wondered how many times you'd have to do it to be declared an unco.

I swam out of the omnivator to the wall of our corridor, and hauled along the net as fast as I could. It felt really good—I almost bruised my hands stopping at the living unit.

Mother was sitting in there, at the reader as always. Usually I'd have said hello, she'd have said hello, and I'd have gone to my room, but this time she pushed the reader away. "How was school today?"

I shrugged. "Mostly okay—it was Compets." I didn't want to tell her about what had happened to Randy; Mother never gives you sympathy when she can give you an interpretation instead.

"I finished the turnover to Mrs. Harrison. She's *very* interesting, but I'm glad I won't have to go back to that office now."

"Oh." I unslung my werpsack and tossed it lightly against Tom's door, letting it bounce into my room. Guess it had been stupid to hope that she'd decide to go back to work.

"She said that a bunch of the other children—a 'real gang,' she said—got together to visit with Theophilus this morning over breakfast. I understand your friend Miriam Baum was with them—"

"Yes, Mother," I said. "I was invited but I thought you wouldn't let me go. You know, breakfast with the family?"

"Well, for something like this, of course I would. If he does it again—"

"I don't think he'll ask me. We're not getting along very well." I plunged into my room; for once I really did want some of that privacy she was always talking about.

Five seconds after I closed the door, she banged on it. "Melpomene."

"Yes?"

"He would really be a good person for you to get in with. He's from Earth, and you could get more of a perspective—"

"You mean a distortion. No thanks. If I want to be an unco, I'll ask for advice here in my own family."

"Melpomene!"

She started to open the door; I kicked it shut. I sat in my chair, rubbing my face. More than anything, I wished my homework was already done—it would have been if it hadn't been for all the nonsense yesterday, and now with this . . . it didn't seem right. Today had been more than long enough already.

After a while Mother tapped on the door.

"Go away," I said.

"I will. I know you need some time by yourself." What I needed was time away from her, but close enough. "Your father and I are going to one of the little cafeterias over in the Mushroom. If you want to come along you can, or you can wait for Tom and go to dinner with him."

"I'll wait for Tom." I could tell from her tone—that was the right answer. "See you."

"All right, Melly. Take care." I heard her and Papa go out; she probably hadn't told him that we'd had a quarrel or that I was upset—she would think it was "none of his business." I'm still not sure I understand what she means when she says that. Since they were gone, I pushed the door open and went out to sit in the sharespace. I could have pulled out the werp and gotten some studying done, or maybe meditated—our family is cyber-tao but it's been at least a year since I've even looked at *Forks in Time.*

There were lots of things that might have been sensible, mature things to do, but fortunately I wasn't so old that I always had to do those things. Instead I turned on the reader and called up a book—good, old, familiar *Beat To Quarters.* After a minute I got myself a hot cup of coffee-and-chocolate, and settled in to read.

I was feeling a lot better half an hour later when Tom got home and called me back to this world with a touch on my shoulder. I guess he was kind of surprised to see me at the reader—he and I usually only use it late at night when we can't sleep, and on weekends and vacations of course. "Something new come in from Earth?"

I raised the reader's screen away from my face, brought the seat back to upright, and turned off the back massager. "No, just something old. I was waiting for you and didn't feel like doing schoolwork. We're on our own for dinner—want to burn some of my discrets and go get a pizza?"

"Baby tilapia and rabbit sausage?" he asked—his favorite kind.

"You drive a tough bargain. Can we skip the fish and just do straight rabbit sausage?"

"It's your treat—but how about mushrooms then, instead of tilapia?"

"Pos-def. Bunny and fungus, large. I'll order; grab whatever you're taking with you." The pizza cafeteria is down in the promenade area beside the entrance from the Mushroom. It would take us a few minutes to get there, so I flashed the request ahead.

We didn't talk much on the way, and a couple of minutes after we settled into a booth the pizza came out of the slot, so there was a long time there of not talking and just being with Tom. That helped too.

"I missed you," I said suddenly, not sure why I had happened to think of it. "All those times you were having dinner with Susan the Rodent." He tensed. "I mean, Susan, your girlfriend."

He shrugged. "I'm sorry." He could have had the decency to say he'd missed me too. "I know you don't like her. But since you bring it up, I'd better mention that we've started seeing each other again. In fact," he leaned forward and winked at me, "part of the reason I was late was we did a quick sneaky."

"Koapy." I was in a nasty mood. "Did you execute the docking maneuver?"

"No, we just had time to touch each other a little. It was fun, though. She's got breasts. Why don't you grow some?"

I stared down at my food and tried to make myself eat.

"I'm sorry," Tom said. He reached over and tagged my shoulder. "I know you don't like Susan. I won't talk about her."

"It's not that. Well, it is, but that's not the big part of it. . . . Things just aren't going very well. They haven't all this week, and they really didn't today."

"I knew something was on your mind," he said. "You've been feuding with Mother a lot."

85

"Yeah." I sighed. "Something really awful happened today, but I don't exactly know how to talk about it." I took another bite. "Theophilus organized an audience for himself and then beat the living shit out of Randy."

"You'd better tell it a little slower."

I did, calmly at first, but then seeing it again in my memory, coming near tears at the end of it. "I never saw anything like it except on vid. I mean, when people hit each other sometimes someone gets bruised or shaken up a little, but he *really* hurt Randy. And he wouldn't accept the apology and be friends afterward or anything. I know a lot of kids are afraid of Randy and they probably liked seeing him get beaten, but this is too much. Theophilus doesn't stop after he's won. . . ."

He chewed his way through his whole next piece before he said, "Bad. Real bad. You talked to Papa, too?"

I nodded. "Last night. He'd been waiting in my room when I went back. Before that he was listening to us at the door."

Tom nodded. "Earning his salary, I guess. Did he say anything about what was going on?"

"I get the impression it's some kind of a bizarre Earth custom. Like human sacrifice and slavery, you know, in the history books. Oh, Tom, it just makes my head spin. I feel bad for Theophilus and for Randy and maybe even for Miriam and I don't know what to do about any of it. Thanks for listening but let's change the subject. How was *your* day?"

He shook his head. "The thing is, I really don't know how it was yet—I'll have to see how it comes out. This should be good news, but I can't just relax and enjoy it—it feels like I'm being set up for something." He stopped to take a big bite. "I got this colony-hold of CSL problems today, and all of a sudden I knew all the answers. Nothing like that ever happened before. I must have p.d.'d ten kids."

"That sounds wonderful," I said. "I always knew you had talent for it—you just never seemed to be able to use your talent."

He shook his head, stuffing in another bite and chewing quickly. I love my brother but the way he eats . . . "The trouble is that I didn't really know how I got any of the answers—I just got them. Flash of light, blind intuition, whatever you want to call that. So there's no guarantee I can ever do it again—"

"And now the machine's going to jack your difficulty level. Ouch."

"Yeah. Ouch. Unless of course they're all going to be like these today."

"Maybe there's some trick all these problems have in common, and you're doing the trick without knowing that you're doing it. If I can figure out what it is, and show it to you—do you remember any of them?"

He gave a gusty little tenth of a laugh. "That's another weird part. I remember them all perfectly. Usually I sweat over a problem for ages, and then I can't remember any of it—but none of these took me as long as a minute, and I could practically recite them all verbatim."

I had him key all the problems onto my werp to look at later. At first glance, there was something strange about them, but I couldn't see what.

"You know," Tom said, out of nowhere, "it sounds like Randy was never very popular before. Your new kid seems to have figured that out in a hurry."

I nodded. "And he's getting a lot of use out of it. But for what? He seems to be after something, but I don't have any idea what it is."

"Maybe he just wants people to accept him," Tom suggested.

"Maybe. But this doesn't seem like the way to do it." I shrugged. "Maybe it'll blow over," I added, trying to talk myself into the idea.

"It might. Do you want that last piece of pizza?"

"Take it, it's yours. You need it for the big toggle race; you have to impress Susan."

He gobbled the last piece of pizza as I watched—or rather, as I avoided watching. "Melpomene, it's okay. You don't have to be nice about Susan. It's even harder to take than when you call her a rodent."

"Sorry. Just trying . . ."

"Yeah. It's okay." He stretched and yawned. "Between the

87

rumors going around about Mother, and the fact that Susan is so impressed by Papa's job that she can't talk when he's around, it's pretty hard to get her to come for a visit to the living unit. And I really wish she would. If you do want to help, just act like you're glad to see her the next time you meet."

"Do or die tryin', bwana," I said.

He leaned forward and kissed me on the cheek. "Were you reading Rider Haggard earlier?"

"C. S. Forester."

"Oh."

We tried to talk about small things after that, but it got more and more awkward. The problem was that Tom was so close to FA that getting it was all he could think about; he'd even lost interest in toggle racing, which at one time I'd have thought could never happen. He was going to stop being a kid in less than ten weeks; I had two years yet to go.

There just wasn't as much to talk about any more. That thought made me really sad, and I got quieter and quieter. At last we went home, not saying much, shy and awkward with each other for the first time I could remember. Tom went straight into his room, and to judge from the noise, the Alien Artifact was progressing nicely.

Papa and Mother were still not back. I didn't care about Mother, but I knew Papa would want to talk about what had happened between Randy and Theophilus—well, I knew I would—and I couldn't afford to be up late two nights in a row.

I got my homework done and they still weren't back. I put a trace on them, and of all things they had gone to Ballroom Dance Club, out on the rim of the Mushroom. When I was little, they'd done that a lot, but it had been years.

Well, if that was their idea of fun, they were welcome to it. We had tried it in rec and the best thing I could say for it was that I got to do an up-close inspection on a couple of boys I kind of liked.

They were sure to be late, but I still wasn't sleepy, so I decided to wait up a while.

Tom had gone to sleep, and it was past Lights Down, so I

couldn't go out, and it was too late to call anyone in A Shift on the com, and I didn't know anyone in B or C. I didn't feel like I had to get way out ahead on my homework either, and though re-reading the old Hornblower had been comforting earlier, I didn't especially want to read any more just now. I wished Tom were awake to talk to.

That reminded me—his problem set. There was nothing else to do, anyway.

When I looked at the problems carefully for the first time, they certainly looked intriguing—difficult and tricky, but not at all beyond me. I was probably doing CSL at higher level than Tom was—birthyear doesn't determine the level of what you study, only who you study with—so I was sure I could do them.

Forty minutes later I was wide awake, and more frustrated than I'd ever been with a set of CSL problems. I had almost forgotten I was waiting up for Papa.

Tom said he had come up with right answers in less than a minute for each problem. So far I hadn't made a dent in even one of them. Yet they were all well within my level. Something was drastically wrong.

I got myself a container of fruit drink from our food dispenser, punctured the top with the straw, and sucked it down, half-finishing before I got back to the screen.

Twenty more minutes, and it was really late, and I still wasn't anywhere. I gave up and tried setting up a feasibility-proof algorithm for every problem. Usually that's the dullest, slowest, and dumbest way to solve a programming problem, but the one way that always works. I hadn't thought of doing it because, if Tom was getting the answers in an intuitive flash, it seemed unlikely he was subconsciously solving the problem by the *slowest* of all possible methods.

It was such a big job that there was actually a little bit of a delay; apparently even with an allocation for four kiloprocessers this was a struggle. When the answer finally came back, it took me completely by surprise; all the problems *did* have something in common.

They were all incomputable.

(The werp just hit me for another explanation. I'm afraid I have trouble remembering you don't take CSL. Well, it's important for things I'm going to tell you about later, so let's try:

There's a thing called Godel's Theorem that shows that not every true proposition can be calculated—some problems can have just one right answer with no logical pathway to it. You can guess a right answer, or you can try lots of answers and hope it happens to be one you try, but you can't really "solve" such problems at all. You can only get answers.)

Somehow or other, Tom, who couldn't do the easiest problems without sweating blood, could just "know" the right answer to all these impossible ones. That had to be what the software was looking for, and it had found it. Well, he could stop worrying about getting harder problems—what he was doing was already impossible.

It didn't make any sense, but not much did any more. God, I was tired. I folded everything up, pulled down the bed, jumped up, stretched, let go, and was asleep before I hit.

CHAPTER SIX

I GOT TO CLASS A LITTLE LATER THAN USUAL FRIDAY MORNING. There had been some changes.

Miriam, who always sat by me, was next to Theophilus. I knew he wanted to be called Ted—Dr. Niwara had even announced it—but somehow I kept calling him Theophilus anyway, maybe mental revenge or something. Gwenny and Kwame and Carole were clustered with her around Miriam and Theophilus. Well, that was no surprise, since Kwame was probably following Miriam, and Carole went wherever Gwenny did.

Usually Randy was a little separated from the rest of us, with only Barry Yang close to him. Randy was in his usual seat, but Barry was across the room from him, in back of Theophilus's crowd.

And there was no one even near where I usually sat.

In a way it was a continuation of No Friends Day, because we started with Individual CSL. My mind was wandering but I got top rank anyway; the problems on the screen just flew by, more like I was just completing sentences than actually figuring anything out. Of course, after I had spent more than an hour the night before trying to do the provably impossible, this stuff was bound to seem easy.

Toward the end of the time, Dr. Niwara notified us through our werps that the afternoon would be pyramid CSL; the screen paused a moment, and then added:

—YOUR PARTNER: CHRISTIAN KIM.

Lim koapy. The guy was dumb as a rock. There went my top standing. . . .

—PAIRED WITH: PADRAIC MONAGHAN AND ANGEL CASTAGHENA.

Well, maybe we could all gang up on him.

I got engrossed in the last bonus problem and was last in line on the way to the cafeteria; I seemed to be about thirty seconds behind the present all the time today. Theophilus and his "real gang"—thinking back to some old flatscreen movies I'd seen I could see why they called it that—were all up front with Dr. Niwara.

While I was thinking about that, the people in front stopped to let a class of little kids get through an intersection, and I bumped into the guy in front of me, suddenly realizing it was Chris Kim. "Sorry," I said. "I wasn't looking where I was going."

"It's okay." He smiled at me, a little shyly. "I guess you're in charge of de-dumbing me on CSL this afternoon." It didn't sound like he was challenging me. I almost wished it had.

"You shouldn't say you're dumb." I was still thinking about Theophilus and his "real gang." That was such a good word for it . . . not like they stuck together out of friendship and loyalty, like the pack of wolves I saw once when my window was tuned to a camera in Denali Worldpark . . . more like a school of sharks . . .

Chris had just said something and I had no idea what it was. "Sorry, I'm completely weirdwired today. What did you say?"

"I said once you see me try CSL you'll say I'm dumb too."

"Well, look, give me a chance to make the discovery for myself. What's so bad about CSL, anyway?"

"Nothing except it's gibberish." He sounded just like Tom.

We went through the door into the cafeteria. Our lunches were waiting for us as always, and somehow, with all that had been happening, that was wonderful. No matter what people thought of you or who you had trouble with, your lunch was always there with your name lettered on top "—because you belong to the ship," I heard Papa's voice say, and I suddenly realized how many times I had been told that when I was younger. Thank the ship for your dinner. Love the ship because it feeds you . . . because it loves you.

Suddenly I knew whatever was in the lunch, I didn't want it. Oh well, everyone always ended up trading anyway. . . . "Ugh. I can't imagine why I ordered guinea pig fried rice."

"Trade you crawfish cakes for it," Chris offered.

"Pos-def."

We took a small table together. I wanted to see if I could figure out what the matter was between him and CSL before he actually had a problem in front of him. I scraped my fried rice onto his tray, and he flipped the crawfish cakes onto mine. "There," I said, "We've pushed out our indifference curves."

He wasn't listening; he was watching Miriam go over to sit with Theophilus. "Uh, what did you say?"

"I said you're hardly indifferent to the way her curves have pushed out."

Chris laughed, a nice big friendly sound, nothing like Theophilus's evil-minded giggle. "Okay. I *did* hear you the first time." He shrugged. "I used to think Mim was a little bit interested in me. It looks like that's over."

I watched too. She was hanging on every word Theophilus said, laughing at all his jokes.

"You're tying a knot in your fork," Chris pointed out helpfully.

I straightened it on the edge of the table, giving it all my attention.

"That Ted person really has changed things around here," Chris added.

I nodded, glumly, and looked around the room. The crowd at Theophilus's table was whispering and talking, and sometimes they'd laugh that funny way that sounded like it was meant to be overheard. Occasionally you'd swear that some of them pointed at you and said something, though you could never guess what.

At the tables around their table there were a lot of other kids, all trying to listen in. Some of them, like Barry Yang and Paul Kyromeides, seemed to be trying hard to get invited to Theophilus's table; others didn't seem as directly interested, but they too tended to lean in to listen whenever there was a roar of laughter from the table.

There were other people, besides Chris and me, who weren't sitting close to the Real Gang. Randy Schwartz was all by himself, across the room from them. His concentration was all on his tray, but his shoulder blades were pulled back like he was expecting an arrow between them. Bekka Hayakawa and Penelope Graham were at another corner. They seemed to be ignoring it, but they both dove into their food whenever the laughter got really loud. Rachel DeLane was all by herself too, reading something on her werp, but now that I thought of it, she had always done that. There were other people scattered away from Theophilus's table, but it seemed to me that all their ears tipped toward it.

Padraic's voice rose a little above the rest of the Real Gang. "Well, he is *kind of* ugly, and *sort of* clumsy, but he makes up for it by being *completely* stupid."

Aside from Randy, he might have been talking about Robert, M'tsu, Ichiro . . . as the roar of laughter came, every one of them tensed up. I looked at Chris, and he was clenched like a fist.

"Even some of us who are friends with Miriam think she's out of her mind," I said. "Some of us still think it's more important for a guy to be kind, and good at a lot of things, and a hard competitor, than it is for him to impress people."

His smile was thin. "Well, I'm a hard competitor, and I'm not *un*kind. But I'm certainly not any good at CSL, or any school stuff."

"Wait till I'm done with you," I said, only half teasing. Dr. Niwara had told me more than once that I was a natural teacher.

Chris was looking off into space, as if he hadn't heard me. "A lot of it probably is that I'm just not motivated, so I get bored. You don't need CSL for agtech. I want to work the aqua side; that just means I have to be able to do a few numbers and read graphs. This other stuff, it's all right I guess, but sometimes it just feels like it's there to make me feel bad. I can't wait to get FA and never have to look at it again—I just want to get down to the tanks and work."

I took a big gulp of milk; I had the urge to ask Chris if he was sure he was smart enough to outwit the oysters. Papa always says there's room for everyone, but some people certainly take theirs up without making it interesting.

After that, the conversation drifted over to sports. That was more fun—I had noticed before that although Chris was small, he was wiry and very agile, but now I realized he had a real eye for strategy, and his opinions about people's hidden strengths in the class and who he would pick if he were a captain (not likely, with his low standings in everything) were really astute. (They agreed with mine almost completely.) He wasn't as dumb as I'd thought, I realized—just not interested in the same things I was.

That thought gave me a little flash of insight. When Chris offered to take both our trays back, I took him up on it. As soon as his back was turned, I called up the Fink Board on the werp.

The Fink Board (the official name is the Shared Instructor Information Bulletin Board) is where you post things you've noticed to help the teacher. It's supposed to be anonymous, but I'm sure the CPB knows whose i.d. things are coming from, just as they monitor the private channel com.

I typed in "C Kim probably more interested in CSL if app problems were from ag ecol & econ esp aqua." I cleared my screen before he turned back my way, and called up next week's schedule as a cover. Sometimes you can really do someone a favor with the Fink Board, but nobody appreciates it.

We talked a little more, mostly about toggle racing and sixwall handball, and then it was time to go back to class. I felt a lot better.

The afternoon did not start badly. Pyramid CSL is always a lot easier on me than any other Pyramid competition. I dug Chris out of a few problems, bailed out some of the others on the team, and once gave Randy a couple of hints—though CSL is usually a good subject for him.

We were milling around outside the classroom at the end of the day, and I was saying some encouraging things to Chris while trying to get him over by Miriam, who was still hanging around with Theophilus, when it started.

"Randy. King Randy. Your Majesty." It was Gwenny that time. Randy ignored her and walked straight toward the omnivators.

"Hey King Randy," Kwame chimed in. "You came in second again, Your Majesty." There was a nasty titter among a lot of kids. I still didn't understand that style of joke, and I was getting to be glad of it.

"Hey Randy." Theophilus stepped out of the crowd. "Randy, boy, I'm talking to you." I didn't know why he stressed "boy" so hard; after all, none of us would even *take* the FA exam for more than a year.

Slowly, as if he'd rather have done anything else, Randy turned around to face Theophilus. "What?" he asked, sullenly, his head down.

I wanted him to hold his head up and stare Theophilus into silence, but Randy just stood there looking at the floor.

Theophilus stepped up to him confidently, waiting for him to look up before he said, "I thought it would be really funny if you did that howling noise for everybody."

I could see Randy didn't know what Theophilus was talking about. Neither moved or said anything for a couple of long breaths.

Then Theophilus, very slowly and deliberately, turned his back on Randy and walked a few steps toward us. He looked around and said, "Since I have to 'get adjusted,' they make me go to this psychiatrist. Randy goes too. His appointment is right before mine. I always hear Randy in there before me, yelling and screaming, and then he makes these lim weird howling noises. So I was wondering if maybe King Randy would do them for all of us to laugh at. . . ."

Randy stood there as silent as if he'd been stunned. Tears ran all over his face. He didn't move to wipe them away.

"Come on, King Randy." Theophilus took a step back toward him. "Don't you remember? It goes like this. . . ." He put his head back and howled—a long squealing inhale erupting into an open-mouthed falsetto moan, sharp sobs and deep grunts breaking into it as it collapsed into a slow, wretched wheeze. Even in Theophilus's mocking imitation, its misery pierced me from throat to gut.

It got so quiet I could hear Randy breathing. Miriam, who ought to be slowly gutted, gave a nervous little laugh. Then a lot of kids did.

Randy wasn't really trying to hit Theophilus, I don't think. I've never asked. It looked more to me like he just charged blindly at him, too furious, too outraged, to make any kind of a real attack.

Theophilus was ready—probably had started out ready. He did another of those pivot-and-kick things, hitting Randy in the face, then stepped in for a solar plexus punch. Randy sat down, hard, and Theophilus grabbed his jaw and slapped him across the face again and again. It sounded like aerocrosse balls slamming into the safety pads, and Randy seemed to fold around the blows like a soggy towel.

I didn't even know I was running toward them. If anybody yelled, or said anything, I didn't hear it. Papa had hammered at me, as soon as I could speak, that whatever I heard or saw of his patients, I was to say nothing to anyone, ever. Chris and Barry have both told me since that I was yelling, not words, just a loud, open-mouthed yell, the whole way to Theophilus; I don't remember doing that either.

I would have hit him squarely in the middle of his back, except that he reached out, grabbed my wrist, snapped it downward as he kicked me high on one thigh, and flung me upside down against the wall.

Papa says they teach all of you how to do that in rec, and it's one more reason I'm never going to visit Earth.

My back stung like being burned, and my thigh was numb, but then I slid down the wall and landed on my head. A dull curtain of pain shut off the world. I was barely aware of Dr. Niwara bursting in on us, and by the time things quit hurting enough for me to focus, Papa was there, sitting with me and Randy in the empty classroom. "I think," he said, "the time has come for a long talk. Randy, I've called your father, and he knows you're with me, so if you'll just come with me . . ."

AFTER EVERYTHING THAT HAD HAPPENED, I WAS EXPECTING some sort of a big revelation, but I was completely disappointed. Papa had just wanted to make sure Randy understood what was happening to him, and he had wanted me there "to supply observations and comments," as he put it. There wasn't much to say. Theophilus Harrison was about as well-established as he could possibly get. What Papa called "adolescent power games" were replacing "the mutually supportive neoconstruct." I'm sure half of it went right by Randy, since a third of it did me and I'm used to Papa.

Finally, Randy said, "Um, Dr. Murray? I can follow most of this—I think—but I don't see what I can do about it. Or Melpomene either. We're just kids, you know."

Papa scratched his head; I always liked the way he did that. The great brown expanse of his bald spot shone as if it had been waxed, and I found myself looking at him and thinking about how old he seemed to be getting, rather than listening to what he was saying.

"—not sure you are 'just kids.' In a lot of ways, you're the only people who really do understand anything." He sighed. "We have a very small number of adults trying to raise a very large number of you into a culture that we just made up, one we don't have any emotional attachment to ourselves. We're doing about as well as anyone does in a completely unprecedented situation. We're screwing up right and left."

Randy scratched his head too. I had the funny image of it being contagious. Since then I've learned that Randy does that when he's trying to find a polite way to tell people to cut the bullshit. "Um, sure. I see. But what can we do?"

Papa leaned back and seemed to be thinking, harder and harder. I had a little time to think myself, and I was losing my temper. This man had programmed both our brains to think what NAC wanted us to think. Now it turned out he'd done it wrong and didn't know what to do. So who did he ask to dig himself, and NAC, out of the mess? You've got it. Us. The people they had crippled with their plan.

So here he was calmly talking about it with Randy as if it were the most natural thing in the world. Then again, Randy was just sitting there listening to it—of all things, having had this done to him by this man, Randy was asking him for advice.

I was about to say something—maybe yell something—when Papa shook his head, as if something sticky had landed on it. "Pfui. I had a bunch of answers and none of them really tells you to do anything—only to 'be this way' or 'be that way.' Typical shrinkspeak. I'll tell you both what I want you to do, and especially you, Melly."

Melly. I hated that.

"Follow your hearts."

Follow *our* hearts? In just what way were they supposed to be ours? "That's it," I said. "This is all I can listen to."

I got up and left; they were too startled to do anything about it. I think my father called my name.

I SCOOTED INTO OUR LIVING UNIT, SLUNG MY WERP INTO ITS bin, and shut the door. I wasn't sure what time it was but I couldn't get up enough ambition to push a button and find out. Instead, I just put the desk and seats up, pulled the bed down, and stretched out on it.

Drained and empty as if I'd cried for a week, I was asleep almost at once.

I always know when I'm dreaming, so nightmares hardly ever frighten me. But this one did.

In my dream, I walked around the outer edge of the Mushroom, along the central corridor that rings the rim. The gravity was too high, somehow, and I'd been walking for a long time, so my feet and ankles and knees were aching. No one else was there.

I was whining to myself—I *never* do that in real life.

At first, I thought, "In this dream I'm going to look for someone and not find them." But I couldn't imagine who I was supposed to be looking for, and besides I'd have been allowed to rest if that was how it worked.

Footsteps behind me. I must not look back and I must not let whoever it was catch me. I always hate chase scenes in the old flatscreen films, and I like them a lot less in my dreams. It seemed to be gaining on me, and I broke into a run, my legs aching and sore from my thighs on down. For some reason I could not turn off into any side corridor either.

At first I seemed to be getting away, but then the footsteps behind me broke into a run and caught up rapidly. I ran harder, gaining space again, and again they caught up. Finally, when I ran as fast as I possibly could, my pursuer also seemed unable to go any faster.

Up ahead, I heard more footsteps, retreating from me. If I could just get to that person, I would be safe. But the footsteps in front of me stayed the same distance away, their source hidden by the upward curve of the floor in front of me. Just as I could not lose the terrifying steps behind me, I could not catch up with the friend I could hear just ahead.

In the same part of my mind that knew I was dreaming, I realized that both sets of footsteps were my own. That didn't stop my running—nothing could. The fear I fled and the hope I chased had to be obeyed, even though the sounds themselves were mere echoes circling the outermost ring of the Mushroom.

In that senseless logic, it was my running that kept the Mushroom turning, like the little animals I had seen on treadmills on the vid. Without my running there would be no grav and our calcium balance would go, our skeletons dissolving. The ache in my legs was from the terrible effort of pushing the great structure, half a kilometer across, a hundred thousand tonnes, with only my two legs.

I saw myself from outside, face darkening, stumbling. Either I would master my irrational fear and hope, and stop, or I would not, and would keep running.

If I stopped, I would fall into an exhausted sleep on the floor. Slowly, as I slept, the Mushroom would run down and stop turning. There would be no more grav, and because it would all be my fault, the disaster of everyone's calcium loss would fall on me all at once. My bones would dissolve, urine white and thick as yogurt pouring from my body, the flesh collapsing. The ribs would soften and bend, and I would wake only in time to feel my chest muscles give their final spasm, the bones crumbling, my lungs collapsing, unable to breathe, to move, even to reach outward, pulsing on the deck, turning blue-black, face and brains sucking down into my windpipe . . .

Or if I kept running, like the "Wonderful One-Hoss Shay" in the poem, my whole body would finally go to pieces at once, every blood vessel ripping along its length, every membrane rupturing, all the tissues turned instantly to thick jam, the skin going next to last as my screaming face dissolved. My juiced body would splatter forward in a long red iron-reeking streak.

I both watched and felt the last of it—the nervous system remained intact. My brain, trailing an immense tangle of nerves, lay in that red pool, dying for hours as pain messages flooded in through the still-intact spaghetti of nerves.

Both my deaths, shapeless collapse and dissolution, were impossible, as impossible as my turning the Mushroom by myself or hearing undistorted footsteps through almost two kilometers of corridors. I said this to myself over and over again, as I said to myself that I was dreaming.

But I didn't stop running and I didn't wake up.

"Uh, Melpomene?"

I sat up screaming into Randy Schwartz's surprised expression, my face sticky with tears.

"Uh," he repeated, staring. "I'm sorry I woke you up if you were sleeping."

"Hi," I said, not sure what else I could say. I grabbed a wipe from the dispenser and rubbed my face frantically.

"Hi. Uh, Dr. Murray . . . you know, your father—"

"That's what Mother says."

"Yes, well, he—what did you say?"

"It's an old joke I heard in an old flatscreen movie, so old it was in monochrome. The movie I mean, not the joke." I blew my nose. I was so glad to be out of the nightmare that I couldn't yet remember what I had been upset about. "Have a seat if you can find one. What did Papa say?"

Randy sat down next to me on the bed. "Well, uh, he wanted me to see if you were okay. He said he was afraid that he would just upset you more, and he didn't want you to have to wait for your brother to get home."

"Well, I am okay," I said, sitting down. "How are *you?* I thought Theophilus was going to kill us both."

"I half wish he would." Randy shook his head. "Kill me, I mean. At least they'd give him some brig time and I wouldn't have to be afraid of him anymore."

"I see what you mean, pos-def. Did Papa say anything after I left?"

"I wanted to go after you but he said you probably needed time by yourself. I thought that was a pretty weird idea, but he's the shrink, so . . ." Randy shrugged again. "Anyway, I'm glad you're okay."

"Did he say anything else?"

"Not about you, exactly." He looked down at the floor and that was the first time I realized that he was shy. "He—um, I guess you know I see Dr. James once a week about some problems I have." He made himself look me in the eye. "I guess everyone knows."

I nodded. "I still like you."

Randy turned two shades redder and I was afraid he was going to cry, but then he smiled this big, beautiful smile—I'd never seen him do that before—and even laughed a little. "Thank you! I'm always afraid people won't like me. Like anything they knew about me would be one more thing to hate me for." He was looking down again. "It's lim weird, Melpomene. It used to be people hated me for being the class bully, and at least I could understand that. Now I'm not much of a bully anymore, and they hate me even more."

"I don't hate you," I said. "As far as I'm concerned, you're real koapy. And I don't think very many other people really hate you either. It's more like Theophilus has invented this new game and everyone wants to play."

He sighed. "Maybe."

I couldn't think of anything more to say, and he looked so tense that I was afraid if I touched him he'd jump headfirst into the ceiling. I sat there for several long breaths, just watching him.

On the other hand, this silence was worse than anything I could possibly say. "You were talking about Dr. James," I said.

"Yeah."

"Are you happy to be changing doctors?"

"Yeah. I don't always get along with Dr. James." He shrugged again. "It might be because he's a pompous lim bokkup and cryo besides. Just for example. But your father—he's pretty koapy, I think, I mean just from meeting him this once, so I asked if I could be his patient instead of Dr. James's."

"That's great," I said. I meant it, because I knew Papa was supposed to be very good, but at the same time it made me remember what I had been angry about. "When are your appointments?"

"Mondays after school. He said if it was okay with you, I could come home from school with you, then he'd see me, and then I would come to dinner with your family?" Randy made it a question, and I could tell he was ready to back out if he thought the idea annoyed me at all.

"Pos-def it's okay," I said. My stomach rumbled, and I remembered. "Speaking of it, have you had dinner?"

"No, I spent a long time talking with your father. He said he didn't want to impose himself on you for a while. I think he and your mother were going somewhere together."

"Well, let's practice for Monday, then," I said. "Let's eat together, maybe some cafeteria where nobody knows us, so we can talk about all this."

"Pos-def." He got up, grabbing his werpsack, and I got mine from the bin.

We decided to go to the cybertao cafeteria out on the Mushroom, Randy because he'd never done Ceremonies and me because I was hoping doing this could get me out of CT on the weekend. Papa and Mother weren't especially strict but I usually found myself at Copy Transference most Sundays, bored and annoyed. Maybe if I bought the guilt off now, I could sleep in on Sunday.

It was fairly far—about as far as back to school—so we caught the omnivator together. When the high grav hit us, down in the outer edge of the Mushroom, I found out how tired I really was, trudging limp and hungry down the hall to the cafeteria. I looked at Randy, and if anything he looked worse.

To my surprise, the attendant at the cybertao cafeteria was Bert van Piet, Sylvestrina's father. Usually the attendant doesn't have much to do, since everything is automated, so after we sat down and ordered meals, he came over to talk with us. "Good to see you here."

"Just wanted to try something new," I said noncommitally. Miriam and I had hung around with Sylvestrina quite a bit when we were younger, but I hadn't really gotten to know her father.

He nodded and smiled. There was something just a bit weird about it, and I was suddenly glad that this was a public place and that Randy was here, even though I wasn't sure why. "Have you done Ceremonies before?" he asked.

"Only on the wire—I'm afraid I don't have them memorized. Is that all right?" I knew it was, but I might as well get authority to confirm it and make Randy comfortable.

"Oh, yes, of course. I take it you liked the Ceremonies or you wouldn't have come back."

"They're very soothing," I said. It was the most neutral, bland remark I could think of.

"You'll find they're even better once you have them from

memory." Obviously he was no better at taking hints than his daughter was. He said it with this big, beaming warmth that looked sort of like Earth politicians on the vid, or come to think of it like Dr. James. Turning to Randy, he asked, "You're Randy Schwartz, aren't you?"

"Yes, sir."

"Silly talks a lot about how much help you give her with her math. We really appreciate that." He had switched to beaming at Randy now.

Silly. And I thought Mother calling me "Melly" was bad. I guess there's always someone worse off. . . .

"She's really pretty good, just lacking some confidence," Randy said. He was lying. She's dumb as a rock and lazy besides. But I guess Randy wasn't going to tell her father that.

I had missed something Mr. van Piet had said. Randy was explaining, "Well, um, actually, Dad is Ecucatholic, kind of, but we don't go to church much."

"Well, if you enjoy yourself this evening, be sure to come back and try it again. And if you do have any questions—"

"I'll be sure to ask." Randy looked at me a little strangely. I realized that he was probably wondering if I had lured him down here to be converted; you don't get many people like Mr. van Piet up here, but there are some everywhere. (Papa says Earth is infested with them.) So maybe Randy thought I was another one. This was getting embarrassing. . . .

Mr. van Piet talked to both of us about trivia for a little longer, then went off to bother someone else. "Sorry about that," I said. "I wasn't really thinking. I should have realized they'd have a Pathmaker in here to try to save us heathens."

"I thought you *were* cybertao."

"Not enough for people like him."

Randy made a strange, sour face. "Maybe this is why Sylvestrina is so quiet. Probably her parents want her to try to make converts, and she's too nice a person to do it, so she just doesn't say anything."

The thought hadn't occurred to me, but it explained a lot. "I guess you never really know what goes on in someone else's

105

family. Dinner will get here soon; if we're going to do Ceremonies, we should start."

"You're the expert here."

That made me laugh. "Just remember this is the infidel leading the heathen." I pulled the earpiece up from under the table. "Pull this out, put it in your ear, and do what it tells you to." I stuck mine in.

He pulled his earpiece up, looked at it curiously for a moment, and put it in. I touched the cue spot. "Tell your companion you are happy to share a meal with him," the voice in my ear said.

"I'm really glad we're eating together," I said. "I hate eating by myself."

Randy listened to his earpiece for a moment, then said, "I'm glad too. It's a real treat to have somebody to talk to."

My earpiece said, "Tell your companion something you like about him."

"I like the way you smile," I said.

He turned purple, but after listening to his earphone he managed to say he thought I was a genius at CSL. It was kind of cute.

It went on like that; the First Ceremony, which a lot of people memorize, is a directed conversation about how much you like each other. Papa says that's what really converted him to cybertao.

At the end of the First Ceremony, the cart rolled up and we took our food. I was surprised at how heavy the trays felt until I remembered the grav was almost .5 here, ten times what it was in the cafeteria where I usually ate dinner. You get used to the idea that breakfast and dinner won't weigh much but lunch will be heavy, and this kind of put everything off rhythm.

"Second Ceremony now," I told Randy, "while we wait for this stuff to cool. Then we eat and talk, and we do Third Ceremony before we get up from the table." We put our earpieces back in.

Second Ceremony is an individual experience, and it's always done on the wire. The machine directs you in a Random Appreciation of Circumstance, which is the official language for sitting there thinking about how the food got to the table, how many people worked in the process, how much the plants and animals and you had to evolve to make this particular meal a possible event, and so forth. "Try to see the wheat in the pasta," or "Remember somehow the table had to get there," or "Consider protein compatibility," are the kinds of things it throws at you, about thirty seconds apart, usually five of them.

I always want to ask what questions other people get, like after a test in school, but that's a Minor Discordance and you aren't supposed to do it. I just hoped Randy wouldn't ask me, because if he did I'd never be able to resist trading information.

He didn't ask, though, so I had no opening as we picked up forks and ate. "It's different, but I like it," Randy said.

"The Ceremonies?"

"Yeah. We 'say grace.' "

"Like in the old flatscreen movies?"

"Yeah."

We went back to eating. I'd never been so hungry. There's nothing like a brawl, an emotional crisis, and a late dinner to boost your appetite.

Finally, Randy said, "Um—Melpomene . . . I guess I ought to talk with you sooner or later about one thing. Your father says you got really upset after he told you about the social engineering for the *Flying Dutchman*. . . ."

I nodded, too unsure of myself to speak. He sat still for a couple of long breaths before saying, softly, "That happened to me, too, but I didn't have anyone to talk to about it."

"Really?"

He nodded, but then there didn't seem to be anything more to say. He made a thorough scrape of his tray for the last of the gravy.

I ate my last couple of bites, and said, "Are you caught up on your homework?"

He looked startled, smiled crookedly, and said "That wasn't exactly what I was expecting you to say."

"I thought maybe we could go do something together where

107

we could talk. It is Friday night, you know. We could get a room
for rec someplace."

"Yeah, I'd like that. Sixwall?"

"Pos-def." Sixwall is a speed and coordination game, where
his being a big guy wasn't going to matter so much.

We talked a little about schoolwork, did the Third Ceremony,
and said a quick goodbye to Mr. van Piet. I was really afraid I
would end up promising to make it to CT and thus blow the
whole point of coming here.

With food in we weren't as tired as we had been, and back in
the Main Body we played sixwall for more than two hours (it was
Friday, so curfew was late), mostly without talking. We were
fairly evenly matched, and it was good to just concentrate on
playing, and to have someone there who was making sense—a
lot of my old friends hadn't lately.

He had won the last two games. I was getting tired, and it was
late. I asked, "Do you want to play more, or is it time to talk?"

"Let's talk." He pulled himself over to a strap. "What was it
like when your father told you about it?"

I told him everything, just letting it spill out, about talking
with Papa, starting with Tom because that seemed to fit in too.
Every so often he stopped to ask me, in detail, what Papa had
said or how he had reacted.

It felt so good to just talk about it and have someone understand me. Sometimes while I talked, I cried; sometimes we
laughed about something together—I don't remember about
what. Finally I wound down, drained and tired, but feeling less
alone than I had in days.

He said, "This is going to sound really bokky."

"If it does, Randy, you're forgiven." I moved over and sat next
to him against the wall, almost touching. He didn't move away,
but he didn't put the arm I'd been hoping for around me either.
He rubbed his face with his hands. "Okay. Here goes. I know this
sounds dumb, but I wish somebody like your father had told me.
Dr. James just told me flat out in the last two minutes of one
appointment. He practically shoved me out the door."

"That's terrible."

"Pos-def. 'Oh, by the way, everything you think and feel is part of the conditioning that NAC designed to make you a good employee. See you next week.' " He shrugged. "Pretty much the same way he does everything. I keep wondering if he's planning to transfer out or something. That's why I'm so glad I'll be your father's patient."

"He didn't do *me* any good. I hurt too."

"Yeah." He nodded once, slowly, looking down at the floor. "I know you do." That was such a stupid thing to say.

"He's a lot better with other people than he is with his own family."

He folded his arms around himself, closing up tightly. "A lot of people are."

"It's not really all that wonderful to get told something like that by your own family, either, you know!" I took off my gloves and kneepads with awkward, fumbling fingers and rammed them into my werpsack.

"I'm sorry."

"You should be."

He stripped off his gear, wadding it up, dropping it carelessly into his werpsack. And we had only half talked—he hadn't really gotten to talk at all. I had really done it this time, absolutely lim bokked.

He closed the werpsack and said, "I'm really sorry I upset you. I'll try not to bother you again."

There was a tear trickling out of his eye. Two people had ever made him cry as far as I knew—Theophilus and me. I felt so stupid. "I'm sorry too." It seemed about the only thing to say. "And you don't bother me at all. I like you. I just lost my temper and got upset, okay? I still want to be friends."

His head dropped, but he said "Yeah, pos-def." He looked at me sideways over his shoulder. "I'm sorry," he said again.

"About what?"

"Um, I just am, I guess, that you got upset."

I was bokking, but I wasn't the only one. "You're upset too," I pointed out. "Can we stop apologizing?"

109

"Maybe *you* can." Randy sighed. "Barry used to say I apologized for everything. . . ."

"He was right. Let's talk about something else, though—anything else."

"Pos-def." So of course we stood there with nothing to say to each other. Miriam had been telling me this always happened with boys and I hadn't believed her.

Finally I thought of something I *had* wanted to say. "Randy?"

"Present, ma'am."

"Cute. Uh. What are we going to do about all this?" Randy looked very startled and embarrassed. It's only now, writing this more than a year later, that I realize what he must have thought—and now *I'm* embarrassed.

I did figure out that he didn't know what I was talking about, so I said, "This whole social engineering thing."

I'm trying to remember now whether he looked relieved or disappointed. Probably it was both.

"I don't know what we could do," he said, sitting back down. "I figured we were just talking about how to live with the idea."

"Well, I'm curious, anyway. I want to know how much they actually hardwired me. Do I *have* any feelings of my own? And there's a bunch of stuff I can't believe they could design, like I don't see why you would design people to be lazy or rude, but some people sure are."

Randy shook his head. "I've been wondering about all those times I got lim weirdwired and started beating on people because I was jealous of them for something. Was I just doing what the CPB wanted me to do? Did they want those kids beaten up? Then why do *I* have to feel guilty for it? Or if they wanted me to have the experience of being a bully, why did the other kids have to get beaten up?"

I took a deep breath; I'd had an idea, and if Randy went along with it I was ready to think it might be a good one. "That's exactly the kind of thing I wonder about. And the other thing is, I don't see how they can even try to do it down to fine structure. Maybe they just did something like set up the Three Laws of Robotics in us, or something—remember those old stories?"

"Yeah. 'An employee cannot harm NAC or through inaction allow NAC to come to harm.' And so forth. But—I just realized. What makes a bunch of groundhogs think they know every situation that can possibly come up? What if someday we all need to be able to leave the ship or something?"

I stared at him, my clever idea gone completely. "You're right. If they've limited the options, sometime in the future that could put the *Flying Dutchman* in danger." It was almost too horrible to think about.

"And now all of a sudden it's not working," Randy said. "Your father told us so." He kicked upwards to the ceiling, flipped over, pushed back down, and bounced between ceiling and floor. If I'd known before that he was a ponger—

Another flag from the werp. All right. Ponging is the same thing as the "pacing" I've seen people do in Earth plays and films, but adapted to low g. It's a way to burn off energy when you're thinking hard. A lot of people do it.

On the other hand, a lot of people get driven crazy by it. "Will you please stop that!"

Sheepishly, he caught a loop and pulled himself to the ceiling. "Sorry, I do that when—"

"When you think. I know. Mim does the same thing." I sighed. "Sorry I snapped at you. I'm a little edgy myself." My idea began to come back to me, but I wasn't sure I wanted to involve Randy in it. "Do you have any ideas, anything we *can* do?"

"No. I just know we need to do something." He shook his head. "I'm sorry."

Randy looked so guilty, and for nothing, that I couldn't help laughing.

"What?!" He glared at me.

"You! If the sun went nova and cooked us all, you'd apologize."

"Well . . ." he looked like he was getting angry, then like he was going to apologize. "Well, um—somebody should."

That was so silly we both laughed, and I felt a million times better. I was about to tell him my idea when the speaker came on. "Attention Melpomene Alice Murray and Randomly Dis-

111

tributed Schwartz. Estimates show you need to check out of the six-walled handball room and begin return trips to your living units within fifteen minutes."

"Acknowledged," we said in unison, and turned to finish packing our werpsacks.

"Tomorrow's Saturday," Randy said. "And next week is languages."

"Yeah." There we were again, standing there without anything to say. "What do you do on weekends?" I asked him, for lack of anything better to ask, and then I realized how perfect my idea was.

"Usually I study," he said. "Barry and I used to get together for glideboarding sometimes, but . . . you know . . ."

He sounded so sad, and there wasn't really time to explain, so I said, "If your studies are caught up enough, do you want to get together for some time tomorrow? I think I have an idea about how we could do something about the problem, and I really only need Sunday to get ready for next week."

"Well—I want to get in a lot of practice on Japanese—"

"I can always use some too. Maybe we could just speak it for a lot of the day?"

"That would help, but I really need to work through the readings." Then he made that strange face again, like he was laughing at himself and not enjoying it. "This is really silly. I'm dying to spend the day with you. I'll find some study time somewhere this weekend. Let's spend Saturday together, and you can tell me all about your idea."

"Better than that, we can actually get started. Let's just meet after breakfast and—oh, no."

"What's the matter?"

"I really have to go to Outside Club tomorrow morning. My brother Tom is toggle racing. It's for the Juniors All-Ship Championship."

Randy gave me an even bigger grin. "That's what I was going to suggest. I've been dying to meet him."

"You follow toggle? Do you do it?"

"I'm no good at it," he said, "but I love to watch. I've seen your brother a lot. He's terrific."

"I think so too." We stood there stupidly.

"Well, then, it's settled," I added after a long pause.

We stood there some more, until Randy said "Yeah. Meet you at the Block A Commons, 0900?"

"That will be fine."

"See you then."

Another very long pause. Then, quite abruptly, he kissed me on the cheek.

I was really startled, and he started to back away, so I hugged him. He hugged back.

It would have been even better if we hadn't both been too embarrassed to look at each other or say anything. Finally the loudspeaker broke in. "Attention Melpomene Alice Murray and Randomly Distributed Schwartz. Estimates show you need to check out of the six-walled handball room and begin return trips to your living units within five minutes."

We let go of each other, both of us smiling and flushed and looking at everything except each other. "Randomly Distributed?" I asked.

"Dad said sooner or later he was bound to lose a paternity suit, and more likely than not it would be to an unfit mother." He seemed to be very serious.

"I think Randy is a really nice name." And that was how I got kissed on the mouth for the first time.

December 23, 2025

To DAY IS BIZARRE.

I've never missed school before.

When I finished writing I had only left myself three hours to sleep. I really did try to get up—crawled almost to the dressing corner before falling asleep again, and now that I'm finally

113

awake, there's less than an hour left in the school day. Bokky thing to do—close to FA exam.

I guess I'll call the postings board, get the assignments, get them done, back to bed. Really wrung out.

Wish I could just sit down and get back to work on this, feels like it's too important not to finish first, but I'm not thinking lim clear just now; might do same thing again, miss two days.

Writing about yourself is addictive. I hope all you kids notice that. If you feel like autobiography, try heroin. Lots safer and easier to control . . .

Schoolwork. And a night's sleep. Then we'll see if I go on. Might be a while.

CHAPTER SEVEN

January 2, 2026

WELL, IT'S BEEN TEN DAYS FOR ME, BUT I DON'T SUPPOSE IT seems like much to you. I've been re-reading all this and it seems like I haven't told you a tenth of what happened, at least not of the important things. And sometimes I've gotten way off the subject. I mean, getting kissed by Randy was my first and all but it happens to a lot of people and it doesn't have much to do with what I was going to try to tell you about.

I guess I started to recognize the problem when I was talking with Dr. Lovell yesterday. She always struck me as 100% cryo, efficient and so on, maybe someone you'd turn to in an emergency but never for sympathy. Yet there I was, sitting in her office, voluntarily putting up with half-gee grav for half an hour after school just so I could talk to her.

"I feel like if I write more I'll say too much."

"There's always that chance. And you might say it wrong."

She leaned forward, looking into my eyes with a sad little half smile.

That wasn't exactly the reassurance I had wanted. I looked at her window; like Papa, she left it always tuned to Outside whether there was anything interesting or not.

Today it was just a black field of stars. "I guess I need some idea about how important this is really supposed to be," I said. "I mean, you asked me to keep writing. Is this therapy, or does the whole future of the *Flying Dutchman* depend on it, or what?"

Her smile widened. "Easy question. Somewhere between."

I wasn't in the mood to be teased and said so. She apologized, but there didn't seem to be anything to say afterwards, so I got away politely and went home.

Tom wasn't in yet but Susan was. That was okay. Usually, if not exactly a source of unending joy, living with Susan is okay. We accept each other and sometimes we even like each other. Later in this I might mention some of the stuff that happened between us in the last year.

She was sitting in the sharespace, in what had been Mother's usual corner, finishing up some report or other on her werp. She's really very talented at what she does—internal logistics architecture—and I guess they think a lot of her in her office. Susan doesn't talk about her work except when I ask, and then only for a minute or so.

She finished an entry, looked up, and said, "Hello, Melpomene."

"Hi. Anything exciting happen in your day?"

She yawned and stretched. "I talked them out of two traffic corridors that they were going to put in. Too much loss of structural strength for too little cargo handling."

"That sounds big to me." I sat down, dropping my werpsack beside me.

She smiled and shrugged. "Yes and no. Remember, the *Flying Dutchman* won't be finished until 2059—and then it probably won't be running at full capacity till 2120 or so. And problems like the ones I solved today won't show up significantly except

116

across several orbits at full capacity. So it's 120 years till what I did today will have any measurable positive effect."

"With what they're finding out about life expectancy enhancement from low grav," I pointed out, "we'll probably both still be alive. I'll buy you dinner."

She winked at me. "I'll hold you to that. All the same, I can't get rotated soon enough, even though my next job is really just the opposite of this one—proposing new structures for my old team to shoot down. Kind of like getting paid to be in Debate Club." She sighed. "And now I'm whining and complaining again. That drives you crazy, doesn't it?"

I know a cue when I hear one. "I like you, anyway."

She got that silly glow she always gets when I say something like that, even if she has to fish for it. It must be awful to need to hear all that reassurance all the time—and to be so shy that you blush when you do get it.

"There were several months last year when you didn't complain at all, and you certainly had a right to," I added. I'm never sure whether I say these things because they are true and I need to remember what a good person Susan is really, or because I know they make her squirm and I enjoy that. Probably both.

For once, she just accepted it and changed the subject. "How's the book going?"

"Not that well. Or too well. It's chewing up a lot of time for something that's not that important."

"It's *not* important?" She sat up straight and looked at me with this lim intensity.

"Well, no. I've got FA exams coming up in fifty-three days." I couldn't believe she could forget that. She could be so dumb sometimes. "That's what I have to focus on," I added, in case she still couldn't see the connection.

She bit her lip, hard enough that mine hurt watching her, and said, "I'm trying not to annoy you."

Oh, god, why did Tom have to have a sensitive kid like her for a lover and a bokkup like me for a sister? "You're not annoying me—I'm just getting annoyed. Much too easily, too. It's the damned FA, I worry about it all the time, but that's not your fault and I'm sorry." By now I was sitting facing her, holding her hands in mine.

We always end up like this, lately, trying to talk around the awkward problem that we both love my brother but we can't talk without drawing blood.

Susan nodded a couple of times, being a good sport because I was trying, I guess. "Melpomene, look, all I meant to say was—listen to me, because I don't always get these things right and I want you to get what I *mean*—when I see you working on that book, you concentrate harder than anyone I've seen, except Tom when he's doing a spatial, maybe. I guess I don't know really if it's that important, but I can certainly tell you feel that way."

I hugged her. "You just said exactly the right thing."

"I *did?*"

"Yeah. Don't let it go to your head." I even kissed her cheek. "And I think I'm going to go work on the book. I've got fifty minutes till Randy meets me at the cafeteria."

"I hope it goes well." She really meant it.

Okay, it shouldn't have been such a big deal to me, but it was. Besides, whose book is this anyway? I felt like telling you about all this stuff, so I did. And Randy is late as usual, so I'll get back to the real story I'm working on now.

BREAKFAST THE NEXT MORNING—I'M BACK TO TELLING YOU about last year again—was amusing, if you're the kind of person who's amused by slow torture. As always, Mother started it. "Are your friends having breakfast together today, Melly? Would you rather have gone with them?"

"I'm meeting a friend after breakfast—we're going to go to Outside Club and then study together. And I thought it was 'important for a real family to eat together.' " Okay, I was being lim snotty . . . but on her part, she was really pulling out all the stops on her deeply-concerned-mother routine.

Papa started another one of his jokes and it died, like they do ninety per cent of the time, so all of us were off to a jolly start.

There was a long pause while we all just shoved food into our mouths, but that was too good to last. "Tom, you're barely eating," Mother said. "Is something wrong?"

"The less I eat now, the less I'll spew onto my faceplate in three hours," Tom said, talking with his mouth full.

"Tom!"

He shrugged. "It's true. And don't tell me I'm spoiling your appetite. You brought it up."

"You are, but I'm less concerned about that than I am about your hostility," Mother said primly. She was getting just what she wanted. "I'm honestly worried about you. You don't eat, you pay so much attention to sports and the Alien Artifacts . . ."

Tom dropped me the slow wink that we've always used to say "Watch this—and back me up if I need it," and looked Mother straight in the eyes without smirking. "It's Art, Mother." You could hear the capital. "It's just going to take a while for you to learn to appreciate it."

Mother was so quiet that at first I thought he had actually stumbled on the magic formula to shut her up.

Finally she sighed. "I suppose you could be right. It *is* in the family. . . ."

And she was off into telling us about her dead kid brother James. James was a poet, which may or may not have involved writing any poetry. He was constantly lonesome and depressed and had no friends. I could easily see why—he made fun of the athletes (I guess in Earth schools only a very small fraction of the students are allowed to play sports, and those kids aren't allowed to study, or something like that—it sounded so stupid I could never make myself listen), and the athletes beat him up. He fell in love with girls who didn't know him at all, and they rejected him. He hung around with the brainy kids, but he annoyed them so much they got rid of him too. (Since according to Mother he refused to learn anything about anything except poetry, I can see why, again.) I'm really not sure that any of that had anything to do with poetry, but Mother seemed to think it did.

It sounded to me like a classic profile of an unco, but of course on Earth it's not a criminal offense so people can't be given the therapy they need. In that way I guess it was kind of sad

119

about James—up here they'd have treated him and he'd probably have been fine.

Anyway, James wrote a lot of things, all very short, in which he talked about being an isolated screaming X in a vast indifferent Y. Like X = pebble, Y = beach; X = tree, Y = desert; X = iceberg, Y = ocean. You get the idea. I know those Xs don't really scream, but Mother says that's part of the point.

In every photo of James I have ever seen, he seems to be wearing the clothes of about a decade before, say of 1985 or so, in gray or black.

Anyway, he was twenty-six when he got mutAIDS and died. It was after the main Die-Off and the Eurowar, so maybe around 2005 or 2006, as if he couldn't bring himself to go with anyone else in any normal way. Probably about seven or eight years before I was born, I'm not really sure.

I think, but I'm not sure, that what my mother was trying to say was that since she had been the only one who understood James's poetry, if there were anything to understand about the Alien Artifacts, she would already have understood it.

Tom got more and more quiet as this went on; Mother seemed encouraged by that. She elaborated on all the ways he was different from James. Apparently the major one was that Tom wasn't "sensitive." Since surely she knew Tom as well as I did, she couldn't have meant any of the normal meanings of that word, but as far as I can tell, she was using it to mean "clumsy and a bad loser," since the reason Tom wasn't sensitive was that he liked sports.

Several times Papa tried to get her going on some other dead person we were related to besides James, but without success. As far as I was concerned, they were all dead groundhogs. What was there to talk about?

Finally, finally, finally, breakfast was really over and we'd had enough home and family values for the day. I'd eaten about half my meal, Tom even less. Papa sort of steered Mother out of the cafeteria to something he said she'd be interested in, mentioning that they would catch Tom's race on the vid.

Tom went down through the Main Body toward the Men's

Suit Room. It was still half an hour before I was due to meet with Randy, and it was sort of on my way, so I went along for company.

The corridors were deserted—no more than half a dozen people in sight. Tom hauled along ahead of me, without looking back.

Finally I asked, "Um, Tom—are the uh, Alien Artifacts *really* art, or did you just say that to hassle Mother?"

"They have to be art, Melpomene. Remember the First Law of Anthropology: if they're doing something you don't understand, it's either an isolated lunatic, a religious ritual, or art. I'm not religious and since I'm the Great Cornelius Murray's son I can't be crazy, so it must be art." His voice was so harsh and so bitter that I thought of just turning and going, but it seemed like everyone was letting Tom down lately, so I couldn't.

Keeping my voice as even as I could, I asked, "Are you worried about the race?"

He squeaked out, "Kind of."

I put an arm around him, and he turned to hug me. We dropped a long way down that corridor before we realized neither of us was hanging on. Luckily we hit feet first and it was only about fifty meters of drop on a low grav day, so it was less than what you'd feel jumping off a chair on Earth. Still, it was a jar, enough to get us out of it.

As he leaned back, he was smiling a little. "I feel better. I'm glad that wasn't our heads. I think we missed our turnoff."

We hauled back up; when we had taken the turn we meant to, he said, "Susan will be watching. She made me promise that if I win, I'll show her the gadget I showed you—how it works and so forth."

He paused. "I've made a lot of changes and improvements and really learned how to use it," he added defensively.

"Has she ever seen any of your other things?"

"All of them." He hauled on ahead of me. I sped up to catch him, since the entry to the Men's Suit Room would be coming up soon.

"Tom."

"What?" He looked back at me. "Do I have to spell it all out? She liked some of the other stuff—she even talks like she understands some of the things I'm trying to do, trying to say. She's the only one who ever did. And this one is the most important one. So, yes, I'm nervous and I'm a little tense. There's a lot riding on this race."

"It will be good work," I said, "whether or not you win the race. You'll see, and so will she."

He didn't speak for a long time, then, just hung there by his hands and feet from the netting, upside down, a few meters from where I sat on the floor of the corridor. "I'm serious," he said at last. "What if Susan doesn't like it?"

"She's going to love it. Then she's going to explain it to me, and *I'll* love it. Really. Now go win the race so you won't have an excuse to put this off any longer."

He gulped, nodded, and hauled away to the Men's Suit Room.

As I headed back up to meet Randy, I found myself thinking that, half an hour after breakfast, it had already been a long day.

Randy was waiting for me at the Block A Commons, a little early but so was I. I suddenly realized we hadn't planned to do anything other than watch Tom race, and we wouldn't have to suit up for that for at least an hour.

Well, based on the experience of the night before, maybe we could stand around awkwardly and stammer. In fact, that was almost certainly what we would do.

As I approached him, weaving my way between tables of chess players and kids studying together, watching out for little kids flipping through the air, I realized he hadn't seen me yet. He was doing about as much ponging as you can get away with in public, bouncing in a little triangle in one corner, rising up half a meter to bump his back on the wall, then turning his back against the other wall, then sinking to the floor; from floor to wall to wall, to floor to wall to wall—after watching him through a few cycles from a few meters away, I was getting dizzy.

He was either thinking really hard or he was really nervous.

I bounced over and said hello. He hit the ceiling. Nervous, I guessed.

"Ouch," he said, rubbing his head as he came back down. "I must have been drifting—you really startled me."

"Let me take a look at your head."

"I'm okay. Koapy. Really."

"How can you tell? Can you see the top of your head?"

He bent down and let me look. There was a red spot showing through the thin fuzz of red-blond hair. "Here?"

"Ow! Don't touch!"

"Must be. Looks like just a bruise—no broken skin and you won't get a bump. Thanks for letting me check, though—otherwise I'd worry about you."

Randy touched the bruise gingerly. "And to think I always wondered what it would be like to have a mother."

"You can have mine if you like. But I warn you I'm not taking her back." It came out much more seriously than I intended it to—all of a sudden we were staring into each others' eyes, and now *he* looked worried.

So we sat down and he heard all about my troubles, and Tom's troubles, with Mother. He listened the way he always did, with his full attention, and somehow after enough of that, although Randy didn't say anything much at all, I began to feel a little silly about all my fighting with Mother.

After a long time I sighed, wiped my eyes, and decided to stop feeling sorry for myself. "Well, now that we're all done with emotional first aid, I guess we should go suit up."

"Yeah." He got up, and without either of us quite intending it—well, I didn't and I don't think he did—he took my hand and held it. I was very proud of not hitting the ceiling myself.

I hoped no one would see us.

I hoped everyone would see us.

Especially Miriam, so she could see what it was like with a *nice* guy.

As we went down to the locker rooms together, I remembered. "I never did tell you my idea, Randy. And it's the kind of thing I think we could talk about better off-radio Outside."

He looked a little puzzled, but he said okay.

I knew I was getting paranoid, and I kept telling myself that, as I suited up and went through medchek. But I had no idea how the CPB or Security would look at what I had in mind, and if they didn't approve we could both be in real trouble. So with so many cameras and microphones around, it just seemed wiser.

As always, the race started late because some of the racers had to be walked through the toggle course extra times. Tom says that's what a toggle racer does when he's losing his nerve but it's too late to back out.

The course is always a zigzag circumnavigation of the Main Body, and it's always nine kilometers, but they change it every time, so it can always be used as an excuse to add more toggle stations to the Outside. I suppose that's a demonstration of how bokky people are—instead of just saying that the people who work Outside can always use more toggle stations, they justify it by recreation.

In the race itself, everyone has a series of stripe-coded toggle lines, and they toggle their way around—

The werp just pointed out that you don't do toggling on Earth.

Well, okay. Toggling is the basic man-powered way of moving around on the surface of the Main Body. A toggle station is a collection of extruded steel poles about five centimeters in diameter, each with a ring on top, about as big around as your fist and as thick as your thumb. A toggle is a simple locking clip that fits over the ring, and a toggle line is a spun monomyl cable with a toggle at each end.

To toggle from station to station, you pick a cable that runs between the two stations. You take the toggle off the ring and clip it to your chest harness; then you clip the replacement cable from your backpack to the ring, and make sure the line is running free so you won't yoyo backwards. (Yoyoing's not a problem for racers, because they don't have to run replacement lines.)

Then you jump straight up and wind in the cable to pull yourself toward your destination station, wrapping the cable onto the lugs on your chest harness and slowly pulling yourself down onto your destination station. When your magnetic boots grab surface at the other end, you flip down the lugs, put the wound-up cable onto your back harness, take the replacement cable off your backpack and toggle it to an empty ring, and there you are. If you need to make multiple jumps to get somewhere, you just keep repeating the process.

Toggle racers have a pre-laid set of cables, one set per racer, forming a nine-km course around the Main Body. Some of the legs are long, some short, because those pose different problems. The objective is to get through all your toggle stations and back to the one you started from first.

There were about fifty spectators today on the surface tram, plus I suppose a couple of hundred others on the vid like my parents. When you see it on the tram, you watch the takeoff, then ride around to some station roughly in the middle of the course, and finally ride back to the starting point to watch them all come in.

While you ride between points, you can either watch the monitors to see the rest of the race, or you can just look out into space, which—sorry Tom!—is what I usually do.

As I came out of the lock, I saw Susan already standing by the tram, boots clinging to the rail, and waved to her. She stood still for a long second, then waved back enthusiastically. I guess she was surprised that I had paid any attention at all to her; well, if being nice to her was what it would take to make Tom happy, I'd be so nice it would choke her.

She jumped over—down, really since the tram is above the lock—with a neat flex of one ankle, the safety line to the tram shaking out behind her, and said "How was he this morning?"

"Jumpy as a fat rabbit before Celebration Feast. How was he last night?"

"Completely impossible." You can't really see faces through the faceplate very well, but I could imagine the face she was making. "Do *you* know what it is he's going to show me if he wins?"

There was an unidentified snicker on the com. Silently, I held up my private link cable; Susan took it and attached it to hers. I tongued from open freke to private link. "Test?"

"Check. Don't you *hate* it when people listen in?"

"Yeah. I suppose someone would get all worked up about it,

though, if we cut his air line or pushed him off and let him walk to Mars."

"That's morbid," she said. It was also from that bokky Earth vid show, *Pirates of the Asteroids,* but I guess she hadn't seen it. "But it's an idea. Anyway, what *is* this big secret of Tom's?"

"It's hard to describe." I hedged because I really didn't know what would be the best thing to say, but that embarrassed me because we were trying to be friends and I thought I should trust her. "It's not like anything he's ever done before, and I don't understand it very well myself, so I don't want to bias you."

She nodded. "But did you *like* anything about it?"

"Oh, pos-def. A lot. But I didn't really know what it was that I was liking." It was an exaggeration, except for the last part, but with a little luck it would be what she had wanted to hear.

She bought my answer, anyway, so I was off that hook. "I just want to make sure *I* like it at first glance."

"Tom said you like a lot of his stuff."

"I do," Susan said. "But this is different. He's got an awful lot wrapped up in this whatever-it-is. And he's decided that how I react is the same as whether it's good or not. So I've *got* to love it. I just thought if you could tell me something about it, I could get myself pre-set. Because he's *got* to stay with it."

"He does?" I said, startled, not just by what she had said, but by the way she was holding both my hands, facing me, and by my realization that I really knew nothing of her beyond my vague impression that she was quiet, always hanging onto Tom, adding nothing, *boring*—and as I saw her now, glad that my suit gloves kept her from crushing my hands, she was someone else entirely. "I know it matters to him," I added, stammering, "but I don't see—"

"I can't explain it. I just feel it. He's doing something we all need, even if we never understand it." She shuddered with frustration. "Shit, if I could explain it, everyone already *would* understand."

So I hugged her. That's very awkward in a suit, but I had absolutely nothing to say otherwise. I'd probably never get to like her but for Tom's sake I was going to love her if it killed me.

There wasn't much to say after that, so we both agreed, in this lim bokked half-conversation that I can't even begin to re-create (it sounded like neither of us had exactly learned to talk yet), that we both hoped he won and we both wanted him to do well. Then we unclipped, tongued back to radio, and got on the tram.

By now almost everyone was on. I felt guilty, as I looked for Randy, that I didn't know what his suit looked like. Most of us have all kinds of patches and markers, especially if we're in Outside Club, and then we do custom coloring, so that the total effect is this patchwork map all over your body.

It's as distinctive as a face, so you can identify people Outside as easily as you can when they're sitting across the table from you.

That is, you can if you know what they look like. And I had no idea what Randy looked like.

Fortunately, at first glance there were only four people Randy's size. I knew who two of them were, and thought vaguely I'd seen another one in the Women's Suit Room. The last one was a kid-sized Outside Crew uniform, vis-orange with no colors, just VWU Junior Auxiliary patches and black hashmarks for Outside experience. I knew, vaguely, that Randy's father did something on Outside Crew, and was in the union. Besides, the kid in the vis-orange suit sat like Randy—all by himself.

I sat down next to him. "They've given them a really complex route," he said, "seventeen stations, but two legs more than a k long. It zags all over the place. One long leg is practically straight down."

"Hunh," I said. With lesser racers, that could be really danger-ous. On a long downward toggle, if you didn't jump right, you could end up "trailing out," unable to wind in before the motion of the ship pulled you down into Main Engine exhaust—the purple glow that eddied and vibrated down below us, ions streaming out a shaved fraction below lightspeed. But this was a Championship, so they must have figured people could take care of themselves. "Tom should be fine, then—he likes drops."

"Yeah, he has that funny trick he works with yanking on the

extended cable. I tried to copy that once and slammed up against the side."

"I can't do it either," I admitted. "He says it's all timing—which is like saying that playing piano is all in the fingers."

Tom's stunt—I had heard, with secret pride, some kids in my class calling it a "Murray takeoff"—was to leap straight back, stretching the cable taut, and then give a hard yank exactly along the line of the cable. If you did it right, you put yourself on a ballistic trajectory for a point close to your destination station. Then, if you wound cable in fast enough, you would again have a taut line when you were near your destination, and could wind in quickly. It was much faster than staying taut the whole way, and going down toward the engines it could be incredibly quick, almost a direct bound.

"The tram will be going out to Station Nine," Randy said, "which is right at the bottom of the longest drop. And the next leg is only two hundred meters, sideways, so we get to see all of that hop too."

Lots of other people were chattering on the com, too, and it was getting hard to hear each other, so we cabled up to talk privately.

The racers came out at last, stretching and bouncing around as they always do before takeoff, on the short tether from their starting rings.

A thought hit me, and I felt stupid again. "You know, Randy, the way you talk about it, you must have been following the whole toggle-racing season for the last fifteen weeks, but I've never noticed you out here."

"I hardly ever talk. I never had anyone to talk to."

"Oh." I didn't know what more to say; his voice had been so flat.

"I go Outside every chance I get. My dad teases me about it, calls me the Junior Space Ranger Five Star Cadet, whatever that means. I go anyway. Do you ever make the Wednesday night excursion?"

"I never have," I said, deciding right then that I would soon. "Isn't it just a tram ride around the Main Body?"

"Yeah." There was a warm enthusiasm in Randy's voice, like he had wanted to say this for a long time. "But they do it with no roof on the tram, and there are so few people, you can just strap onto the bench and look straight out from the ship the whole way. It's just—well, I don't know how to describe it. Koapy. You'll have to see it for yourself."

"Now that you've told me about it, I *will* have to," I said. "It sounds beautiful, but it must get pretty lonely."

"Actually that's part of the attraction."

"Um—well, anyway, if we're not both too loaded down with homework on Wednesday night, let's do it. I really want to." I hoped Randy wouldn't notice that I was sounding like a moron.

There was a soft chime in the earpieces. "Race begins in two minutes. Racers prepare for toggle check."

Mother always said Tom's suit looked like he'd stolen it from a poor family's scarecrow, though why anyone would own both a scarecrow and a space suit is beyond me. Anyway I knew what she meant. The whole surface had so many patches attached, and had been re-colored so many times over the old patches, that except for two recent ones—"Shift A Glee Club '24" and "Block A Commons Redecoration 4-2-24"—there couldn't have been five contiguous square centimeters of the same color or patch. Tom preferred shimmery re-colorings and shiny patches, so in the glare of Outside sunlight, the total effect was iridescent.

The main opponent he'd have to worry about was the B Shift Champion, Karol Kysmini. Karol was a big, strong guy who favored heavy horizontal lines on his suit—he always looked like a piece of heavy machinery to me—but B Shift had lost the spin, so the race started four hours earlier than Karol would ordinarily have gotten up. Furthermore, Karol wasn't very clever. Tom always said he must have put a lot of time into perfecting his headstop.

C Shift had won the spin, and was competing in their early evening hours, but their champion, Inga Blanc, was really just the best of their weak field. She might have been a little stronger than Tom, and she was surely smarter than Karol, but she wouldn't have made third on the A or B Shift teams. Her suit was patched only from waist to shoulder on her right side, with the rest re-colored silver-gray. She wasn't much of a competitor, but she looked lim koapy.

I didn't know any of the other racers from B or C Shifts. The other A Shift racers were Tswana Carmen at second, a girl from Tom's class who I thought had a good chance at second overall, and Levi Yang, one of Barry's older brothers. "I wonder where Barry is," I said. "You'd think with a racer in his family——"

"They hate each other," Randy said. "Levi is the Yang family 'good kid.' Except for him, none of the Yang kids spend any more time in their living unit than they can help."

The opencast spoke again. "Racers to starting stations please." There was a little flurry of motion, and the starting position lights rolled over from red to yellow at each station.

"Racers signal ready please." Nine right arms went up. "Get set. On green——go." The lights went green.

Tom and Tswana shot straight out seventy meters from the side of the ship, snubbing at almost exactly the same distance. Their lines snapped taut, they heaved, and they plunged toward the horizon of the Main Body. In less than ten seconds their lines formed graceful curves in the sunlight with darker dots at their tips. I clicked up my distance lenses and looked at Tom. He was winding the loose cable in quickly and steadily. He would probably only have to wind under tension for the last twenty meters or so.

Meanwhile, Karol had bounded up only about thirty meters from the *Flying Dutchman*. He yanked hard, but it was obvious that he'd have to do more than half the trip on tension rather than ballistically.

Everyone else took off in the old diving style, leaping forward rather than back and winding under tension close to the surface. "Bokky, lim bokky," Randy noted. "Levi even knows how to do your brother's takeoff but he won't because his father said 'You can jump further with your feet than your arms.' Brains don't exactly run in that family——they sort of dribble slowly away."

I laughed, and then realized, "That's the same kind of joke that Theophilus and the Real Gang have been making," I said.

He made the "shot through the chest" gesture and admitted, "I've always *thought* things like that. I bet other people have too. We just never used to say them till Theophilus came up. Probably in a few months even the little kids will be doing it."

The tram started its slow crawl around the outside of the Main Body, gliding a few centimeters above the iron track so slowly and evenly that most of us only noticed we were moving by the slow motions of the stars. "Well, midpoint next," I said. "I always think coming in is more exciting than takeoff anyway."

"Yeah. More to see. Um—we're on private link and it will be a while. Do you have time to tell me about this plan of yours?"

I sighed. "I wish it were more than it is. I was just thinking that if there really is some kind of master plan or design for the society they're fitting us to, then there must be a copy of it somewhere, probably in the CPB's files."

"Those are *private!*" I had been afraid he would be shocked.

I gave him the argument I had used on myself. "Are they really? They're *about* everyone, they concern everyone—that seems pretty public to me."

Usually suits hide headshakes or nods, but he was shaking his head so hard I could see it plainly. "No, *no,* Melpomene. It's— well, it's not like—well, shit. I understand what you said, but that's not how you decide whether files are private. It's not."

He was stammering like a moron, and I hated to hear that, because it made me realize how much I had upset him. But if I backed out now, we might never find out. And I still thought we had been right the night before—this might be important for the whole future of the ship. "What makes a file private?" I asked him, stalling while I thought of more arguments.

He didn't answer for a long time. "All right, Melpomene. I don't know why you're making me explain something everyone knows by the time they're six, but all right. A file is private because the person who created it says so. That's the only way there can *be* any privacy. If anyone else were to decide, they'd have to look at it, and then it wouldn't be private, would it? So if the creator says it's private, it's private, and that's all there is to it."

By now I had thought of a lot of arguments. I could have asked whether I could copy one of his files, label it private, delete his original, and then say he couldn't read it. I could have pointed out we were mad at the adults exactly because they wouldn't tell us anything. I could even have insisted he back me up because we were friends. Lonely as he was, that would have worked, though I'd have felt like an unco for it.

I didn't say any of those things. You can't really win an argument against somebody's feeling that something is just plain wrong. Papa always says that.

So I let the whole thing drop. I leaned over against Randy and watched the stars wheel around us. After a minute he dropped an arm around me. "Sorry, Melpomene."

"For what?"

"Oh, getting upset, lecturing you, being a bokkup, being born. Things like that."

"I'm glad you're here, anyway." I attempted the nearly impossible—snuggling in spacesuits. It must have worked; he seemed to relax and we just watched the stars and talked about some of the recent races as the tram crept around to the dark side of the ship.

The Earth and moon were still visible, low downship as we crossed into the shadow; the Earth was a half-disk, the moon a rounded dot. Together, they were the size of a pea and the period on this screen, a handsbreadth apart and an arm's length away.

Then they fell below the horizon. A few minutes later Mars rose upship, a bright red light not yet showing any disk.

"Tell you what," Randy said. "Let's go there next."

"Pos-def. It's a lim koapy red. Wonder if it will turn green or blue when they're done with it?"

"We had a problem set on that in my old class. It's supposed to depend on how much water they put into it. If they do fill all the big lakes they're talking about and use cloud cover to hold heat, it will probably turn white sometimes the way Earth seems to. But it's going to stay at least half desert, so all that will still be red."

"I did some numbers on my own, and I think we'll be in

position to see the first comet strike on Mars. That will really be a sight." I drifted off into a daydream, happy thinking about watching that with Randy . . . and with all my other friends, even with Susan—and then I remembered Miriam, and I thought about how much trouble there was, and that got me back to Papa and the way they'd engineered us, and in two minutes I wanted to cry. I couldn't imagine how it could all work out.

The tram glided into place, and we all turned to watch the ship horizon for the racers. "This toggle station is really far down toward the engines," Randy said, breaking me out of feeling sorry for myself. "And the leg is almost the full length of the ship, nearly vertical. They're putting a lot of challenge into the course, even for an All-Ship Championship."

"I guess they figure they can handle it." I had a brief twinge of concern for Tom, but he was better on the toggle than most people, and not the type for idle risks.

Still, the ship length was more than a kilometer, and a lot could happen in that distance.

The opencast spoke. "Racers are now arriving at the previous station, and can be expected to be visible within two minutes. First racer down at the previous station: Thomas Murray, A Shift Champion. Second: Karol Kysmini, B Shift Champion. Third: Tswana Carmen, A Shift Second."

Probably it was just family arrogance but I was so sure Tom would win that I was actually worried more about Tswana's chances for second place. How had Karol gotten ahead of her, anyway?

We clicked up distance lenses, set them for infinity, and watched the upward horizon.

The first indication that anything was wrong was how fast Tom rose over the upward horizon. He shot up like a linerocket does during a rendezvous, appearing to go straight out from the side of the ship.

Whole seconds crawled by as Tom reached an impossibly high peak. Then Karol and Tswana bobbed slowly up over the horizon, arms wheeling slowly as they wound on cable, and another few seconds went by before slower racers, using the old

133

technique, came into view low on the horizon, wrapping cable quickly to keep it taut.

I looked upward again to see what Tom was doing and I couldn't find him at all. "Where——"

"Near Cygnus's head," Randy said, his voice low but tense. "He must be five hundred meters out from the side at least. What's he doing?"

"I don't know." Now that Randy had pointed him out, I could see Tom dimly when I clicked in for a closer look. I saw that he was winding his toggle line with both hands, not in the big easy loops he usually used, but keeping it hard and tight on the lugs by pulling it taut with one hand and winding with the other. I had no idea why he thought he would want neat, tight wrapping— his takeoff technique was effective because he didn't have to put much muscular effort into winding against tension. And he wasn't even getting the benefit of winding in—he was shortening the line, but it still hung limp, and in fact he had to use his free hand to keep it pulled taut as he wound it on the lugs.

The other racers neared the station. Tom continued at that amazing distance from the ship. Everyone watched him.

"Look at his line," Randy said quietly.

Near us, it was visible in the ship's floodlights. It was no longer completely limp, nor taut yet either, but bulged in a long, single, unwinding curve.

"There must be some kind of potential energy in that," Randy said, "but I can't see what it is."

I told him how Tom was winding it tightly for no apparent reason. "He's up to something, but it had better work fast—Karol and Tswana aren't long from coming in."

I had never seen a toggle race so hard to follow. Normally all the racers are in one small area of the sky, lighted by the sun or the floods depending on which side of the ship it is, not more than one hundred meters out. But Tom was ninety degrees or more away from the rest, and where they were mostly within fifty meters of the surface, he was out at around three hundred, covering only three percent as much sky and reflecting only three percent as much light.

Randy gulped audibly.

"What?"

"The cable. Look now."

It was still bowed—but now downward toward the engines. Tom had dropped down below the station and would have to work his way back up.

This couldn't be some new tactic. My brother had bokked and was certain to finish last. I felt terrible for him, even for Susan . . .

As I thought this, he brightened against the sky. A weird, flickering light suddenly played across his suit, multicolored fire dancing on its iridescence.

"What—" Randy began.

I knew. "Main Engine exhaust. The light from it." I had seen it through vid cameras and on dinghy excursions—but now the light of its flickering, dancing sheets of thin plasma played over Tom's body. My stomach felt like I had swallowed a brick of iron. "He's got too much line left. He's going to trail off into the exhaust."

I heard Randy's breath catch. Tom was now very bright in the exhaust glow, flickering and shining. Just before he trailed off he would probably pass out of the ship's shadow and I would see him flare in the sunlight before he dropped into that deadly radiation bath.

"The cable looks like—" Randy began.

Tom jerked, hard, with his whole body.

He leaped upward, back toward the station. He jerked again, and again. Abruptly, the flicker of Main Engine exhaust over his body stopped as he shot back into the shadow of the ship.

Randy laughed, a weird torn sound of relief. "God, your brother has nerve. He timed that snub perfectly, yanked the cable right at the bottom. Just like he does in that takeoff. And it catapulted him forward. Want to bet he lands fully ballistic?"

"No." I was breathing again myself. "He jerked more than once—I guess he could catch the line because he could see it in the exhaust glow."

"Watch the station!"

135

Karol and Tswana were within a few seconds of landing, with the rest of the racers trailing. Karol was a bit higher up than Tswana, and I gave her the edge—

Tom shot straight in, almost perpendicular to the side of the ship, landing so hard his heels seemed to bump his butt. In an eyeblink he had handed off his coiled cable to ground crew, reclipped, sprung upward, and snapped the new line hard. He shot forward and slightly upward toward the next station, a short leg of only about one hundred meters.

Before Tswana even came in, Tom was halfway to the next station. She did a neat turnover, and Karol came in as she launched herself. Before either of them had finished the short leg, Tom had come in again, taken off, and gotten over the horizon.

The rest of the field was just straggling into the station in front of us.

"That's the most amazing thing I've ever seen," Randy said. "He might even beat the tram to the finish line."

As if the group super had had the same thought, the tram started. Since there was little more to look at, we spent most of the trip to the last station arguing about the physics of what Tom had done. Randy eventually got me convinced that he was right—all the advantage came from the added acceleration of dropping below the finish station, so it was only likely to be effective on really long downward legs.

When we got to the last station, we had to wait less than a minute before Tom hurtled in, far ahead of everyone, and made a neat landing by his station, boots clamping to the side of the ship. The clock registered his time—not a record for the nine kilometer toggle, because the course had been unusually tough. Still, he had come in before the rest of them cleared the horizon, which had to be a record lead, anyway.

He shoved his card into the reader, registering out, and came over to join Susan. From the way he waved to me, I guessed he was pretty happy.

The rest of the racers came in with Tswana leading Karol by four full seconds. As the racers and spectators gathered around and on the tram, Randy and I clicked over to listen on the general band.

They were all talking about Tom's maneuver, some of them making him explain slowly to them what Randy and I had already worked out. Apparently the really dedicated people who watched the whole race on vid had seen him do the same thing on another long downhill leg. He had to explain the basic idea several times—that the long free fall past the toggle station stored up a lot of energy, and all of it could be redirected by snubbing hard because monomyl line was so elastic. The additional energy was large enough to more than make up for the longer path if some formula he had worked out was satisfied—it depended, obviously, on the length of the leg, the extent to which it ran downward, and the acceleration of the ship.

The opencast's voice crackled in our ears. "Announcement of standing for today's toggle race. First place and All-Ship Champion: Tswana Carmen. Second place: Karol Kysmini. Third place—"

The machine read through all the placings, down to the last straggler from C Shift, before it finally said, "And one special judges' ruling. By unanimous verdict, Thomas Murray is disqualified by use of a dangerous technique. The judges' ruling has been posted for inclusion in RULES FOR TOGGLE RACING in the following form: 'No racer may at any point pass below a plane extending perpendicular to the ship from a line drawn around its circumference equidistant from the lowest station and the highest engine exhaust port.' Text copies of the rule will be available for examination and comment on the Outdoor Sports Bulletin Board, available via commoncast."

My head hurt. Everyone was talking. I couldn't sort out the comm. Randy gestured to me, I clicked over, and we went back on private link. "Test."

"Check. Melpomene, that's so crazy. They just stole the race from him. And that technique is no more dangerous than being out here in the first place is."

"Yeah." I was numb. "I guess I should try to talk with him or at least—"

Susan was suddenly there, standing in front of us. She extended her private line, and we piggybacked it on my clip so she could join the conversation. "Tom is going in to get out of his suit. I'm going to catch him on his way out. Do you want to meet us at the pizza cafeteria? I think it would help if you did."

"Pos-def," I said, as Randy started to say "If you want—"

"Both of you," Susan emphasized, knocking her standing hyperbolic with me. "We'll probably need to gang up on him. He's going to be in an awful mood."

"We'll be there," I said. "Be sure you catch him—when he's really upset, especially when he's been badly p.d.'d, he goes off and hides."

"You're talking about him like he's four years old." Her voice was back to its normal pouty whine. Maybe she was embarrassed at having behaved graciously or something.

"Whatever. But he'll try to go off and hide. We'd all better get moving before he gets a lead on you."

She unclipped and went, not saying anything more. Maybe she was angry. I hoped, though, that she had taken me seriously, and was hurrying.

"Well, Randy, I guess you've been invited to a family crisis."

"You *do* want me along?"

"*Pos-def.*" I was surprised at how much I emphasized that, and then embarrassed at having shown so much. "Meet you at the big viewing lounge, soon as we both get out?" It was about equidistant from our Suit Rooms.

"Right. See you there." Randy unclipped and the roar of chatter on the general freke came back. He brushed me with his arm—probably an intended hug—and we both headed in.

It takes a while to check a suit back in because you have to put all the fittings through pressure check and all the pieces through the UV sterilizer. Furthermore, there were a lot of people ahead of me, and worse yet some were adults, who never trust the machines for some stupid reason, so they always double and triple check everything and bother the attendants with dumb questions about how to tell if something needs replacing. (The suiting room administrators won't even *let* you use up ten percent of the rated duration on a component.)

Anyway, at least Susan was up near the head of the line with no adults ahead of her. She waved at me as we waited. Naked as we were, with our suits in our bags, I could see she was really developed, even more than Miriam, and though I guess I was glad for Tom, I felt my little-girl body more acutely than ever. I knew Susan was older than I was and for all I knew when I hit that age I'd look like that too, but right now I was so tired of looking like a kid.

Susan got through checkout, and waved again. I waved back. She really did support Tom, and he seemed to like her. And I hadn't thought of her as The Rodent for almost an hour, either.

She bounced off to get dressed, my envy following. Maybe puberty would hit me instantaneously and I'd just wake up looking like that.

When I got to the viewing lounge, Randy wasn't there yet and the place was deserted except for one adult couple sitting at one of the small screens. They weren't tuned to an outside camera or telescope—they were watching the view from a Mars polar orbiter, a low one.

I had noticed a lot of adults doing that lately. Maybe there was a contagious Mars fetish going around or something. Usually hardly anyone except old people like Papa and Dr. Lovell ever look at the Outside very often. A couple times a week does it for me and I bet I look more than most people.

Randy finally turned up and we grabbed net and hauled up to the Mushroom.

The pizza cafeteria is crowded most of the time, and it's worse on weekends, so it's not easy to find anyone there. We made one complete trip around the room before Susan spotted us and managed to get our attention, among all the other people waving and shouting at *their* friends.

When we sat down, I sort of officially introduced Randy, since Tom had only heard of him and Susan had only met him in a spacesuit. Tom surprised me by winking and flashing me a covert thumbs up.

"Just to get it on record," I said, "they really robbed you."

Susan glared at me and I felt bokky, but Tom just said, "Yeah, but they do have a point." He shrugged. "It *is* tricky and dangerous to do that. But I'm glad I developed the technique, because sometimes they need to get around fast out there and the risk be damned."

Randy nodded. "My father's been using your takeoff for months. I'm sure he'll be excited about this trick too."

I had a sudden embarrassing sensation. "You know, Randy, I don't actually know what your father does."

"Vacuum extrusion. Mostly he works Outside."

Tom said, "Tell him to be careful if he does use the new trick. There was a lot of darkening on my film badge when they confiscated it—apparently you get a lot more sidescatter rads than I thought you would. And if somebody didn't practice enough beforehand, they *could* trail off and get roasted. It's probably just as well that they won't let people mess with it." He got up. "I'm going to hit the head before the pizza gets here. Hope you don't mind if it's—"

"Baby tilapia and rabbit sausage," I said, "the same as you've had on every pizza since you could pronounce it."

He grinned at me. "Ah, but I've been reformed. Susan has a bunny allergy. It's sliced quail and mushroom." He kissed her on the forehead and was gone.

She smiled. "I do hope you don't mind."

"No problem," I said. Quail tastes like an old boiled sock without the flavor.

"I'll eat almost anything," Randy said. Since then, I've realized he was lying too, about the "almost." "Do we need to throw in discrets?"

"Tom insisted it was his treat," she said. "I'm—well, you know him, Melpomene. He's really acting weird. He was taking off to hide, just like you told me he would, when I caught up with him. He said today was the only day the museum was open for general visitors and he wanted to see it."

I couldn't help laughing. The museum is where they keep a lot of old junk from Earth, pictures and clothes and so forth.

Nobody our age goes there, except when they force us to, in school.

Susan obviously didn't think it was funny at all. I thought she might start whining at me.

"I'm sorry." I swallowed several painful giggles. "It's just I've been tracking down his hideouts ever since I was a little girl and that's the strangest one he's ever picked."

She nodded, looking a little thoughtful. "Well, then it's one more really strange thing he's done. I was dragging him back here and he was being really sullen, and then something, some idea or something, just hit him and he got all weirdwired. But very cheerful and excited, too, which really didn't make any sense."

"I don't know him," Randy said, "but isn't it true that when some people get really hurt, they'll kind of react the opposite?"

"Yes," I said slowly, "and Tom does that."

We were all quiet for a long time. Then Randy said, "I still don't understand it. There's half a dozen moves that are legal in toggle racing that all have some serious risk of trailing off. Why did they pick on this one, especially when it's so effective and gives such a big advantage to the best athletes and the people with the most guts? The ruling itself just doesn't make any sense. The reasoning behind it is silly. It doesn't really fit in with the other rules for similar situations. What made them decide to do that to him?"

I wanted to get Susan back to how Tom was acting. "I don't think it was personal."

Randy nodded, but I saw his mind went elsewhere. He was thinking really hard about something, but I had no idea what.

"Did Tom say anything about why he was feeling better?" I asked. Normally when he's in a good mood he dumps his heart out to everyone about everything.

"No, and that's not like him either. I even had to ask what he was thinking about, and I've never had to before because he tells you right away—"

I was afraid she was going to pout. "What did he say?"

"Either he was crazy or everything was fine. That's exactly

141

what he said. And that he had to work on it. And all of a sudden that thing he was going to show me that I asked you about— well, I guess he still is going to show me—he said he was sure I'd like it and he wasn't worried and we'd probably just do it this afternoon. And that's all except he's been sort of happy and silly and disconnected ever since." She paused and took a sip of water. "Could he really have cracked up from disappointment or something?" She gnawed her lower lip again. With those thin lips, it looked really rabbity.

I quoted Papa. " 'Just because people do go crazy doesn't mean they do it often.' Maybe he's just come up with a new Alien Artifact?"

Susan seemed startled. "You call them that too?"

"Yes, why?"

"It hurts his feelings when your mother does. He's told me so a lot of times."

I felt like a cockroach.

"I'm sorry!" Susan said.

"No. It's okay. I'm just glad I found out."

Then one of them changed the subject, I'm not sure to what or which one of them it was, but after a while I quit feeling guilty and joined in. We just talked about trivia like school and families.

Since Susan had four brothers and five sisters, she naturally did most of the talking about families. I found myself thinking, as I often had, how odd it was on the *Flying Dutchman* for Tom and I to be the only two kids in our family. And now that I thought of it, I hadn't heard Randy mention any brothers or sisters at all. Hadn't he said he'd wondered what having a mother was like?

Just when I was really beginning to lose the thread of the conversation, Tom got back, even more obviously cheerful. Then the pizza arrived, and we all ate quietly for a while.

Or it would have been quiet if it hadn't been for the strange little thoughtful "hmms," "aahs," and "yes!es" Tom was making.

We finished up with the guys making such a fuss over trying to give each other the last piece that Susan abruptly snagged and gobbled it. At that moment I really loved her.

142

We talked about the latest batch of movies up from Earth for a while, all of us watching Tom closely, until, out of nowhere, as if he had finally given in and agreed to surprise us, he said, "You all really should see Main Engine exhaust."

He looked around the table; none of us said anything. "That must have sounded lim bokky."

"Pos-def," I said.

Susan asked, "You mean the glow——"

"Yeah, but not on a vid or from an excursion dinghy a kilometer away. The way I did. The glow is——well, hard to describe. That's why you should see it." He sounded like he was politely trying to explain something obvious to a very small child.

That seemed to end the conversation. Presently Tom dragged Susan off to go see the gadget. He wasn't making much sense, but he still seemed happy.

"That was the weirdest I've ever seen him," I said, after he'd gone.

"Well, not knowing him," Randy said, "I'd have to say he was either a saint or completely crazy. I mean, he's too smart not to see that they're doing something to him."

"Doing something?"

"Yeah, pos-def they are. They're really working him over for some reason." Randy wasn't looking at me. He seemed to be squirming, and I wondered if our day together was about to get cut in half. "Would you mind if I ordered another small pizza and ate it, as long as we're here? I didn't get much of that last one."

"Me either," I said, "how about splitting a medium? Anything as long as it's not bird-and-fungus again." We settled on rabbit sausage with extra cheese; it came fast, so the awkward silence didn't last long after we'd ordered, and then we could just concentrate on eating. Mother always said the great thing about young love is that when you run out of things to do or say you can always eat. Maybe this was the first sign of love . . . or maybe not being able to talk was.

After a while, I decided to just tackle it head-on, the way Papa would. "Randy, I think you're one of the smartest people I've ever met, and I like you, and I trust you. So even though it obviously

143

makes you uncomfortable, I wish you would tell me what you think is being done to Tom."

He took an enormous bite of pizza and chewed it very slowly. After swallowing a couple of times, he seemed about to speak, but then he took another big bite, chewed it, swallowed . . . drank some water . . . at last, he sighed.

"There's not exactly a word for it. But if they arrange so much of what happens to us, why are they arranging such bad luck for him?" Another drink of water. My fingers felt like drumming, but I didn't let them.

I saw him force himself to look into my eyes. I looked back as steadily as I could.

"You know how I really felt when Dr. James told me about the social engineering they've done on us? Scared and mad." He said it with almost no expression, like he was typing it onto a screen. "A lot of times when I feel like this I just start looking for someone to hit. Like if I could just hit the right people and hurt them bad enough, they'd have to stop."

"Stop what?"

"The thing I can't name. That I just feel they're doing. Whoever they are." He sighed again. I was getting to hate the sound of it. "That's what the world needs, more responsible people to hit, I guess. I don't know.

"About your brother. Number one—when have you ever seen a new rule announced as a disqualifier? I know they *can,* but have you ever seen them do it? They watch everyone practicing so they won't have to. If anyone does anything they don't like, they warn them way in advance. And that couldn't have been the first time Tom ever did that. So they knew he was going to try that long-drop-and-bounce-back maneuver. And they gave him no warning. On a technique they claim is too dangerous?

"They can't dropline fast enough to make that look right." He tore into another piece of pizza, as if trying to murder it with his teeth.

"Don't choke on that," I said. "I'll wait to hear the rest."

"Grmph." He swallowed. "Sorry. When I don't hit people, I eat. The two basic solutions for all problems. Okay, so the judges' ruling doesn't make any sense, and all by itself that looks like they're out to get Tom. Now, put on top of it that you tell me he's been really upset by the CSL problems they give him—and it turns out they've been giving him *impossible* problems. And all this right before his FA."

"He did those problems."

"I would bet they didn't know he'd be able to. I think they were really trying to throw him for good, have him get a zil he couldn't work out of." I had seen Randy angry lots of times, but always before it had been a wild lashing-out. Now he sat here, talking to me without raising his voice or tensing a muscle, but angrier than I had ever seen him. "Probably fifteen weeks ago Tom was a real leader in his class, lim high standing, am I right?"

"Pos-def. Except CSL he was terrific at everything."

"I wonder how they held his CSL scores down—"

That sounded just plain paranoid. "Maybe he just doesn't have the knack."

He snorted and shook his head. I hated the twist that came into his smile.

"It could be." I insisted.

"How? At least nine-tenths of CSL overlaps math and language, and you told me he's good at those. And everyone knows CSL performance has big correlations with music, art, and science performance. Remember what it says in the fourth year CSL text—'in a sense, doing CSL is synonymous with being intelligent'? So how can he possibly be doing so well at everything that overlaps CSL, and so badly at CSL itself?" He crammed in more pizza, gulped more water.

"You're going to make yourself sick."

"Yeah." He drank again, more slowly. "Or something will. About your idea, to look at those files . . . have you ever tried anything like that before?"

"Not really. It didn't seem like it would be difficult."

"It's much harder than it looks. I know. I'd hate to see you get in trouble because you didn't know some of the tricks."

I nodded. "Thank you."

"If we're both done eating, let's go back to my living unit. We won't be interrupted."

The whole way there we didn't talk much, but for some reason I felt very close to him, and better and safer than I had all week. And that was truly strange. You'd think I'd have been afraid of all that fury I could feel in him.

CHAPTER EIGHT

RANDY'S LIVING UNIT WAS REALLY SMALL, AND OF COURSE SINCE it was Saturday and most of B Block was asleep or just getting up we had to stay fairly quiet, too. So it was natural to keep our voices really low. It made me feel like a secret agent in one of those silly flatscreen movies we get up from Earth.

He slung his werpsack into the bin in his room, saying "It's easier to wipe i.d. off a house terminal, so we'll use that."

His room was completely undecorated, and everything he had visible was standard issue—not one thing an extra discret would be spent on. It was clean and neat, but there was no Randy in it at all.

We went back to the sharespace. "Where's the rest of your family?" I blurted out, feeling stupid as I said it.

It didn't seem to be a sensitive subject, though. "Dad's probably with the Earth Sports Club, watching soccer or baseball or something, so he'll be gone all day. And there's just me and him."

147

We sat down at the house terminal, and in about ten minutes I realized that though I might be better at CSL in theory, Randy knew far more about the ship's system than I did, because I had rarely gotten into anything restricted or prohibited.

"I hate to ask and show you how dumb I am, but why are we doing this?" I asked after a while.

Randy put touched my shoulder lightly. "I'm certainly glad I'm your guide on this one, Kemo Sabe."

"Who?"

"Old flatscreen. Lone Ranger. Show you some time." His fingers were flying over the keys, pausing only to grab the mouse and roll it. "Just meant you'd have been in lim deep shit if you'd tried it on your own." He sat back and gestured at the screen. "Now it's running a program to set up a chain of virtual terminals. Each virtual terminal controls another one on out to a few hundred of them."

"What's it for?"

"Well, you can't use your own terminal because they read i.d. and attach it to everything in every dialog, right?"

It was right, now that he pointed it out. I'd have been caught right away. I leaned a little closer to him. "Okay, so why so many?"

"The sys register for this class of terminal only tracks virtual parents fifteen deep, but you can chain up to 511 of them. So when it's chained out to a couple of hundred, we're disidentified. And at that point we're free to mess around."

"Why not just sixteen terminals in the chain?" This was getting interesting; maybe Randy's CSL talents were as sharp as mine, just differently directed.

"Well, there has to be a bridgeburner in the chain if we don't want to get caught. So we'll work at a depth of 250 and set the bridgeburner to start at number eighteen." He pounded at the keys again; he must have been replacing his keyboard every week.

I was dying to know what a bridgeburner was, but I felt like I'd bokked enough already. By watching what he did, anyway, I figured out that a bridgeburner watched events further down the chain. The register showed only the last fifteen terminals in the chain, so you couldn't get caught in a direct jump, but Security could still trace you back in jumps of sixteen. If they started, the bridgeburner would destroy all the other virtual terminals, leaving no pathway back to the controlling terminal.

It was lim clever, and sneaky too. "That's brilliant," I said. "Where'd you learn all this?"

"A lot of techs pick it up. Self-defense against management, you know. It helps to have the real numbers at contract time. And B Shift has most of the techs. Any knowledge that's any kind of use transpires after a while." He brought up a dump of the registers, studied it, and nodded. "That's a good start. But if we're going to try to penetrate the CPB's files, we better load on some other stuff too, say a pepper shaker and a false continuation."

I took a large bit of my pride and swallowed as hard as I could. "I don't know what they are."

"The AIs that trace chains of virtual terminals are called bloodhounds. A pepper shaker viruses the bloodhound, turns on all its error bits, and reports it as damaged code to the system, so the immunity AIs attack it. It can take as much as eight milliseconds for the bloodhound to get back on the track, and by that time the bridgeburner has us out of there."

I watched as he set it up. "Shouldn't you optimize the algorithm more?"

"Where can I?"

"That induction engine should use a discrete geometric in its comparison space, instead of a continuous one." At last I felt almost sort of useful. "And in that case you can change the comparison from numeric to linked-OR, and the matrix will be a tenth the size."

"Yeah—got you." We worked on it together for a few minutes. When we had a finished version, Randy installed the pepper shaker in a dozen virtual terminals. "Mind if I post it too?"

"Post it? Where?"

"The *Unofficial Organ*. It's a good trick, and other people could use it."

"Sure." I didn't really know what I'd agreed to, but he obviously thought I should do it. I had heard of the *Unofficial Organ* a few times, but always as a pun in a punchline. I had no idea what it was.

He tapped out a key sequence and a couple of unfamiliar icons appeared. He triggered two of them, and a copy went somewhere.

I could also help with the next step: corrupting a newly copied generic AI to do the penetration. That's tricky—you have to override some deep-level prohibitions, because if an AI is smart enough to do the penetration it's smart enough to suspect something and call Security.

The real barrier is supposed to be the password, but in fact we were already past the hard part. Password protection up here isn't all that effective because everyone's complete bio is required to be available online to anyone. So you can always find mothers' maiden names, relatives' names, what a person reads, anything that would normally be there in a person's Security dossier.

For example, from some past minor tinkering, I knew that when Papa was in "high school" on Earth, his friends sometimes called him Horny Corny, and that on his first date with Mother he had been arrested by Sergeant Joseph Clifford for driving at sixty-four miles per hour in a forty-five mile per hour zone. (I converted those numbers to kilometers and decided everything moves much too fast on Earth.)

So you could set up another corrupted AI to search relevant biographies and see what it could pull out. Besides, very few files were password-protected. Most people figured the "private" flag was enough, even on a file where they had recorded some higher level password.

We were into the files of the clerical staff at CPB almost at once, and sure enough, some of them had recorded passwords for more secure files there.

As soon as we got into the high-secure CPB stuff Randy said, "Okay, now for a false continuation. In fact, we can make it do something really clever. . . ."

It was clever—and with a little help from me it was elegant. CPB has the highest clearance on the system. So Randy extended the virtual terminal chain out from CPB and into Security, using the CPB's high-level clearance to override Security's protections, and put monitors on the ends of the chain. In effect, he bugged the police station.

We ended up with lots of time to work because of that. First we pulled copies of twenty or so files that we thought might contain something we'd want to know, and downloaded copies onto my werp's backup memory block, where Central wouldn't be able to see that we had them. Then we went through more systematically, picking up any file that shared more than eight keywords with the ones we'd gathered. Finally, mostly for amusement, we pulled the files on ourselves, Tom, Theophilus, Miriam, Gwenny Mori, and Barry Yang. "Let's pick up Susan the Rodent while we're here," I suggested.

Randy laughed. "Who?"

"Susan Rodenski. We had lunch with her and Tom."

"One rodent added to the menu." The file copy dumped it into memory.

The living unit door opened.

My heart bulged against my larynx. We were in lim shit—it would take almost a minute to fully close down.

Randy squeezed my hand with his right hand and worked the mouse with his left. An icon spun up—an old-fashioned cartoon burglar, wearing a black mask and carrying a bag. Randy clicked again.

We were looking at a reading assignment in Japanese, with a notepad below.

In Japanese, Randy typed "all clear" and wiped the screen, bringing up the next page. He passed the keyboard to me.

"Hi Dad," he said, as calmly as if we had really been doing homework.

Mr. Schwartz was *huge*—close to two meters tall, and heavy as well. I suspected two of me could have sat comfortably on one of his shoulders.

He was wearing one of the standish vis-orange coveralls most techs seem to prefer. It had a bunch of really koapy patches, mostly construction project ones, going back to Quito Geosync

151

Cable in 2009 and right on up to the *Flying Dutchman* Outside construction patch, the Vacuum Workers Union, and a couple of union office badges. On the left front, just below the seam, was a black XV with two bars underneath—seventeen years total time in space.

I wondered if it bothered him that Randy and I already had twelve.

"Hello, company, I see."

"Dad, this is Melpomene Murray. Melpomene, this is my father. She's a friend from school, and she's single-handedly saving my Japanese grade."

"Brave young lady."

"It's nice to meet you," I said. "And Randy doesn't need that much saving."

Mr. Schwartz nodded, smiling, and said to Randy, "If you can believe it, they're showing four hours of cycle pursuit. Can't stand to watch a bunch of guys in tight shorts chase each others' butts, so I thought I'd get a scrub and a change." He nodded to me again. "Nice to meet you."

He reached into his room, pulled out a small bag and a change of clothes, slung them over his shoulder, and bounced out the door in one neat motion, letting it autodog behind him.

"I hope I didn't just chase your father out of his own living unit."

"No, he always goes to the public baths anyway. He likes to have people to hang around with—most techs are that way."

I sort of knew that the baths were there, but I had the impression from Mother that there was something disreputable about them. "Do you go there?"

"Sometimes. There aren't many people our age. Your friend Miriam is there with her folks now and then."

So he had seen Miriam naked, but not me.

Yet.

I was annoyed with myself for feeling so jealous, so I said, "Well, let's see what we caught while we were burgling. And where did you find that coverup program?"

"Just a little trick from the *Unofficial Organ*. I'm surprised you know computing so well and you've never run across any of the good tricks. Most of the real wizards are——" The funny expression that crossed his face bothered me, and the nervous laugh bothered me more. He took my hand. "You don't know why."

I felt hurt, but had no idea why. I shrugged and shook my head.

"Your father's on the CPB."

I couldn't have been more surprised if he'd said the problem was my horns and cloven feet. "What's that got to do with it?"

Randy gestured at the list of secret files on the screen.

"Oh." There must be millions of things no one had ever told me because of that. I must have been left out of stuff for years. Suddenly I could remember lots of times I had felt like a conversation died when I came up to join it.

I cried. It went on for a long time. He held me, and rubbed my back and neck gently, and after a while I stopped, but still we sat there for a long while, holding hands facing each other and saying nothing.

Finally, Randy said, "There's snot or something hanging from your nose. Would you like a wipe?"

"Y-yes." I sighed—and it turned into a giggle. "Ah me, what a romantic you are, sir."

He bounced over to the wall dispenser and fetched a wipe, handing it to me with an exaggerated bow.

I felt morally obligated to honk, which got him laughing too. When we finally calmed down, I said, "Now maybe we'd better take a look at those files we've gotten."

The CPB has a lot of strange jargon. Scanning keyword lists and abstracts didn't do us much good. Finally we just worked through it sequentially.

Most of the afternoon went by as we alternately read and argued about what it all meant. It's not easy to turn shrinkspeak into English—"Japanese would be easier," Randy said. "A lot easier."

"Hai soo-desu, ne? At least it's *starting* to make sense. And it's not as bad as we were afraid it would be——"

"I don't know about that, Melpomene, there's stuff that would make a lot of techs explode." He was pointing at the list of "Values for Inclusion in Semiotic System at Age 8."

"I thought that was just a list of platitudes."

"Looked like it to me, too, at first. But look at number three: 'On a space ship or in a society, the fundamental interests of everyone are the same. We must all cooperate with corporate policies and directives regardless of position, rank, standing, or title, to fulfill the objectives of the ship.' How do you square joining a union with that? In fact if you take away the high principles, it boils down to 'everyone should shut up and do what NAC tells them.' "

I read it over and over, trying to see what he meant. "I guess you could read it that way. The applications list on that value would probably tell us whether that's the intention. Do we have any docs of the rule applications it refs?" I hit a few keys and the list came up. "Looks like we do—two abstract reports, our case reports, and Tom's case report."

"That's weird. Why us three and not any of the others?"

We found out in about five minutes that that was the key to all of it. This is where NAC will probably erase everything I write, so I'll just put it down for my own sake:

Unions were supposed to disappear within twenty-five years.

Elections would be replaced by an "organically developed consensus process" before 2040. (We were thrown off the track at first by "organically developed." We thought that must mean it was up to the people on the *Flying Dutchman.* After enough poking around in the supplementary material, we realized it really meant that the CPB wasn't sure what people would accept yet, so they were going to wing it when they had a better idea.)

And most importantly, when we began to examine our own files, we found that Randy, Tom, and I were all labelled "Special Category."

"What *do* we have to do with all this?" Randy asked. "There's the mystery."

But just as we brought up the file and began to read, the door latch turned. We had to flip back over to the Japanese assignment.

I swallowed hard for one second. I suppose I imagined Papa and the whole CPB bursting in with guns blazing or something. Of course it was just Mr. Schwartz again.

"Hi. Hope you got a lot done. Anyone want to get some dinner before the party starts?"

I hadn't heard anything about a party. I looked at Randy. He was blushing a deeper red than I'd ever seen.

Mr. Schwartz looked back and forth between us a couple of times and broke into a broad grin. Then he whooped, bounded up to the ceiling in a tight flip, shot straight back down, caught himself on his hands and kipped back upright. He was roaring with laughter.

Randy was almost purple, looking down at his lap.

"So you didn't get around to it," Mr. Schwartz said.

Randy shook his head.

"Randy?" His voice was suddenly gentler.

Randy didn't move or speak.

"Umm. Uh, sorry." He turned back to the door. "Uh—" he winked, but Randy didn't look up to see it—"I just remembered I have to go check the vacuum hold to make sure the vacuum isn't leaking out into space. So I'll be back in maybe ten minutes or so, okay?"

Randy nodded.

"I'm sorry. I really am. Don't feel like *you* have to act like an idiot just because your old man does. It's not a big family tradition or anything."

Randy looked up, finally forcing a sort of wan smile. "Pos-def. See you in a few."

Mr. Schwartz was out the door in a single bound and had it dogged faster than you could say it. You'd have thought there was a francium hydroxide spill in the room or something.

I didn't really know what was wrong with Randy, so I put an arm around him. He moved a little and then settled back. I waited.

"See?" he said, finally. "This is his idea of lim hilarious." He snuffled. "I can never bring anyone home. He's always going to barge in and say something stupid. Always. He's so fucking bokky. And it's like it rubs off on me."

I bounced up, grabbed a wipe from the wall dispenser, and handed it to him. He blew his nose and sighed. "You'd think I'd be used to him. I mean, I know he thinks he's the life of the party. But somehow or other I always end up in a corner looking at the floor while he laughs at me. If I could just look up once and explain—I don't think he'd even hear me." He blew his nose again. This was a big day for crying. "The truth is I just forgot. I meant to, but I forgot. It wasn't because I was scared or anything, but he's going to make it into a funny story now—"

I handed him another wipe, and watched him wipe his eyes. "Forgot what?"

"Oh . . ." He started to turn red again. "Tonight, or this afternoon and night, on B time—well anyway, it starts in a couple of hours . . ."

He took a deep breath and started over.

"It's the B Block party, the big one they have after every perihelion and aphelion. Because after an Earthpass or a Mars-pass, the big rush is over—most of the Outside crews and techs are on B Shift. It's kind of a big thing, I mean, everyone goes, all my old friends will be there, and I kind of thought . . .

"Well, you know, I don't eat with Dad that often, maybe once a week at most, but this morning we had breakfast together, and for once we were talking, really getting along. And he was asking about school and friends and things. I wasn't going to tell him about Ted and getting beaten up, and so I mostly talked about . . . you, Melpomene."

I gave myself a mental hug. "So what did he say?"

"It's what I said. Well, kind of. He started teasing me—I mean, not really cruel the way he does sometimes, but just teasing me like a friend—about asking you to go to the B Block party with me. . . ."

I hugged him, hard, and said. "And you forgot to because we got so involved in everything else. Well, it's okay, I accept."

He started crying again, harder. Guys can be really weird.

I grabbed another wipe and handed it to him. "I mean I

accept if you still plan to ask me. For both dinner and the party. But I'd really appreciate about forty-five minutes to get present-able. Since all your old friends will be there, I think the least I can do is be devastating, don't you? Or should we settle for stunning?"

He finally started to laugh, which was a relief because I wasn't sure how long I could keep this line of nonsense up. "Okay, formally, Melpomene, do you want to go the B Block party with me?"

"Pos-def."

He sighed. "Well, it wasn't exactly what I imagined it would be like, but it worked anyway. I feel like a moron."

"But you're such a *likable* moron." I kissed him on the cheek. "See you in a little bit."

So I zoomed back to my living unit, probably flattening fifty little kids without seeing them, heart pounding, practically sing-ing, plunged into the shower, and finally found myself pulling out the new white coverall I had been saving to break in on School Awards Day.

Papa and Mother came in as I was looking at myself in the mirror, trying to think of something else I could do along the lines of looking wonderful. Crewcut, coverall, and blue slippers wasn't much to work with. . . . I kept trying to decide whether I wanted to wear a belt or a sash.

Papa headed straight for the bathroom. Mother stood and watched me for a while.

She finally said "Melly, if I didn't know it was impossible, I would swear you were primping."

I don't know why I thought that was funny, even with the "Melly," but anyway I laughed and told her what was on the queue.

She seemed a bit startled, but then she smiled at me, this great big wonderful smile that I hadn't seen in years. "Melpomene—dear—no doubt this will come as a complete surprise to you, but I do believe you have a *date.*"

"Oh, Mother, I'm really just going to a party . . . uh, with a guy, to meet all his old friends . . . hunh. Maybe I do." There didn't seem to be much else to say. "Well, umm."

She looked me over. "Not a bad effect, a little different from what was fashionable in my day, but skirts aren't really practical in low g and heels always hurt my feet anyway. Let's see what we can add—"

"What else is there?" I asked.

"Hold on for just a minute." She darted into their room; in a moment she was back with a small box. "Let's see what we have."

I gaped at the box. "It's wood. Natural wood. Not tank-grown."

"Yep, brought from Earth." She passed it to me carefully, and I took it with a strange sensation that there was something terribly important there. "That box, and what's in it, was about ten percent of my weight allowance," she added, nervously, as if afraid I'd laugh.

"It's so smooth. But the grain is so . . . swirly, random, like a picture in a fractal geometry lesson. And so warm to the touch . . ."

"I got it from my grandmother when I was a little girl. The clasp slides to the right. It's silver."

I had never seen so much silver in one place, even in the chem lab. It was a strange shape that I couldn't quite name, but had probably seen in a biology text. A leaf or a seashell or something. I pushed it over to the right and gently lifted the lid.

"Jewelry! I saw some when our class went to the museum. I never even knew you had this. . . ."

"It wasn't time yet. Or something. I'm not really sure why I didn't show it to you before." She took it back carefully. "You know, you and I really have similar features, so all this should work for you, but you don't have pierced ears or long hair, so . . . let's see. This pin was my grandmother's." She lifted out a little rose of metal and fastened it gently on my chest, a few centimeters below my left shoulder. "And—hah. Of course, I'd almost forgotten it, but it's perfect."

She pulled something tiny and crumpled from a little compartment in the box. "Short hair, really short hair, was very in fashion a couple of years before we came up. Your father gave me this."

It looked like a tiny piece of metal netting. "What is it?"

"They called it a 'coleman.' Maybe that was the designer's name or it was based on something coal miners wore, or something." She held it loosely in her fist and breathed over it several times. "Once it gets warm . . ."

She eased it out; now it was a rumpled flat sheet the size and shape of Nathan Roswald's yarmulke. She spread it out and laid it on the left side of my head, just to the side of the crown. It gave me an odd prickly feeling in my hair. "Now shake your head, hard."

I did.

"Good." She breathed on it again, her breath warm and moist on my scalp, and waited a few seconds. "Shake your head again. Right. Okay, one more time . . ." Her breath was warm on my scalp. "Wait . . . now shake." I bobbed my head around vigorously; I could no longer feel the coleman. "Is it still binding anywhere?"

"No."

"Now it will stay on as long as you want it to, and it won't pull your hair. They respond to temperature differences somehow—I don't really understand it. Have a look at yourself in the mirror."

I was amazed—the whorl of shining metal spread against my dark hair like a tiny galaxy, catching fire from the oval gleams on the rose-shaped pin. . . . "It's beautiful."

"You are." Mother said it briskly, as if correcting me. "It's a family trait. Now hurry—traditionally you're supposed to be a little late, but up here five minutes is a long time."

"How late did you used to be?"

"Just as long as you will. Exactly long enough for him to really want to see you, and not one second longer . . . unless you're absolutely determined on a career as la belle dame sans merci."

I laughed, but her expression just got stranger. "Do you know . . . do you know that you look, oh, five years older? Like a woman?"

I felt something swirl in my stomach. "Like a very small woman, maybe," I said, and felt how flat the joke was.

But she smiled anyway, and we hugged. It had probably been at least a year since we had done that.

I took an omnivator by myself, partly because I was running a little late and mostly because I wanted Randy to see me before anyone else did.

He opened the door right away. He had changed too—into his company uniform. NAC insists we all have them in case our parents have to entertain some plutock tourist and pass us all off as real corporados. I guess a lot of groundhogs who come on Ship Tour think we wear those all the time.

Randy, like everyone else, wore a kidsized version of his same-sex parent's uniform. For Randy that was vis-orange separate shirt and pants, broad black cloth stretch belt, black slippers, and black neckerchief. My father always called it the "Halloween Boy Scout look," for some reason, and referred to our light-green professional uniforms as the "Hospital Boy Scout look." Sometimes adults don't make any sense at all.

Randy looked terrific, very grown up and handsome. The only thing that spoiled the effect was that he seemed to be staring at me. "You look really . . . good," he stammered, after a moment.

"Try not to be so surprised. You look great yourself," I told him.

There was a long, awkward silence, before Mr. Schwartz spoke from somewhere behind Randy. "Your next line, son, is, 'Come in.' "

From the way Randy blushed, I guess it embarrassed him, but he stammered out the invitation and I came in.

Mr. Schwartz was in uniform too. He was holding a camera and grinning. "You two stand together."

So we did, and he took pictures of us.

It was so startling we both laughed. He laughed too, but he kept shooting pictures. He set the camera into the reader slot in the house terminal, and hardcopies rolled out. He bent to tap at the keys for a moment. "Might as well send your mother the full set, Melpomene," he said.

"My mother?" I asked, startled.

"She called while you were on your way over. The pictures were her idea, but I thought it was a great one. So the hardcopies are for me." Then he tapped at the keyboard for a couple of minutes. "Soon as I get this last thing done, we'll go to dinner. Hope you guys don't mind hitting the Soup Bar." He finished whatever he was typing and picked up one of the pictures. "I've saved permanent copies, but you guys really should take a look at this." He held it up.

I saw what my mother meant about looking five years older. Believe me, when you're twelve, that's lim koapy.

I had only rarely been to the Soup Bar. The first thing I noticed was that there were a lot of Outside techs in there. When his father went up for his fourth refill, Randy explained, "You know how dry your throat is after two hours of Outside Club? And how hot and sweaty your suit gets if you have to piss while you're Outside? Well, they don't drink anything for several hours before going Outside, and they work most of the day on just sips of water. So they really get dried out. I always make up a couple liters of flavored gelatin and put it in the living unit refrigerator as soon as I get home from school—and he gulps half of it down as soon as he gets in."

"Here's another thing that's weird," I said. "If we're all supposed to be so equal, how come I don't know anything about techs?"

Randy's father, coming back, heard this, and after he'd had a few more spoonfuls of soup, he said, "Well, in theory the ship is supposed to be classless, but it doesn't work that way. People just experience life differently, depending on what their work is. Life feels different if you get sweaty every day or if you've always got to look good, or depending on whether management cares about what you do in your offtime." He snorted. "Perfect example right there. When I think 'work,' I think of being managed—I never think of managing as work."

Mr. Schwartz finished his soup. A thought came into my mind from what we'd just learned from the stolen files. "I know one big difference between tech and professional. All the techs are in the unions, but I don't think anyone I've ever known, except Randy, has liked unions."

"Or their parents haven't," Mr. Schwartz agreed. "Most kids just echo their parents. Randy's lucky enough to have figured out his old man's a fool at an earlier age than most people do. Some of 'em'll change their minds when they're working."

I hoped he'd go on, so I said, "I guess I've never heard the case *for* unions. The official NAC channel isn't very sympathetic."

"Well, you can't expect them to be. I suppose it's—" he glanced sideways at Randy. "Hey, I don't want to take up your first date talking economics with your girl. You ought to kick me under the table or something."

From the way Randy jumped, I guess that was when *he* realized it was a date. "To tell the truth, Dad, I'm interested myself. I've probably been in three or four fights on behalf of the union, and I don't really know what it's all about."

Mr. Schwartz sighed. "I swear it's something in the schooling they give you kids. And maybe it doesn't matter, because with your grades and all, Randy, I think you're more likely to go professional. But anyway, I see it like this. As long as people do different jobs they have different interests. Sure, sometimes, in a real crisis, like a sea-ship in a storm or a small company about to go bankrupt, everyone's interests really are the same, because saving the whole thing is more important than any one part of it.

"But most of the time it's a lot more complicated." He paused to take a sip of coffee. "See, if you're on top, it's easy to think that what's good for you is what's good for the organization. In the short run it might even be—a company does better if it gets more work for less wages paid, or if it spends less on health and safety.

"In the longer run, though, workers do the work. Management doesn't. If workers are sick, hurt, pissed off, or broke, they don't work as well."

As Papa's daughter, I'm a pretty good debater myself, and cross ex is one of my strong points. "But then there's no problem. Doesn't the company have an interest in keeping the workers working?"

"Sure—but for as little as possible. Suppose a manager got us all to work two extra hours per day for half pay. Who would get the added profit?"

"NAC," I admitted.

"Well, that's what I'm trying to say. Management works for the employer, and at least in the short run your employer's interests are exactly opposite yours. No matter how nice a guy your manager is, he still gets paid to be your enemy.

"But that's not the whole story. Otherwise I suppose they'd just make slaves of us or we'd kill them. The fact is, they don't dare win—because if they destroy the worker, who will make the product or buy it? The union limits how much management can win. So in a sense the union looks after the long run. Or justice, which might be the same thing."

He finished his coffee. "That's all I'm going to say. Actually I kind of hope neither of you ever needs to join one—as far as I can tell, management and professional jobs are a lot softer. And in the long run I don't think there will be many of us working with our hands in space, anyway, so maybe no one will be union in a few decades. But the family's been union for four generations, Randy, and I guess you're entitled to have some idea why." He stirred his coffee; there was something sad about him, like the way my mother gets when she talks about Grandpa or Miriam's father does when he talks about Manhattan before it was domed. "Now let's get going. You kids need to dazzle your friends, and I need to prove I'm not too goddam old to some of the young snots on my crew."

We hauled down the corridor to the party together, going comfortably slowly so we could talk. Mr. Schwartz told us about things years ago, jobs he'd been on, like how they hung the geosync cables, and about Earth before the Die-Off. He had run away from home when he was ten, in February of 1994, and managed to wander thousands of kilometers around North America, just as the old society was collapsing. When he decided to go back home, that June, his parents, like so many others, were dead of mutAIDS. We'd heard mutAIDS stories before, of course, but it shocked us that things could get bad enough to make you go out the door and take your chances.

He shrugged. "No psych intervention teams, no CPB, and it was an unscreened population—up here the rottenest apples are a lot less common. Just one of a lot of ways it's a lot better up here. Still, Randy, I wish you could have seen San Francisco or New Orleans or even Cleveland before the domes, or just taken a trip on the old interstates through the industrial belts. The lights and flames from the mills, factories, and refineries used to glow like dawn—it was beautiful, just beautiful."

"I've never even seen dawn," Randy pointed out.

"Well, you *will* have to see Earth someday. I'm sure they still have dawn. But the factories are gone. Now it's just a dome every few hundred kilometers and everything falling to rust since heavy industry moved up to orbit. The old highways are empty except for freight disksters, and the undomed towns are empty except for the crazies." He sighed. "A lot of people used to think the old cities were ugly—but they were *human*. It's like people are disappearing from the world."

Then he grinned again. "So here you are hanging on the nets listening to an old geezer reminisce. You kids today sure know how to have a good time. Anyway, let's get there before I'm senile."

"Have a good time, Dad," Randy said as we reached the entryway.

"It's been very nice meeting you," I added.

"You too. I'll be over on the gaffer side if you need me for anything." And he was gone.

Randy shook his head. "Well, you sure bring out the charm in him. He was practically human." He took my hand as we floated over toward a crowd of people our age. "Whatever it was, I'm glad it happened—I'm angry at him a lot of the time but I do want you to like him."

Shit! Shit! Shit! Shit!

I set the werp to give me a warning bell when it got too late, so I wouldn't miss school again. So of course it went off right when I was getting to the good part.

And it *is* pretty late. I was going to go a little longer but now my concentration is gone, too. And all of a sudden I feel like I'm lying to you. I write down what I remember, but I think I'm "remembering" things in much more detail than I probably really perceived. Like I don't think Mr. Schwartz really said everything exactly the way I wrote it down, but I'm sure I'm pretty close, so I'm not sure whether that's false or not. A lot can turn on one or two words or on an intonation that might not show up at all. Not exactly *not* true, but not *lim* true either, if you see what I mean.

And the trouble gets worse telling you about the B Block party, because I remember all kinds of things perfectly, which ought to make it easier except I really can't remember the order they happened in, or how they all connected.

And if I can't write it down just like it happened I don't want to write this part at all. Because I've noticed I'm starting to remember things the way I wrote them even when I know they happened differently. Like every so often I improve somebody's joke, or sometimes I make somebody say what the whole problem is when actually he just sat there and sobbed and sniffled until I practically had to beat it out of him. And then after I've done that, when I think about it again, I seem to hear them saying the words I wrote just as if it had really happened that way.

And when it comes to the B Block party, I want all my memories to be real. It was the only completely good thing in all that bokky lim stupid time.

So there's no order, but I'm quite sure I remember people running up to say hi to Randy; resting my head on Randy's shoulder while we danced (and finally being grateful that they made us learn how in rec); Mr. Schwartz doing the Boink or some other prehistoric dance with some older tech, both of them laughing and her very drunk; Randy just touching my face lightly like he didn't think I was real and wanted to be sure; talking with two of his old friends while he was getting us drinks, both Terry and Henri trying so hard to be superpolite and superintelligent as if impressing me was the most important thing in the world.

I remember the way the music sounded louder than any I'd heard before and I could feel it pulsing down in my belly, and the gentle pull of the magnets in my slippers against the floor while we danced. That funny warm smell from a crowd that big, every one of them with a fresh shower—they must have really put a strain on the water budget.

It was so strange to look down and notice we were on the Blue Spot, in the same Big Commons where we play aerocrosse.

The punch tingled and foamed in my mouth; Randy's father roared with laughter as he held some woman over his head.

Whorls and spins of soft color drifted lazily across the floor.

One wonderful rich maroon color shone at me through Randy's hair, giving him a halo close to his head. I laughed at it because I was so happy, and he looked so confused I had to explain, and I couldn't, and that was very funny too.

I was giddy and dizzy a lot.

When our pocket phones went off to let us know we had half an hour to get home, we both jumped half a meter. It took us by surprise because the party wasn't going to end for another six hours—after all, most of these folks were on B Shift—but more surprising than that, we had lost track of the time.

Mother says it happened to her a lot when she was a girl. But it never happens up here—you live by the clock. It would be like forgetting to breathe.

Nevertheless, we did it.

Now it *really* is late. Setting a warning bell doesn't do much good if you ignore it when it goes off.

Anyway, Randy took me home, and we decided the next day we'd study Japanese together, and he kissed me good night at the door.

I feel like making up the detail that he whistled as he clambered away on the net, but that's not true. He ponged from side to side of the corridor a couple of times, but he didn't whistle.

I went in and everyone—Mother, Papa, Tom, and Susan—was sitting in there with these silly smiles. I had one myself, probably.

Late. Late. Late. Well, maybe I should have another talk with Dr. Lovell about doing this stuff. It's beginning to weirdwire me.

WERP: MAKE NOTE. get appt Lovell tomorrow. END NOTE.

I'm going to bed now.

CHAPTER NINE

January 3, 2026

T ODAY DR. LOVELL TRIED TO TALK TO ME ABOUT THE WRITING and the FA. I got so upset I wasn't really sure what it was about, to tell the truth. As far as I could get it, maybe they don't know what to do with me. I think that's what she meant but I could be wrong.

She said, I think—god, why couldn't I stop crying long enough to listen?—she said I should put in as much time writing as I want, and I don't have to come to class anymore.

That's not what upset me so much as what I learned—if you're Special Category, like me and Randy, your FA doesn't really count. They make us take it so we share the experience with our peers, but they expect our hobbies or quirks to take over and make us whatever we're supposed to be, the way Tom's did.

When I think about it, I should have known after last year, but I guess the idea didn't sink in or something. But it makes sense.

I mean, they don't raise us like everyone else, why should they treat us like everyone else?

Maybe the trouble is that now I get what it means. It's like a fairy tale. Once upon a time there was an ugly duckling. Everyone made fun of her. She was miserable because she had no friends. Then one day she saved the whole flock from a tiger or whatever it is that eats ducks. And everyone said, "Wow! What a duck!" And they were much more polite to her.

But she still didn't have any friends, because when you come right down to it, she was still an ugly duck.

Maybe I'll write later. Just now I don't feel like it.

I̲T'S BEEN AN HOUR SINCE I LAST WROTE. THERE WAS A WERP flag in some of the text before this, but I want to tell you about this before I get back to the stuff that happened last year.

Tom came in. He's been teaching Mandelbrot Pointilist technique to an adult art class in C Shift. Susan was taking a nap, having given up on trying to be nice to me, and I don't blame her.

When he saw me sitting there looking miserable and asked what the matter was, I told him as best I could, and he acted like a complete moron, trying to tell me how I shouldn't feel that way because it was "better and freer" to be a "real individual." "Even if you feel like no one understands you. Especially then. Because that's when you can see things no one else sees, *understand* things and bring them into being for everyone else. You're really important and special—"

I burst into tears. It's the best defense ever found against well-meaning people who are telling you something stupid "for your own good." He stammered, patted my arm, hovered around ineffectually, and, when the sobs got louder, fled into his and Susan's room, closing the door behind him. I went into the bathroom to dry my eyes.

After a good look at myself, I decided the rest could use work too, so I stripped, threw my clothes into the freshener, got into the shower stall, and turned on the spray and vacuum. I was about a day and a half early for a shower, but I felt like I needed it now. The warm, sudsy water-alcohol mix felt wonderful as it squirted in over my head and slurped away through the screen by my feet. It was early in the week, so the charge was fresh and didn't yet smell of other people—Tom had used this only once before me, and Susan only twice.

I clicked the filter into place and stood in the warm rinse, swishing it over me and letting the unhappiness wash away. I pushed the finish button and the mix went back to the storage tank.

The towel smelled like Tom. He must have showered right after a workout again. The scavenger just can't seem to handle that.

I clicked on the vid to get some news while I dried myself. Everyone was rich and getting richer and everyone was happy. NAC was lying again—once we're far enough out from Earth, the onship independent news channels have no way of getting information except from NACFlash. Supposedly someday Tass or the BBC will set up directional channels out to the ships and the bases, and we'll get accurate news all the time, but we've been up here a lot of orbits and it hasn't happened yet.

Why they think all we should get from Earth is "HappiNews" and "Progress!" is beyond me. Maybe I didn't steal the right file to find out.

I tossed the towel into the scavenger and put my freshened clothes back on. Susan was waiting in the sharespace. "I sent Tom on ahead to dinner. I'm meeting him there—you can join us if you like or I can pick up a workmeal for you."

"What would I do with a workmeal? They as good as told me not to bother doing schoolwork anymore. And I don't really feel like eating." I pushed off and glided toward my room.

She intercepted me in a sort of gentle version of a flyball tackle, hugging me and bringing me up against the wall. "No you don't. I'm sorry you feel bad but you're not going into your room to feel sorry for yourself. Tom doesn't get to do that any more and neither do you."

I really cried then, no strategy about it. I hated her.

But it was so comforting to be held that I didn't try to get away.

"It's going to be all right. It is. Now, listen, I know I don't really understand you, but I do know that for a couple of days after you get some writing done you're easier to live with and you don't seem to hate yourself so much. And I think all that's because you're happy.

"I want you to be happy.

"So sit down and write. You'll be hungry in about an hour and a half and by then I'll be back with a workmeal. No arguments. Just do it." She gave me another hard squeeze on the arms and let go, pushing back and looking at me for a moment from the entry. "By the way, right now Tom thinks he's solved all the problems in his life. So he's really unbearable to anyone who's at all unhappy. You might want to stay away from him until he gets over it."

Then she popped out the door.

So I'm here at the werp again, anyway, and I just realized that what it flagged before was my reference to Special Category.

That even fits into the story, but I guess I'll get there when I get there. For right now I'm just setting things down in the right order and hoping it will mean something. Here goes.

THE NEXT DAY, SUNDAY, SHORTLY AFTER BREAKFAST, PAPA RE-treated into his office and Tom to his room. They said they couldn't take any more.

Mother and I had started talking about the B Block party at breakfast and continued it all the way home and back into the living unit. I told her what everyone wore, and who danced with who as far as I could remember. She seemed to have almost guessed everything that had happened as if she'd been there.

Papa muttered something unpleasant about "girl talk" just before he disappeared. "Don't forget you married one," Mother called after him.

"I *can't possibly* forget," he groaned, and went in.

That was wonderful. We must have laughed for five minutes. Anyway, while we were laughing, Tom got away too.

I was having such a good time I was actually asking Mother about when she was a girl.

She had a recording of all her old family photo album, and we looked at pictures of her going to "proms" and stuff like that. It was funny to think that probably all the buildings in the picture were crumbling now, or already collapsed—her home town was too small to dome.

But she didn't dwell on that or get all maudlin as she so often did. This time she had a lot of stories to tell that were really funny, not disguised sermons about how bad it was up here. And not like I was being entrusted with some big important "family heritage" or any nonsense like that. These were more like things she would just share with a friend.

We finally had to quit the "girl talk" because it was time for me to go over to Randy's to study. When I left, she was bringing one of that Olson woman's books up on the screen, but it didn't bother me like it usually did.

The whole way to B Block I kept thinking of things I wanted to ask her about when she'd been a girl. What wearing skirts was like—maybe Randy and I could take Ballroom Dance, down in the bottom of the Mushroom. They wore skirts for that. And what would it be like to breathe open air and see the sky at the same time, or have no temperature control and animals wandering around wherever they wanted?

Mr. Schwartz was out again, leaving Randy by himself. In case the CPB had been monitoring us and might be suspicious, we decided to do our schoolwork first.

So we talked in Japanese, Spanish, and Esperanto for a while, and we got some papers written, and spent a lot of time just holding hands and reading. When lunchtime came, we went up to A Block cafeteria, picked up workmeals, and came directly back to work some more.

About 1400, Randy stretched his arms, reaching high over his head, and said, "Well, do you want to tackle the stuff we got yesterday?"

I tickled his extended belly, which made him jerk so hard he bounced up a meter. He squawked, flipped over, came back down, and wrestled me into an armlock. "Ar there, me pretty, now I've got yer, ye scurvy wench——"

It didn't seem possible but his pirate accent was worse than his Japanese accent.

"Unh-unh," I said. "You've got to finish the pillaging first. Those are the rules."

"Well, scuttle me barnacles, the wench is right," he said, rolling off me and letting me go. He suddenly sat up, jerking awkwardly at his coverall.

"Are you okay?"

"Uh, yeah, just something surprised me. Do you want to take a look at those files?"

"Pos-def."

We called them up, and started looking to see what a "Special Category" was. "As far as I can tell," Randy said, "it's a person without more than one brother or sister. So we both are I guess. But I don't see what difference it's supposed to make."

I was shuffling my way through the technical papers. "This is like learning a whole new subject. Supposedly we get some of every subject in school, and we're close to graduation—so why does this all look so unfamiliar?"

It was another hour of arguing and trying to understand, and we still hadn't gotten around to reading our own files, before we pieced it all together.

What we found was this:

In a society that really works by consensus, no one wants to lead, because the job has none of the privileges it does in a more hierarchic or representational society. And nobody raised that way wants to act until they know what other people want. So even though you need a vast majority of consensus-seekers, if you are going to have any ability to make a difficult decision quickly, or to delegate an important job, you need a few eccentric cases—the "Special Category" children.

Almost by definition they have to be able to function without popular support, make hard choices, and rely on their own judgment. It's great when they're right, but when they're wrong (and if a society is basically functional, the eccentric individual will be wrong most of the time) they're what we call uncos. They may have friends, and a few of them might even be popular, but they're never secure in their friendship the way kids who grew up normally are. They question every decision, the group's and their own. They often try to do something differently just to be contrary.

But even though they're a public nuisance, you always have to overproduce them, because some of them are going to end up too weird, too bokky, too predatory—*uncos.* And besides you need to have alternatives for jobs like captain, chief agronomist, mayor, and so forth.

What happens to the extras, the ones you produce and don't need?

A few really do become uncos or some other kind of criminal. More of them become miserable people who do their jobs badly. Many end up work addicts, doing a good job but hating everyone.

There's a great demonstration of this available—Earth doesn't try to control the number of "Special Category" people, and if you look at the way they live down there, you can see they really overproduce them. Which explains practically all of Earth history if you ask me.

You create people like me and Randy and Tom (and probably people like you, if you're from Earth) by using some stuff they found in the 50s and 60s of the last century. Apparently the USA was going through some kind of national spasm about the disappearance of "individualism," whatever they meant by that, and they thought they needed more uncos or something. Anyway, they found out how to make uncos: Raise kids in small families so they get more attention, think of themselves as special, and don't learn to share. Force them to spend a lot of time alone when they're young. Manipulate their social lives so that their status with their peers changes a lot and they get used to "earning" the acceptance most people just get naturally. Give them to articulate parents with deviant values so that they grow up distrusting other people's ideas.

I don't really remember what we talked about after we read that. Or even if we talked. I think we were kind of stunned.

Finally we got up, washed our faces, and decided that since the academic work was done and we both felt like the whole world had p.d.'d us, maybe we'd just go to dinner and then do some rec. It might all look better in the morning. I called Mother to let her know we were going to dinner; she dropped a big wink at me, and suddenly I felt better without really knowing why.

At dinner, we were sort of practicing Japanese offhandedly, telling every silly joke we knew, and giggling a lot, when Randy suddenly switched to English and said, "I was snooping a little before you got there. Remember Dad was typing something after he took the pictures? It turns out he sent copies of them, and a letter, to my mother."

"Where is she?"

"Supra Berlin. She's married to some plutock that moved up permanently. I haven't seen her since I was five, when she came up to visit during Earthpass, and I don't really remember her. She used to dance in the zero-g clubs for tips." He took a swallow of milk. "Usually I only think about her around Christmas, when she transfers some money to buy me a new coverall and a new uniform, and Dad makes me write a thank-you note. He wishes I'd write more, I know, but she never writes back when I do.

"I think Dad really wanted her to come along and marry him, but she didn't want any kids. At least that was what she said at the time. I've got two half-brothers now; Dad says when the oldest gets to be about five I should start writing to them. I can never remember their names, though. . . .

"Anyway, I was being a typically nosy kid, checking in the recent activity file, and I found a transmit copy addressed to my mother, so I pulled it up to read. It was real short—I can recite it. 'Just wanted you to know he's growing fast and he's a good kid. I'm very proud of how he's turning out. Write for details.' " Randy shrugged. "Anyway, I thought it was neat. It was about as nice as anything he ever does, you know, the way he is—rude but well-meaning." He looked off to the side, at the wall.

"He upsets you a lot." I tried to say it as plainly and gently as I could, the way Papa talks to patients a lot of the time when he meets them socially. And I hated myself for being so shrinkspeak with Randy.

"Yeah, he upsets me," Randy said. "Things are a lot better since we both got into therapy. Just not as much better as I wish they were. But we talk now." He stretched. "Dad was so nice this weekend. You know? I mean I kind of saw him through your eyes. Maybe that made all the difference. He can be really charming when he wants to. The thing is, it made me think about the way it used to be when he'd just suddenly hit me—"

"He *hits* you?"

"Hey, quieter. I want to tell you about it for some reason, but I'm not going to tell the whole cafeteria. And he doesn't hit me anymore—that's part of what getting therapy was about. But yeah, he used to."

I was still so shocked I blurted out a really stupid, irrelevant question. "Where?"

"Uh, usually a slap across the face."

I tried to imagine it. I'd been hit a few times by other kids. When I was ten, Gwenny Mori and I had traded black eyes. But the idea of an adult, a big strong man like Mr. Schwartz . . .

Randy took my hand. "Look," he said, "it's not so bad anymore. I know it sounds pretty terrible, but it was just something that happened. Okay? Dad feels a lot worse than I do about it, I think. It's just, back when it was happening, right around the time we had to change shifts, I felt really bad because there was no one I could tell. I wanted someone to tell it to, you know, a real friend. So now . . . anyway, it isn't going to happen again. He's a lot better since we started therapy and I feel safe around him again. Okay?"

I nodded and squeezed his hand hard. "I just don't want anything bad to happen to you, ever. Even stuff that's already happened."

"I feel the same way about you." He sighed. "But I don't think we're going to have much control over it. Well, want to go play for a while?"

"Sure." We held hands walking out of the cafeteria. I felt like I was more alive than I had ever been, and the whole way to the Free Rec Lobby, it seemed like every time I grasped a line my whole body sang like a guitar string.

We played a couple of good games, and we kissed goodnight again. We were really getting good at it. I knew Miriam would have teased me—she'd been doing sneakies since she was ten, and she claimed she'd actually completed the docking maneuver with three guys—but it was wonderful to me and I wasn't in any hurry. It's not how far you go but how much fun you have on the way.

HEY! IT'S STILL EARLY! I WROTE A WHOLE DAY UP IN JUST A FEW hours. I'm going to pop out into the sharespace and talk with Susan a little, and then get to bed so I can go to school tomorrow.

Maybe I'll have another talk with Dr. Lovell. Or maybe I'll just sit in the back of the room and make obnoxious noises. Since it's not supposed to make any difference, maybe I'll just try to find a way to enjoy it.

More tomorrow, pos-def, okay?

CHAPTER TEN

THE NEXT WEEK WAS A LANGUAGES WEEK, AND MONDAY WAS mostly conversation practice. That's kind of a holiday if you're any good, because it's just talking. When your birth family language comes up, you join a group to work on your optional language, which is the most fun since you don't get graded on that at all. My optional is Swahili, and I'm really good at it; it's a lot easier than Japanese and more interesting than Esperanto and Spanish. Theophilus, I was relieved to see, was over in the French group, away from me and from Randy (who does Russian).

I'm really lousy at translating, but I'll try. There were only four of us in Swahili that day, and M'tsu and Lisa got into this lim boring argument about the airgym, so Miriam and I were left facing each other. You have to talk—that's about the only requirement there is—so we were stuck.

At first we started to just talk about class work and tell old jokes, but suddenly Miriam said, "I don't know what's happened."

"You were telling me about—"

"I mean what's happened—you know, with being friends." She looked down at the desk. "I can't believe some of the things I've said to you. Or what I keep doing."

I said it was all right. We both knew I was lying. I wanted to ask her how Theophilus fit into all this, but I couldn't think of a way to ask without starting a fight, and after all we had forty-five minutes left in the practice. "Sometimes things change," I said, hoping it would get us to a safer topic.

She looked like tears were coming up in her eyes. "Did you ever just want people to notice you? I mean lots of people? The way they used to notice Randy, or the way they notice Ted now?"

I nodded. "We probably all do."

She shook her head. "I really want it a lot. I always have." She looked down at the desk. "I'm sorry about everything," she said again. "I really am, Mel."

There wasn't much to say to that, so I said it was all right again and changed the subject. After a while we were talking about all the usual trivia, and it was almost like it had been.

That afternoon was Individuals Japanese composition, which is always a battle for everyone, even our three Japanese kids.

That kept us busy most of the day, except during rec, which was in the airgym—board hockey this time.

Theophilus was their goalie, and I drove one in past him, to my deep satisfaction. Randy and Theophilus were nominally teammates, but they were avoiding each other.

I had almost forgotten that Randy had an appointment with Papa. We didn't say much on the way there; I think he was nervous.

Papa was waiting for Randy, and they went straight into the office. I tried to get some work done in my room before dinner. Every so often I heard Randy's voice, which meant he was getting pretty loud since Papa's office is soundproofed.

A half hour had gone by while I sat there, idly daydreaming about Randy and not getting any work done. I couldn't afford that—I had a fourdeep report to get written and multitranslated by Friday. With a sigh, I replugged the search program and started calling up papers from the library again, slotting them into the bottommost level and putting their keywords up as markers in the third. It's pretty brainless work but it certainly takes plenty of time and attention, and that was what I needed.

Miriam had been about to tell me something, a couple of times, in that conversation. I was sure of it. Probably it was something important, but what?

Maybe she just wanted to be friends again. I forced my attention back to the paper I was working on.

I had most of the plan for the paper laid out and most of the notes in place and was beginning to get a little bit of work done on the second level when Randy came out. His eyes were red-rimmed and there were tearstains on his cheeks, but he seemed all right now, maybe even a little calmer than usual.

"Well," Mother said. "Since we are all here, let's go to dinner." She sounded formal somehow. "Randy, we usually eat at our local cafeteria and the whole family eats together. We use the local cafeteria because it's not quite so crowded, and we can have a whole table for just our family." There was something about the way she was talking that I didn't like, but I couldn't quite identify what. I took along my werpsack, instead of just my phone, so Randy and I could compare homework over dinner. Tom brought his werp too; Mother always talked about the family being all together, but a lot of times we were all just using werps and readers while sitting at the same table.

The corridors were almost deserted and we had the netting to ourselves; most people went to dinner right at the end of their shift's Work Period II, and this was more than an hour after that for A Shift. At the cafeteria we took a table for five.

That night it was a rare treat—chicken!—so nobody said much as we ate, except the usual comments about wishing ag would get better at all this.

When we finished, Mother said, "Randy, how many brothers and sisters do you have?"

"I'm it," he said. "I'm an only child."

"Oh. Your parents must have——"

"No." He shook his head. "It's just me and Dad."

Mother smiled. "And what does your father do?"

"He's on Outside crew. Vacuum extrusion. And he's been vice-president and secretary of the VWU local off and on."

It sounded like Mother was leading into p.d.'ing Randy's standing, but that's a game only kids play—never adults or at least never in front of us.

Papa broke in with a long funny story—at least I think it was supposed to be funny, though none of us laughed—and then he and Mother were off into one of those quiet fights that never looks like a fight unless you know them as well as I do. That meant they'd be ignoring the rest of the world for a couple of hours.

"Say," I said, "Tom, do you know what was interesting about those problems of yours?"

"No, what?"

"I looked them over and they all turned out to be incomputable."

Tom snorted. "And people wonder why I have problems with CSL. How can the problems be incomputable when I computed them?"

I shook my head. "No, that's just the point. You didn't. You just knew the answers—there was no rational, computable way for you to get the answer. You just got it."

Tom shrugged. "You mean like the proofs of incomputability in the book. I never have been able to do one of those. In fact I don't see how a problem that has an answer can even be incomputable."

I looked at Randy for support; he was looking up, apparently at the Roswalds dining overhead but probably at something in the back of his head. "Let's go through this slowly," Randy said. "You got a whole assignment of incomputable problems? Not just determine solvability, but they actually asked you to solve them—no labels or warnings? Nothing to tell you there was anything unusual?"

"No sign at all," Tom said. "Looked like any other assignment to me."

"And you solved them. Hmm. Do you have a copy, Melpomene?"

I did. Randy scanned my proofs. At last he said, "Well, those certainly are incomputable problems."

"I still don't see how you can know that," Tom said, "especially not when the answers are obvious."

That got us both into trying to explain the idea to him. By that time, Mother and Papa had wound down the fight. As many times as I've seen it, I still don't quite understand how when they're out in public they can have these fascinating arguments where they both keep smiling and talk so softly.

We all went back to the living unit together. I think Mother was a little surprised (and maybe not pleased) that Randy stayed with Tom and me, but since all of us went back to Tom's room there wasn't much for her to say about it.

For an hour, Randy set up various incomputable problems in math, and I set them up in CSL, and Tom got answers to them in five minutes or so, just sitting there and thinking at them. It was the weirdest thing we'd ever seen—weirder still because he couldn't understand how we wrote the problems. "They just seem like puzzles with only one piece missing," he said. "Of course you know what shape it is and what picture's on it—what else could it be? But how you guys come up with these—all those steps you write—that I can't follow at all."

So we started to show him, and on the way I learned a lot of math from Randy, not so much the procedures themselves, which I knew fairly well, but just how he looked at a problem. Randy claims I did some of the same thing for his CSL, which is not only nice of him but probably true.

For some reason, Tom responded a lot better to Randy and me than he did to me by myself; we really got somewhere with him. "Hmmm," he said, after working several problems successfully for the first time in his life, "I think I'm beginning to get the hang of this. You guys ought to think about being teachers or professors or something . . . you make a great team."

I don't know why Randy blushed; I don't even know why I felt so embarrassed. But Tom didn't manage to notice either of us. He was wading into yet another problem. "I can probably do a dozen more of these before bedtime. If you guys want to get on with your own work—"

Randy looked as sheepish as I felt. "I didn't start my presentation for Esperanto tomorrow yet."

"Me either," I confessed.

Tom looked at the clock in the corner of his screen; it showed barely an hour till Lights Down. "I'm sorry! I really kept you guys!" Now *he* was embarrassed. "What do you have to get done?"

"We each have to give a five minute talk in Esperanto tomorrow," I said. "It has to be arguing for or against stepping up the cargo bay building schedule. We have datasets on it, so it wouldn't be so bad, but we have to hand Dr. Niwara a copy of the speech before we give it."

"You don't have to have it memorized, do you?" he asked.

"No, we can read from a prompter screen, but neither of us writes Esperanto very well," Randy explained.

"Well, I'm top in my class at Esperanto comp," Tom said. "You're allowed to use a rough translator, right?"

"Sure."

"Okay, hack out something in English, rough translate it, and I'll help you polish for style. It's the least I can do."

So that's what we did. In English I'm just fine—remember they decided I should write this silly book—and Randy's okay, so we got done quickly; then we ran them through the rough translator and they came out in Esperanto. That doesn't work well with any other source-to-target language combination, but English has a very linear structure, and Esperanto is perfectly regular, so it was very close to right. Tom made a few corrections and adjusted them for style and we were done.

Central flashed Lights Down warning to Randy just after we got our final drafts into our pocket werps. "I'll have to go," he said, with a little regret in his voice. "See you tomorrow in class, Melpomene. Nice to see you again, Tom."

Tom smiled. "This was a big help, for me anyway. I'm glad we'll be seeing you at least once a week—and I wouldn't mind if Melpomene brought you home more often."

I wasn't sure whether I wanted to hug my brother or kick him; Randy flushed again. We all kind of shrugged and said good-night, and he went home.

I was going over my presentation when I heard my parents arguing; I know that even Papa doesn't like it when I listen in on them, but after all he listens in on people professionally, and besides it says right on the sign in the classroom that "the concern of one is the concern of all." I don't see why that shouldn't be true in your family, if it's true for the ship.

Papa had that ultra-reasonable voice he puts on when he's afraid Mother is going to start shouting. "Helen, you always knew this was possible when you signed up. Remember, you were the one that quoted to me the fable about the fox and the lion. Well, this is the kind of experience that's going to produce lions. I know they're not as attractive as other kids—"

"Not as attractive! That Schwartz kid is a bully, and his father beats him. Sounds like he deserves it, too! Wendy Harrison told me all about Randy Schwartz. I had to talk with her on the com for an hour today." I heard her breath rasping in her throat. "What kind of pair-up is that for Melpomene?"

Papa sighed. "Keep your voice down—these kids have nothing like our idea of privacy."

"That's another thing! Melpomene—"

"Is a moderately well-adjusted kid for the environment. With a big need to be liked, too much empathy to ever be very happy, and a certain amount of quiet charisma. That's the kind of personality our mayor is supposed to have when the ship's fully operational. And being on warm terms—"

"Warm terms!" There were two thuds about a breath apart; when Mother is really upset, she stamps her foot, forgetting that the floor is hard and her slippers are thin, and that in low grav that slams her right up against the ceiling. I imagined she had hurt herself, and was trying to rub her foot and head at the same time, waving off Papa as he hovered over her. I almost didn't hear the

next thing she said. "Why don't you just admit it? You've made your daughter neurotic on purpose, and now you're going to pander her off to a psychotic kid."

Papa's voice was getting lower, which usually means he's about to be angry. "Helen, we're not just talking about the plan here. No one is going to hold a gun to Melpomene's head and make her marry anyone, any more than we're going to run her for mayor without her consent. And we aren't going to brainwash her, either. She is just what either of us is—a product of her experiences. The only difference—the *only* difference—is that more of hers have been planned for a particular effect. If you went into her room right now and asked her what she'd really like to do in 2038 or 2040, she might very well say run for Council—to get ready to run for mayor in the 2050s. And if she hasn't thought of it yet, she will. We may have planned her decisions—but she's still making them. I doubt she'd be upset if I walked in and told her what we'd done."

That showed how little he knew me. I was furious! If he had even halfway explained things, Randy and I might never have gone to the difficulty and risk of snooping. One thing was for sure—when I was mayor, there wasn't going to be any of this stupid privacy business anymore. No more private files. If I could get people to go along with it, we'd take all the doors off living units and rooms.

I almost missed the next thing Papa said.

"And as for Randy—he's a good kid. The best, really. We've hyperstressed him to the limit the last year or so, and the worst he's developed is a little extra aggression. When we shift things over to give him more acceptance, his personality should just about match the ideal profile for ship's officer. If you've got to play matchmaker, think about him as a future captain."

"Ha. Extra aggression? Wendy said that he—"

"Yes, he does get into fights with her son. Small wonder. Just at the moment, little Ted Harrison is, in my opinion as a mental health professional, an asshole."

Mother snorted. "You really don't pay any attention to anything, as much as you like to lecture me. I can't believe you've looked at the Harrison family profile——"

"Yes, I have, and it *explains* why that kid is an asshole. But he'll get socialized eventually. What's happening now is just that our kids are scraping the stink of Earth off of him, teaching him what they've learned from birth——the hard way, because he needs to learn fast."

The idea that we were affecting Theophilus more than he was affecting us lim weirdwired me. I couldn't see anything like that. I was half tempted to barge out there and tell Papa how wrong he was, but I had a feeling they'd both get all upset.

Pos-def it would have been the wrong time. Mother was crying and yelling at him, that yammering whining that she goes into when she's lost an argument, and Papa was just trying to get a word in edgewise. When she gets like that, I can barely understand her even if I'm in the same room, but Papa usually seems to be able to.

When she'd gotten down to just sobbing, he finally said, "Helen, what do you want me to do? Or all of us to do? Earth is gone, the Earth we knew anyway. Nothing will ever look like it did before the Die-Off and the Eurowar. And these kids don't have any obligation to make it look like that, just because their parents miss it."

She mumbled something, sniffling, and I barely caught any of it, just fragments about "freedom" and "human spirit" and a lot of other words.

"That's a question to leave to them. Maybe you're right and people can't live like this for very long. But the best evidence—— with so many people dead, and so much lost——is that they can't live the old way at all. Individualism is dead because it didn't work."

I heard her leap into their room. The door slammed. I knew Papa was in the sharespace by himself. I should have gone out to him, but I could think of nothing to say.

John Barnes

January 5, 2026

I SHOWED ALL THAT STUFF TO DR. LOVELL. "YOU REALLY THINK we should just let this come out this way? I mean, for a whole planet of uncos to get upset by?" (Sorry, if you're from Earth. But all the stuff I've read says practically all of you are.)

She shrugged. "Other people can decide that, Melpomene. How do *you* feel?"

"About writing it? It kind of brought a lot back. At first, I thought I'd explode with happiness. My god—mayor, if I just stayed on course. And maybe the captaincy for Randy."

She nodded a couple of times. "Why didn't you?"

"Oh, a lot of things. I got weirdwired, maybe, lim angry because of everything that had happened. And on top of that I just didn't think much of the plan anymore. Maybe I didn't want to get it like that."

"You wrote at the beginning you were going to be mayor." She sat directly in front of me, looking me in the eye. "What was that about?"

"I *am* going to be mayor. Just not the way they had scripted. I like the story but I think us kids will write it better for ourselves."

She nodded, reached forward, and squeezed my hands. "Here's what I'm wondering about, Melpomene. Is it possible that after what happened the next day—which was sort of when you and Randy got a taste of the leader's job—you decided you just don't want to do it, and this is just a way to lose it gracefully? Are you kidding yourself now?"

That was the first time I remembered that Dr. Lovell didn't seem phony to me. So I really had to think about what she had said, and that's what I've been doing all this evening, instead of writing. Susan and Tom are already in bed, and it's close to Lights Down, and I still don't have an answer.

So tomorrow I'll tell you about the next thing that happened, and how I felt, and maybe that will help me figure out what I really want to do.

CHAPTER ELEVEN

January 6, 2026

I STILL DON'T HAVE ANY IDEA. DR. LOVELL'S QUESTION REALLY did something strange in my brain. So here's what happened. Maybe you can decide.

THE NEXT DAY IN CLASS WE DID OUR REPORTS—BOTH RANDY'S and mine went okay. Then Dr. Niwara weirdwired us all by announcing that there would be a speed math contest to find out who team captains would be for aerocrosse. Every so often they do that—make you do math in the middle of a verbal week. I guess it's supposed to keep us on our guard or something.

It was going to be seven teams of four again. Since team captains had been chosen in a math contest, I wasn't really expecting any surprises. Sure enough, Theophilus was made captain for Team One, and Randy for Team Two—he stiffened suddenly when Barry Yang whispered, "Team color should be Royal Blue." I mentally marked Barry for a good, hard body check.

Gwenny Mori was captain for Team Three, Kwame for Team Four, and Padraic for Team Five. You could really tell who had been hanging around with who lately—little as I liked Theophilus I had to admit he was a math wizard, and obviously a good coach as well.

"Team Six," Dr. Niwara said. "Miriam Baum." Another friend of Theophilus. He really could teach.

"Team Seven, Melpomene Murray."

Miriam getting it was pretty good; *me* getting it was beyond belief. But there it was—I would have Team Seven, the team that started without a goal. Some of Randy must have copied over to me.

Then we did Pairs Esperanto composition, and finally went to lunch. I was a little late getting into line, so I was one of the last ones out, behind Chris Kim, who tended to trail behind anyway. I had been sort of talking with him—I had already decided to make him my first choice for my team, because he was a much better player than most people realized—so I dragged him along when I went to join Randy at a table in the corner of the lunchroom.

That put the three of us sort of off by ourselves. Theophilus and the Real Gang were occupying the center table. Most other people were packed around that, some in close to pretend to be part of it, others farther away but close enough so that they could still hear. One thing you could say for Theophilus, since he had gotten here we'd all had a lot more to talk about.

We sat down and talked about homework and assignments, in Esperanto because it was a good way to lube Dr. Niwara, who always wandered around the lunchroom listening in.

Chris had always been a little afraid of Randy, I think, but now he was more afraid of Theophilus; after all, he wasn't going to get a math score Randy would beat him up for, but anybody could be the target of those nasty jokes.

After a while, the two of them warmed up to each other. It

turned out they both were going to play airball for the VWU Youth Auxiliary team, and they both agreed that their coach, Bob Mori, was still thinking too much in terms of two baskets and playing on a plane.

I was excited from coming in so high in math and getting picked for captain, and—how I knew this, I'm not sure, but I was sure of it—Chris and Randy were both excited about becoming friends. We were all talking and laughing really loud and getting kind of silly.

I happened to look over toward Theophilus's table and saw Miriam look at me for a second; she looked really upset. What I'd been thinking of as the "inner circle," Theophilus plus Kwame, Gwenny, and Miriam, were all whispering to each other and ignoring everyone else. I didn't think much of that at the time—it was common enough, after all.

After lunch we had to go back and do dialogging—lim boring!

—HOW ARE YOU FEELING, TODAY, MELPOMENE?

—JUST FINE, THANK YOU.

—IS ANYTHING SPECIAL ON YOUR MIND?

—I'M VERY EXCITED ABOUT THE AEROCROSSE GAME TODAY.

—WHAT ABOUT THE AEROCROSSE GAME IS SO EXCITING?

—I'M A TEAM CAPTAIN.

—GERMANE? (I hate that! The stupid AI didn't see what being captain had to do with being excited.)

—TEAM CAPTAIN IS A POSITION IN AEROCROSSE. I AM VERY EXCITED TO HOLD THAT POSITION.

—APPROVED. (Gee, thanks.) WHY DO YOU LIKE BEING TEAM CAPTAIN?

After an hour of that, we all jumped up pretty fast when Dr. Niwara announced time for aerocrosse.

Since Team Seven got to pick last in each round, the only real luck I had was I got Chris. I picked Penelope Graham because I thought she would be okay, not special but a good team player, and Dmitri Onegin because he was the only one left. He tried hard but he was just kind of clumsy

Randy, with Team Two, got Barry Yang, certainly one of the best players in the class, even if he'd sort of betrayed Randy's friendship in the last few days. His second pick was Rachel DeLane, who can throw straight as a laser all the way from bottom to top of the Big Commons. He also got Rebecca Hayakawa, which was odd because she usually got picked much earlier for her strength and brains.

Things got weird within two minutes of the start. Normally the high-numbered team faces a hard defense, but there was something beyond that, as if everyone was waiting for something that I didn't know about.

The headset crackled in my ear. Captains get both a common channel to their team and a channel to all the other captains; that way we can cut deals. We listen to both channels all the time but we can pick which one we want to talk on.

It was Miriam. "Hey, Melpomene. If Seven wants to gang on Two, Six is holding two balls." We were holding the other one at the moment and just trying to pick a target—one ball is pretty easy to defend against.

"You got it, Mim."

We bracketed Two's goal pretty well, closing in tight on it right out in the center.

The captain had posted the grav at .0006, and nothing was moving much—you could really swim. Even from a standing start treading air, it was no work at all to kick your way upward.

Miriam detailed M'tsu to guard Team Six's goal, and he took it down below where he could also help retrieve stray balls—a moderately risky move that could turn sour if the alliance broke or someone else got a ball. With that done, Teams Six and Seven were all around Two's goal, taking shots in when we could and passing the balls among seven of us. Everyone else had scattered themselves around the top of the Commons, far away from us in case we decided to do anything tricky.

It was really fine play—Randy's team was hard pressed to do anything but keep getting in the way of the balls, and I knew they'd have some bruises to show later. I was busy being captain, and the game is what counts, but I still had to admire the way Randy kept Team Two in position—I don't think I could have held goal, even with a team that good, for half that long.

Chris justified my faith in him beautifully; he kipped over suddenly, intercepted a pass from me to Dmitri, and snapped a shot in past Barry Yang. The bright "7" replaced the "2" on the goal, and Randy's team dove away from it, doing reversals on the platforms and shooting up to where the big concentration of targets was, hoping to get lucky soon since all the balls were temporarily in the crosses of Miriam's Six and my Seven.

I caught the carom shot, noted that Penelope had grabbed another ball, and clicked captain's freke off so Miriam wouldn't hear what came next.

"Dmitri and Chris, take the goal up to the top and guard it, right now. Penny, we're going to doublecross Six. Get on a catcher platform like you're going to do a long jump up, but dive on Team Six's goal when I signal. I'll take the other side—let's see if we can take it and pull off a cross-catch."

Miriam's voice crackled in my ear. "Okay, Mel, let's take your goal up to the top. We're bringing ours up too."

She really should have known better than that. We were the first team to score, which meant we had a temporary lead—we had one, Randy's Two had minus one, and everyone else including Miriam's Six had zero. You always try to widen a lead.

Well, if she was going to be that dumb, we might as well use it. "You got it," I said. I clicked my mike over so I was talking privately with my team again; Chris and Dmitri moved our goal up, safely out of range.

I let myself drift down and over to one of the platforms, as if I were going to one-jump it as well. Penelope was already in place and nearly invisible, flattening herself back against the wall.

I flipped to captain's freke again. "Hey, Mim, why don't you just pass that goal straight up?"

A second later, and M'tsu threw the goal up toward Miriam.

It drifted up slowly toward her, and she treaded air more slowly, sinking to meet it. I flipped my mike back to team freke.

"Penny, ready?"

"Ready!"

"One, two, *go!*"

We both kicked off and headed straight for the goal, its big green "6" glowing at us. Miriam caught on fast, but she was centered and had no way to work up speed but swimming as hard as she could. We had kicked from the wall, and in one deep breath we were on top of the unguarded goal as it drifted lazily upward.

"Don't throw, Penny, we'll just tag it." She acknowledged and locked the ball into her cross just before she spread-eagled and caught the goal, drifting with it toward me. I spread-eagled too and met her, the goal squishing between us for an instant before my slightly greater momentum carried it.

It was now hopeless for Miriam—we had a big lateral motion, plus an upward one we were adding to with our kicking, and we had the goal about two-thirds wrapped between us. She couldn't possibly get enough speed from swimming to catch us, and because we hadn't tagged her goal yet, hitting it with the ball she was holding wouldn't change the situation.

So she snapped her ball as hard as she could into the back of my helmet, and I found out first hand what I had done to Randy a few days before—my ears rang, my neck ached, and my teeth tingled where they had slammed together. I didn't see where the ball caromed off to.

Penelope popped the ball out of her cross and touched the goal, making it ours officially, then retrapped her ball. "You okay, Mel?"

"Yeah. A bit shook up."

"Cheap shot. She aimed right at your head. She wasn't even trying for the goal. She couldn't have been."

"It's legal," I said.

"Still . . ." she let it hang as we reached the platform. "Which way?"

"Straight up—wrap it and bounce on three." I counted off and we shot up toward the top.

"Melpomene, that was the last straw." It was Miriam's voice; she was mad, but after all, doublecrosses are a big part of the game. "I tried to get you in with everyone, and you stuck me in the back. You could have been on the same side with everyone else against Two and all you could think about was getting a cheap point."

I was starting to get irritated. "It was pretty expensive for you," I pointed out.

"Not as expensive as it's going to be for you," Theophilus chimed in.

I didn't see what Theophilus had to do with it, and his having spoken made me even angrier. Penelope and I were kicking hard, gaining speed as we approached the top, and the big yellow "1" of Theophilus's goal was directly overhead. I killed my mike entirely. "Penny, do you think we could get lucky and rivet One's goal before they caught on?"

"It's just a game of aerocrosse, Mel. Why not?"

I nodded and said, "Wait till we close in, then we'll give them both balls and see how they hop."

At that moment, all but one of Team One dove straight down at us. There was no sign that they were trying to kidnap the goal, grab it physically and try to get a ball to claim it with later. To do that you push off the top and then spread-eagle. They were flutter kicking straight down at us, getting speed for a really hard body check.

I let them get closer. "Now!" We both threw as hard as we could; I'm not sure which ball got past, but the yellow One rolled over to our Seven.

Three goals—if we could keep them.

We waited another breath, then braced our feet against the goal, and when I said "Now" we pushed off, downward and outward. Team One shot past without managing to check either of us, and the goal wobbled on up to the top, where Dmitri grabbed it.

I saw all that as I shot across the space, head first, toward the

193

wall. I flipped over and treaded air against the motion, slowing down before I hit between two platforms. I slapped feet on the wall, caught myself with my hands on the underside of the upper platform, shoved myself down, and pushed off hard back upward toward the goal we'd just zapped from One.

Penelope, I saw, was headed the same way, and Chris and Dmitri were bumping the other two goals along to join us. It wouldn't be easy to hang onto all those goals, even up at the top.

I knew our two balls had caromed wildly and were shooting around down below, as members of several teams tried to get one. But where had the third ball gone after bouncing off my helmet?

There wasn't time to give it much thought. Penelope and I, with Chris and Dmitri, got our three goals penned up against the ceiling as tight as possible, as you have to do when you're guarding short-handed. None of us would get a chance to catch a strap and rest.

The teams who still had goals, Three, Four, and Five, scattered wildly away from us, swimming hard to push their goals against air resistance. When they caught the balls down below, we would be the focus of attack.

That was when the third ball showed up. Randy's Team Two dove out of nowhere on Kwame's Team Four. Randy and Barry plowed into them in hard body checks, sending Kwame and two of his teammates spinning down toward the bottom, and Bekka sailed in and tore the goal from Sylvestrina's arms. Then Rachel DeLane nailed it with the ball, and Randy grabbed the ball on the carom as he returned from a catcher platform—a beautiful play.

But it could have been a lot more beautiful. Randy whipped a pass to Barry, who took a shot at the exposed upper side of Three's goal—but it whizzed past the goal, past Gwenny, and into the cross of Theophilus.

I didn't quite understand what I saw. Very plainly, to me anyway, Theophilus and Barry nodded to each other. It just didn't look right—they weren't on the same team, and Barry wasn't a captain. Communication goes only through the captains, normally, though when teams are allied sometimes you'll talk to someone within earshot.

I didn't have much time to think because suddenly Theophilus's team had all three balls and was swimming up at us fast. They couldn't get as much momentum as you can get in a dive, of course, but they were building up speed pretty well and besides we had a lot to do with keeping three goals penned in the small space.

"Hey, Seven—alliance?" Randy's voice crackled in my earphones.

"Pos-def. Pull on in," I said, and clicked on private freke. "Okay guys, Team Two has joined us." Rebecca and Rachel pushed the goal into our cluster and we turned to face Team One, which was still rising.

Theophilus still didn't know the game at all well; he threw much too early, probably not listening to his teammates. The ball was slowing down, and I was closing in on it. "Yours," Randy said, next to me. I reached for it—

Something hit me in the back. Randy and I both lost our positions and tumbled as Barry Yang shouted "Got it" and grabbed for it, knocking us away.

He tried to catch it with his hand—real dumb because it doesn't change the marker on the ball—and it glanced off and took one of my team's goals.

I righted myself—Randy was still next to me, but we had tumbled about four meters. I heard an "oof" as Theophilus crashed into Rachel, knocking her up against the top and scattering the goals despite our best efforts. In a moment, Team One had gotten all of them.

Something finally connected. I flutter kicked over to Randy and leaned into his ear, turning off both frekes. "Randy, I saw Theophilus give Barry a signal. Barry bokked on purpose."

Randy stared at me. "I saw it," I said. "It's true."

Randy clicked on his team freke. "Barry, get to me right now," he said into the mike. "Melpomene, if you could . . ."

I nodded and started to take off, but Barry swam up and grabbed my arm. "What did she tell you?"

I flipped over, twisting out of his grip, and turned to face him. "I saw you get that nod from Theophilus when you passed the ball to him. And you tipped their ball into your own team's goal on purpose."

Barry started to say something, but Randy said, "I believe Melpomene, so don't bother. But what really gets me—"

"Are you going to hit me?"

"I don't hit people any more."

"Ha." Barry was starting to snivel; his eyes were wet.

"I haven't hit you yet and I'm not going to. Now listen. What I really can't stand is that I picked you for the team because—" Randy gulped and I saw his eyes were starting to run too— "Because you—I wanted to be friends again. We used to be friends. . . ."

Barry started to cry. I felt really awful for him and looked away. My head still hurt from Miriam's ball, and I thought I was bringing up a couple of bruises from where Barry had hit me from behind. We were flat at zero along with most other teams, Randy's team trailed, with minus one, and Team One now had four goals.

But the other teams weren't attacking. Team One was holding all the balls, and it took me a while to realize they were "sitting on their lead"—I've seen teams do that in the Earth sports flash-channel, but never here.

It was really a groundhog thing to do, acting like the final score mattered more than the game, p.d.'ing the other side's numbers without having to really compete with them team to team.

I knew, without being quite sure how, that if Theophilus won the game the way he had planned to, there would be a lot more quarrels, a lot more bad feeling, a lot more getting left out.

I turned on the emergency open channel on the helmet. Usually a captain's supposed to use that only for an injury or something like that, but this didn't seem like a good time to worry about the rules. "Barry Yang has just admitted that he was helping Team One against his own team. We don't know if he was the only one doing that. You'd better make sure that all your teammates are playing on the same side you are—and watch your captains especially. We all know who they're friends with."

There was a long, long silence. Then Theophilus's voice came in on the emergency freke. "You know she's never liked me ever since she found out I liked her friend Miriam better. She's even friends with the class bully now because she hates me so much. She's just complaining because she isn't popular . . .*she just doesn't belong.* She's just not one of the crowd, and she's mad about that."

My eyes stung with tears—

And Barry Yang came off a catcher platform in a hard swimming dive that slammed Theophilus spinning, clawing crazily at the air to get back his balance before he hit the wall. His head hit the edge of a platform with a nasty, sharp thump, and he tumbled back out into the middle.

And then suddenly everyone was hitting him, kicking at him, diving in from all sides to shove him and throw him against the wall. Even the ones who had been in his crowd, Kwame, Gwenny, all of them except Miriam, were on him, slapping him and punching him, keeping him spinning and dizzy and unable to defend himself or even get to the wall. Blood squirted from his nose in a corkscrewing trail, and I could hear him sobbing hysterically.

The ones who were hitting him were laughing, an ugly aggressive fuck-you-in-your-face sound I'd never heard before.

I had never seen anything like that before in my life. I hope I won't see it again. I clicked both captain's and private freke on. "Randy, we've got to get him out of there. I'm going to try to dive in and get his belt. Chris and Dmitri, come along too. We have to get him to the Blue Spot." Half of me was still in the game—the Blue Spot was where injured players went until time out could be called and they could get out. I don't know why, given what was happening, I expected anyone to respect it.

We did get him out. It wasn't easy because he was scared and he was hurt pretty badly—bleeding from some cuts and bruised all over. No one hit his kidneys or his neck hard enough to do any permanent damage, but he was a mess.

197

When Chris, Dmitri, and I caught hold of him, the other kids started cheering. I didn't know what it was about so I ignored it; as soon as we had him halfway stable we started moving him. He was struggling and fighting with us—probably so scared and disoriented he thought we were going to beat him up too.

When they saw what we were doing, people all talked at once, their voices very tight and high, echoing around the space. Then they all swam toward us, some of them very fast. Every one of them had the same strange expression, as if they were all running a copy of the same program.

Randy dove between us and the crowd, Rachel, Penelope, and Bekka following him. They hit the rebound boards and rose to meet the crowd head-on. Randy's voice came over the emergency open freke. "No, no, no more. Leave him alone."

I wasn't sure what he said after that, but it was pretty soothing; he sounded like he was really in charge of everything. He kept talking and we got Theophilus down into the Blue Spot; once he had a firm surface he was less panicked and we could hold him and try to calm him down.

Meanwhile Randy had gotten the others to go to the locker room and change out, sending Bekka and Penelope along to make sure they did. He came back with Rachel to see how Theophilus was—which surprised Theophilus a lot, I could tell, but he didn't say anything. We called a med capsule, put Theophilus in it, and sent him to the infirmary.

Another reason I'll always love Randy—he saw me home. I really needed someone with me, because I was having a lot of trouble remembering what I should be doing. I didn't even change out of my gym clothes, which is really rude when you're going to be out in public. He put his arm around me and hugged me at the door, then went home himself.

Mother was waiting for me. "What happened?" she demanded.

"I don't know. I don't know where Dr. Niwara was or why she didn't do anything," I said, starting to cry, "and I don't know how it happened at all. I just—"

"You beat that boy so badly he had to go into the hospital!"

She shouted it into my face; I was so surprised that I didn't even try to explain. "I keep hearing about what healthy little fuckers you are. Just different. Just a little more socialized. You ganged up on that little boy and you would have killed him if you could. And you're supposed to be—you're the ones who are going to—" She was gasping for breath.

She grabbed my shoulders and shook me so hard my neck hurt. "I should have done this a long time ago!"

And then—well, I'll write it, but I hope you don't believe it even though it's true: she turned me around, grabbed my gym shorts, and pulled them down. I screamed. The neighbors heard it even through the soundproofing.

And then she forced my head down over the house terminal and slapped my bare buttocks again and again, harder and harder. She was yelling at me, calling me names, and sobbing while she did it. I felt naked, more naked than I'd known I could feel, and powerless, and completely humiliated. I wanted to vomit, faint, die, anything but this.

And then all of a sudden Papa was there, and I got away and pulled my pants back up and tucked up in a little ball to cover myself, and then med capsules came, two of them, one for Mother and one for me.

THEY RELEASED ME THAT EVENING; SHE HADN'T HIT ME VERY hard, and there wasn't even a bruise, but they gave me a bottle of happy pills to take for the next couple of days. They were mad at Papa—I could tell, though of course they tried to hide it in front of the "boss's daughter." I figured out after a while that they didn't think he should be doing my counseling; it was against all the theories and so forth. The nurse seemed to be angriest of all; I heard him outside the door. "What kind of responsibility is that? He's been shielding his wife for years and now even after his little girl gets beaten up—" They shushed him and tried to move him farther down the hall. "I don't care what the Plan calls for," I heard him say, and then there was some more low, urgent talking to him, and I heard him again. "I don't give a fuck about the fucking Plan, it's not right." There was more talking, and then silence; they left me alone till Papa came and got me. I was drifting in and out on the happy pills, thinking about being mayor and about Randy being captain, wondering if we should visit Theophilus or something, as long as we were here . . . but of course it was just me here; Randy would be coming to visit me, though, and maybe then we could go down the hall—

I was asleep when Papa finally showed up. He woke me up and handed me my clothes; I got dressed without saying much, and we went home. Mother wasn't there. "She'll be along in about three or four days," Papa said. "She'll need a lot of patience and understanding; she's feeling very guilty right now, and they've got her under light hypnotherapy to boost her acceptance."

I nodded; the year before, when I had gotten caught masturbating in the restroom and the other girls had made fun of me for weeks, I had gone through that. They just give you a light dose of drugs to calm you down, stick you in a sensory deprivation tank, and play a recording of your own voice reading the things they told you to—mine were "I'm perfectly normal," "I enjoy touching myself and I'm not ashamed of it," and "They don't mean to hurt me. If I politely tell them they're hurting me, they will stop teasing."

Of course I was wondering what they had Mother listening to. "I enjoy hitting people and I'm not ashamed?" So I almost missed what Papa was saying, and had to ask him to repeat it.

"I'm sorry, Melpomene," he said. "I didn't realize you—"

"I'm okay," I said. "Just daydreaming. Why did she do it?"

He sat back and looked at me. "Why do you think she did it?"

I hate shrink games. "Because she's crazy."

He nodded. "I can see that it might look that way to you."

"Like shit." I was only beginning to realize how angry I was. "That was the most humiliating thing that ever happened to me, and you want me to see her side of it? Well, forget it. As far as I'm concerned, she's crazy and a moron and if the guilt is bothering her, it should."

He sat quietly, then, for a long time. Finally he said, "I don't really know what answer I can give you, Melpomene. There's nothing much I can say that will make any sense to you."

He pushed up from his chair and kicked over to the view-screen, switching it on. The stars hung still in the darkness; I could see the red glow of Mars, not to be a disk for another couple of months, in the lower corner. He *never* does that. Shrinks don't avoid looking at you, not the good ones, anyway. . . . I didn't know what was wrong with Papa. I didn't know what was wrong, at all.

"Melpomene," he said finally, "I know you got into the CPB Plan files. On Earth, information like what's in the files—if it were published—would result in rioting. Revolution. Anarchy in the streets. What do you think would happen here?"

I shook my head. "I don't know."

"I don't either." He held out his arms, as if to hug me. "Try to understand your mother. She thinks like the people back home—back on Earth, I mean. She sees the world the way they do. That was part of why she was your ideal mother . . . she helped you get more individuated. Theophilus might well have been killed if you and Randy hadn't been there."

"I suppose it's possible."

He nodded. "So what are you going to do if you're mayor? Give good jobs to all your friends and have them get you re-elected?"

"Why?" I asked. "Are they going to be the best people for their jobs?"

He shook his head. "I mean, just give them to them. Because they're your friends."

"Why would they want them if they're not the right people?"

He smiled at me, but I could see tears glistening in his eyes. "Melly," he said softly, "I love you."

It was a strange thing to say, but at least I knew the right answer to it. "I love you too, Papa."

He nodded. "I—twenty years ago, when I was just out of school and NAC hired me, this was doomed to happen. But I never understood it up to now." He was smiling, still, and I hugged him again. "There's something you probably should hit me for," he said. "But I have to tell you about it."

"I don't think I'll hit you for it this time. Whatever it is."

"Dr. Niwara was ordered not to be in the Big Commons. We heard Theophilus and his friends on the mike at lunch time, planning it all out, and we needed to see how you kids would handle the situation with no adult guidance."

I sat back and stared at him. "You *knew* that was going to happen?"

"Not at all. We didn't have the slightest idea how offended most of your classmates would be." He held up his hand to stop me from interrupting; I hadn't actually had anything to say. "Melpomene, I just thought you should know that we fucked up very badly. And as more of you kids have been getting older, we've understood you less and less and fucked up more and more. So . . . well, we're debating something. And this is something I shouldn't even ask you, but you're my daughter, and I find I have to know this before I can begin to think reasonably about it.

"What if we said you *weren't* going to be the mayor?"

"Well, if it's better for the ship . . . I mean, I'd be disappointed but if the *Flying Dutchman* needs someone else—"

"What if we didn't *pick* anyone else? What if we just gave up the whole idea of the Plan, because it's clear we don't know what we're doing, and turned things over to you kids—because you understand more than we do?"

I was stunned. My head spun. "Would you really do that?"

Very softly, tears began to run down Papa's face. "If it's the best thing . . . I guess we'll have to. But oh, Melpomene, it won't ever be as simple as that. . . ."

Then I hugged him again, and he sighed a lot, and stopped crying and dried his eyes. I had all kinds of questions, but I didn't ask them. We just sat there for a long time.

There was a pounding on the door. Papa keyed it open, and there was Tom, grinning like a maniac. "I did it! I did it!"

"Did what?"

"Top score in CSL! The best in my class!" I heard Papa suck in his breath, but I didn't know what the matter was. Anyway, I was too happy for Tom. Papa congratulated Tom, and said he and I were done, so I went out to join Tom.

"Call Randy," he said. "Let's celebrate together somehow. You guys coached me—that's the only reason I got it at all. It was just like a light going on—all of a sudden I understood all this stuff that had been a complete mystery."

"Call Randy?" I said. "It must be close to Lights Down."

"Just 1903," he said.

Then I realized; I'd left school early, and hadn't been asleep for all that long at the hospital. "Sure!" So I called Randy on the com and we all went down to the snack facility in the Mushroom and had pizza, splurging on our discrets to add a bunch of ingredients. I even enjoyed being around Susan, which at the time I thought was amazing.

CHAPTER TWELVE

THE NEXT DAY IN CLASS WE WERE BACK TO WORKING ON JAPA-
nese verb constructions. I'm told those have simplified a lot in the
last couple of centuries—no offense if you're Japanese, but I'm
certainly glad. Randy and I were sitting with each other, not
because we were trying to exclude anybody, but because no one
else seemed to feel comfortable sitting next to us. After a while,
Miriam came over and joined us; it was kind of strained, but we
did talk. I wondered if anyone had seen that she got some help—
what had happened the day before must have been terrible for
her—but I didn't quite feel comfortable asking in front of Randy.

Miriam must have broken the ice or something, because in
short order Chris and Dmitri joined us, and then Rachel. After the
first awkwardness, it was kind of nice to be in a group of friends.

Miriam's Japanese is pretty good, so we did pretty well on the
oral competition—she was a captain and picked all of us, plus
Penelope and Bekka.

I was kind of afraid we were launching our own Real Gang but that's not what happened. Everyone was very quiet and no one seemed to want to talk much, but by lunch time people were at least smiling back when I smiled at them, and in the locker room, getting dressed for the airgym, Gwenny made a point of talking to me and Bekka.

It looked like things would eventually heal. The rest of the day went by quietly; I went home, did homework, talked to Randy and Miriam on the com for a while, and got to bed on time. It was lim normal—which was completely koapy with me.

The next morning, B Shift's bedtime and C Shift's noon, they made the Plan available for anyone to read it who wanted to. There were a lot of arguments and I guess some people were pretty upset, but within a week or so it was just one more ship's policy question on exams. Dr. Niwara had us write papers about it. You'd have thought Randy's and my head start would have helped, but it didn't seem to at all.

Within a month everyone was bored with it, and the Committee to Draft a New Plan, made up of people from the first couple of birthyears to grow up here, quit meeting after six weeks due to lack of interest.

I⊤ WAS ABOUT A WEEK AFTER THE AEROCROSSE RIOT, WHICH was what everyone was calling it. Mother had come home a couple of days before, so I was avoiding our living unit most of the time. Tonight's excuse was that Randy, Miriam, and I needed to go to the infirmary for Psych Wing visiting hours. "Did you tell him we're coming?" Randy asked Miriam for only about the eighth time.

"Yes," she said, "I really did. He knows you kept the crowd off him, Randy. He's not angry with you. He just said he wanted to see you and Mel, so I asked you two to come. That's all there is to it."

The three of us were sitting in the snack bar burning discrets and waiting for infirmary visiting hours to start. Randy was about as nervous as I'd ever seen him.

"Fidgeting like that isn't going to make it any easier, especially not for Ted," Miriam said.

Randy grimaced. "I know. I'll be fine once we go in there. But right now I'm thinking about all the ways things could be really unpleasant, and getting myself generally worked up over nothing."

"As usual," I said, squeezing his thigh under the table.

"Thank you, Dr. Murray. Your whole family keeps telling me to relax. If I took one tenth of your advice I'd be comatose."

"If you took any of it, we wouldn't have to give it."

"Hey, no brawling, kids. Don't start something and get us all brigged." Miriam winked at me; at least we were sort of getting Randy's mind off it.

"That's a bizarre thought," I said. "Even though everyone makes jokes about it, I've never known anyone personally who actually went to the brig. Have you?"

Miriam shook her head, but Randy said, "My father."

We both stared at him, and my stomach sank like a lead ball in ten. "Really?"

"No big deal," he said. "Last year when he was really angry, sometimes he would hit first and think later. So when he felt like he was going to have a real bad night, he would go to Security and have them lock him up for the night."

I was trying to think of something to say when Miriam said, "He must really love you a lot to have himself locked up that way."

Randy nodded, slowly, and seemed to relax. I decided that I had always had superb taste in friends, all along.

We didn't say much after that; a few minutes later, Miriam's werp beeped, letting us know that visiting hours were about to start. We got up and walked down the stairs; they had thought Theophilus would re-orient a little better in the high-grav infirmary, with over a quarter gee weighing him down. That seemed strange to us, of course, but I guess if I visited Earth and got hurt, I'd want to go to a hospital at Supra New York or someplace where the gravity wouldn't bother me while I was recovering.

The bruises were faded to a nasty yellow-brown. I still couldn't believe how many of them there were.

"Hi," Miriam said. "I brought some friends."

He smiled, making a special point of smiling at Randy. "I'm glad you came."

"I hope you're feeling better, Ted."

"Quite a bit." He sat up. "How are things with you? Still holding the top of the class in math?"

Randy stammered something, choked, then laughed at himself.

"You know, that was one of the worst things you could have asked. Gwenny Mori just took over first standing, and I think she's going to get a permanent resident contract on it."

"Not after I get back she's not. And if you want to work together, I'd love to have you come down here for evening visiting—you wouldn't believe how tired I am of hearing my father talk about balancing the B-complex in the new strain of tilapia."

"After you get back?" Miriam said. "Dr. Niwara said—"

"Yeah, I know what they decided. But they didn't ask me about it, Mim. How am I supposed to be able to work with any of you after I get FA, if the last time you saw me . . . well, you know."

"So you'll be back," I said. "That's going to be tough for everyone for a little while, but I guess you're right."

Randy added, "I'm glad. I really am."

Theophilus sighed and stretched; his arms stuck out of the bed bag he was in, and we could see more bruises. He saw us staring and quietly tucked his hands back in. "It's okay," Randy said. "Sorry we were rude."

"That's all right." Theophilus sat very quietly for quite a while; none of us could think of anything to say. I was trying to imagine what the first day with him back would be like; maybe like having a new kid but a hundred times worse? How would the ones who had hit him—especially Barry Yang, who had started it, or Gwenny Mori and Kwame van Dyke, who had been his friends—how would they react?

Then he cleared his throat. "I have something to say. Back on

Earth . . . well, back in Georgia. At my school in the Atlanta Dome
. . . I sort of had a special role in my class. You know what it was?

"I was the class jerk.

"That's Earth slang, and kind of old fashioned. I guess you'd
say I was the class unco. I put a lot of effort into lubing the
teacher, and a lot of time into hiding from kids who wanted to
beat me up. I hurt people's feelings, I sneered at everyone, I was
lim superior because I was better at school stuff than they were.
. . . I was the outsider. Always. I didn't have any friends except
a couple of ding-y weird kids who followed me around, and who
I picked on harder than anyone else.

"When I came here . . ." He turned toward us; tears were
streaking down his face. "At first I thought it was all a fresh start,
and here I was with a class I could run. I could be the popular
kid. But I found out the same kind of things happen—especially
if . . . if . . ." He gave a long sigh. "You know something? I wasn't
really called Ted back in Georgia. They called me Theo. I hated
that name."

"Would you rather be called Ted?" I asked.

He nodded.

"Then you're Ted to us."

He started to turn away, but Randy asked, "Are you going to
do stuff like that again?"

"No."

"Then it doesn't matter. As long as you stop doing it, and try
your best to make up for the damage you did, it doesn't matter
what you used to do." Randy squatted on his heels by the bed so he
could look directly into Theophilus's eyes. "Trust me, Ted. I have
experience. I get along fine with people now, but I used to hit them."

We all tried to laugh, but we weren't quite ready to. We will
one of these days, though, I think.

I GOT INTO ANOTHER ARGUMENT WITH DR. LOVELL. SHE SEEMS
to have moved from teacher to shrink to book critic in one short

month. "But all that stuff afterward is boring," I said. "And it was all bound to happen if you just think about it. The Plan was dead, and anyone who would be interested in this book is going to know who Tom is. 'Fountains of Dark Vacuum' has been seen all over the place."

"It's popular right now," she agreed. "And it may well stay popular for a long time. But I think people are going to want to know how your story really came out."

"Okay, I'll tell them in two paragraphs. Two sentences. One: 'When the Plan broke, NAC decided to transfer all the adults to the Mars Terraforming Project and turned the ship over to us, so they're doing it, and by the third Marspass from now, everyone left on the *Flying Dutchman* will have been born here.' Two: 'Tom got famous because he came up with this moving light sculpture that forms interactively with a piece of music, so the whole thing looks like Main Engine exhaust and sounds a little like Beethoven.' I write that down, and I'm done."

I got up to go, but she put her hand out to hold the door closed. *"Are* you done? What's this book *about,* anyway?"

"I don't know. How things happened I guess. Or what happened. Or just what I happened to write down."

"That's all? Things just happened? Don't they mean more to you than that?" Without quite knowing how I knew, I suddenly realized something I'd never have imagined—I was one of Dr. Lovell's favorite students. Somehow that made me feel like I owed her something, but I didn't have any real answer.

So—like Papa says, when in doubt, tell the truth. "A lot did just happen," I said. "But while it's happening, you're too busy to think, and after it's happened, you don't know really know what you were thinking anymore. That's all. Like at the B Block party, I know I spent some time thinking about my calculus homework, so maybe I was bored for a while, even though I made it sound like it was exciting all evening. Or in the middle of the riot, when Randy came in to stand down the crowd so we could get Theophilus out of there, I know part of the reason it worked was because Bekka and Penelope and Rachel were all there backing him up, and nobody wanted to fight all of them at once. I mean, it took courage for him to do it, and he was the leader, but they had to be smart and brave enough to follow him. And see, if I told it all, it wouldn't mean anything. I mean, am I supposed to write about every time I urinated that week or something? It would all disappear in the details.

"So I'm not going to write those last things. I see what you mean that it's supposed to be what the whole book leads up to—how my brother Tom got to be an artist, the first professional artist born in space and all that stuff Time-Murdoch and OBSR-CHANL and NACFlash hung on him. And about how the adults left and we ended up in charge a decade before we were supposed to, because we were the people who belonged here and they were the aliens. But now that it's obvious, why write the scene?"

She sighed. "All I'm really asking you to do is write two more scenes. And I know you'll write them well. Besides, that visit to Theophilus in the infirmary was part of what it all led up to, so you could say you're one-third done with the ending already. Why don't you want this book to have an ending?"

I shrugged. "What the book is about doesn't have an ending. If the low grav life extension research is right, we'll all live for several more centuries. There's so much in front of us. The story will keep going because we'll keep going. So putting an end on—well, it's a lie. A bigger lie than all the lies I told when I cleaned up the story. And it's my book and I don't want any lies that big in it."

She shook her head. "But it's not just *your* book. It's for the good of the ship. It's supposed to introduce Earth people to the new culture that's developed up here, so they'll sympathize with it and understand it. So far it's all right, I think—it will work for NAC the way they want it to—but how can you cheat your readers like that and expect them to like it? They want to see where it all leads, and see that it all makes sense. That's part of your responsibility, to them and to the ship."

I thought about that one for a long time. It made sense, I guess, but I still don't want to write those last scenes. There's no point in describing art, and you know enough about me and

Randy and Susan to know how happy we all were when Tom's project swept the awards for Projects Day and then went on to that special exhibit and all those broadcasts. We had kind of a party for him, and everyone danced and talked a lot.

And as for the adults leaving . . . well, Tom and I had a long, upsetting talk with Mother and Papa about it, the same talk all the kids did with their parents, really, because there wasn't anything else to do. The CPB's final report showed what you'd expect, when you think about it.

People get older. They get more independent, more different. You can't plan what they'll do so well anymore. Then it's either point a gun at them and make them follow the Plan, or turn it over to them and let them do it their way. You can't make people grown-up at fourteen and then tell them they won't get any real say in things till they're sixty.

Especially not when they really know their environment, the way fish know the sea, and you're the immigrant, the one who came as an adult.

So what else were they going to do, if they loved us? What else was NAC going to do, if they wanted us to work?

I guess maybe there is one last scene I want to write, though. Because now I just made it sound like we all sat down and made the decision calmly and carried it out and that was that.

Of course that's not exactly what happened. It's just what we told ourselves afterwards.

ALL THEIR STUFF—INCLUDING THAT POOR SILLY OLD COPY OF *Catcher in the Rye* that once belonged to Mother's father—had already gone into the shuttle. "One of the big advantages of living up here," Papa said, hefting his duffel bag, "is that you never acquire enough stuff to have any trouble packing." I think he was having trouble believing that small bag was all that was left.

Mother was dabbing her eyes and looking terribly confused. "You'll take care of your sister?" she asked for the twentieth time.

"Right up to midnight, June 30, 2026," Tom assured her.

"After that, she's the problem of the *Flying Dutchman* as a whole."

I had been afraid he'd be insufferable once he got Full Adult, but in fact he'd been a lot easier to get along with—he was under so much less pressure since they'd created the job of "Resident Artist" for him.

Since Mother and Papa were leaving, Susan would be moving in on a renewable trial contract—something Mother didn't quite approve of but could only talk about obliquely, mentioning that Living Unit Six would stay in the family and I could keep my room; Papa's office would become Tom's studio.

Now we all stood there feeling uncomfortable, trying to think of some last thing to say that would make sense.

"Vidphone whenever you can," Mother said.

"I'll even wash my face before I get in front of the camera," I said.

"Oh, you." She hugged me; as she pulled away I saw tear tracks on her coverall and realized I must be crying.

"It's okay," she said. "I know we don't get along, but I'll miss you too."

Then Tom had to hug her, and then I hugged Papa, and after that we all just babbled about how much we wanted each other to do well.

"Send me a picture of your first garden!" I said to her.

She laughed. "I'll be eighty before we have that, and it will look like green refrigerator scudge. We won't even be moving down from orbit for twenty years."

I nodded. "You'll just have to live a long time."

She smiled. "Come visit. It won't be as pretty as Earth, but at least you'll get to see a sky and some plants growing outdoors."

I promised I would. That was silly, of course—a ticket to visit another station or ship cost more than a year's salary, and I could hardly imagine what they would charge me to visit the Mars Terraforming Project's surface colony once it was built. But I'd never really had to say good-bye to anyone before, and I said a lot of dumb things.

Papa was growling a lot of advice at Tom, mostly in fun.

"Remember, you're the Chaucer for these people; try to occasionally get your mind out of the gutter."

"Chaucer didn't."

"And Anglo-American history shows it," Papa pointed out. "And no political satires about your sister, either." Tom looked baffled; Papa winked at me. "Don't tell him. Let it come as an appalling shock."

Tom looked from me to Papa and back again, scratching the back of his head. "Well, it'll certainly be easier dealing with just one of you." He stuck out his hand and Papa shook it. "But I'll miss you a lot."

That got us all crying and hanging onto each other again. No one else in the boarding bay had any dignity either, though.

Finally it was time. Mother kissed me one more time and said, "You won't think I mean it, but I do. Just do what your heart tells you—I know it's a good one."

I held her for a long time. "I hope you're happy on Mars," I said.

"Even if I'm not, I promise I'll do my best there. I'm not going to even look at another Olson book until I've got a corn crop of my own!" She let go of me. "Good-bye, Melly—Melpomene. I love you."

"I love you too."

Then I hugged Papa and words wouldn't come at all, so neither of us said "I love you." But we knew.

They picked up their duffels and went in through a door in the side of the big passenger compartment on the shuttle, among the first in a long line going aboard. Dr. Niwara went in a little after them; Randy's father was far back in the line. I had come here to say good-bye to a lot of people, but in the end I talked only to Papa and Mother.

Later, when I talked to other kids, I found out exactly the same thing had happened to all of them. In fact, Randy and his father hadn't said a single word—just held onto each other and wept for the whole hour while Mr. Schwartz waited to board.

The last of them went in, and the siren sounded. We all went out through the big freight doors and back to our business.

An hour later, the brief shuddering of the *Flying Dutchman* told us that the catapult had cycled, and they were on their way. Even though it was against the rules, Randy and I held hands the rest of the afternoon, under the desk.

February 2, 2026

Papa says on earth you all get raised like randy and me and Tom, maybe even more so. You're kind of all Special Categories.

It's nice that we're needed more up here, because there are so few of us—but I can't pretend it doesn't make us lonely. Really lonely, sometimes, even having each other to count on. So I *am* going to get this in shape for Scholastic or some publisher, or if that doesn't work I'm going to self-publish it on the Copy Access channel.

And then I'm going to ask you to write to me, okay? Even with as many friends as I have shipboard, more are always nice.

With love,

Melpomene Murray